GUERILLA SEASON

Paul Thomas was born in the United Kingdom and grew up in New Zealand. He graduated from the University of Auckland and subsequently worked in journalism and public relations in Auckland, London, Toulouse and Sydney. He has written several books on sport. *Inside Dope*, his first novel, was joint winner of the 1996 Ned Kelly Award for best Australian crime novel. His second, *Dirty Laundry* is also available in Vista.

PAUL THOMAS

GUERILLA SEASON

VISTA

First published in New Zealand 1996
by Hodder Moa Beckett

This Vista edition published 1998
Vista is an imprint of the Cassell Group
Wellington House, 125 Strand, London WC2R 0BB

A catalogue record for this book is
available from the British Library.

ISBN 0 575 60395 X

Printed and bound in Great Britain by
Caledonian International Book Manufacturing Ltd, Glasgow

98 99   10 9 8 7 6 5 4 3 2 1

ONE

Cowards, wrote Shakespeare, die many times before their deaths. So do hypochondriacs.

The radio talkback star Fred 'the Freckle' Freckleton had both strings to his bow; in his imagination, he'd suffered most of the fates known to medical science and the insurance industry. Even at his most creatively morbid, however, it hadn't occurred to him to worry about urban terrorism.

At half past midnight on Tuesday, 22 August, Freckleton dropped his empty beer can into a wastepaper basket, said goodnight to his producer, and took the lift to the basement car park. He felt drained but it was the weary satisfaction of a job well done.

It'd been a top show; he'd sparked, the all-important maniac factor was right up there, and the new gimmick had been a big hit. This was a sound effect of a flushing toilet which he used to terminate callers who didn't enter into the spirit of things: the temperate, the tolerant, and – worst of all – the well-informed. Late in the show, he'd preceded the flush by telling one particularly dogged dissenter to, 'Get back where you belong – with all the other turds.' It was a good line; he'd use it again.

The previous year, forty years old and a self-diagnosed burn-out after fifteen years on the breakfast shift, the Freckle had taken a sabbatical to fulfil his long-held ambition of driving coast-to-coast across the USA in a Detroit convertible the size of Sylvester Stallone's swimming pool. Along the way, he got acquainted with the ebullient and ultra-conservative talk-radio sensation, Rush Limbaugh. Limbaugh, so he'd read in a magazine, earned around US$25 million a year for saying pretty much the sort of stuff Freckleton himself came out with after a few beers. As he pondered the Limbaugh phenomenon, it slowly dawned on Freckleton that he'd stumbled on the solution to his mid-life crisis.

Back in Auckland, Freckleton talked his network's owners into taking over a struggling easy listening station. It was renamed Radio Mainstream – The Station for Real Kiwis, and given a news/talkback format, alleviated only by the odd classic hit. Each weeknight, from eight till midnight, Mainstream's star turn, Fred Freckleton: The Bloke Who Speaks Your Language, vented his spleen on feminists, gays, Maori radicals, left-wing politicans, environmentalists, trade-union leaders, welfare beneficiaries – in short, anyone whose agenda, activities or mere existence was likely to annoy the suburban heartland, that majority which, thanks to talkback radio, can no longer be described as silent.

In empathising with this audience, Freckleton skated over his quarter of a million dollar salary, his lavishly renovated villa with harbour views, his Porsche, his atheism, his childless marriages – both messy failures – and his heavy use of Benzedrine. Instead, he dwelt on his Little House on the Dairy Flat upbringing, the subtext to his tirades against welfare recipients.

A sample: 'You know what really gets my goat? It's when the bleeding-heart mob, the moaners and the bleaters – you know who I'm talking about – tell the government it's got to raise taxes, in other words, grab even more of our hard-earned dough, so they can devote more resources – don't you love that line? – to the less fortunate. Now what that means, in plain English, is taking money off people who work and giving it to people who don't – ninety-nine per cent of the time because they simply can't be stuffed. Let's be clear what these turkeys are on about: they want to take more of your money – the money from that extra bit of overtime, the money you'd put aside for the kids' Christmas presents or the summer holiday or to chip away at the mortgage – and give it to the bludgers and the scroungers and the no-hopers and the parasites. And what do you reckon they'll do with it? Well, for a start, they'll piss a fair chunk of it up against the wall; some of it'll go to the TAB, some on Lotto, some on dirty videos, some on cigarettes. What's left will go on junk food because even though they don't do a stroke of work from one month to the next, they're still too bloody lazy to make a proper meal.

'Well, I'd just like to ask one question: what's stopping these bludgers from getting off their arses – fat arses too, most of 'em: it's all that booze and junk food – and doing something for themselves? My old man was a fitter and turner in a dairy factory. He didn't go to the pub after work and drink himself pie-eyed; he came home, dog-tired and covered in muck, and went straight out to feed the chooks and work in his vegetable garden. Mum, God bless her, baked every day – cakes, biscuits, even her own bread. Every biscuit, every cake, every egg, every vegetable eaten at the Freckletons' was home-grown. But try telling the scroungers to grow a few spuds or bake a cake and you'll get called every name in the book. Why? Because of this crazy mentality that it's not up to them to help themselves, it's not their responsibility. You know how it goes: society has to look after them and when things go wrong, society is to blame. Well, society is you and me; speaking for myself, I've got a lot better things to do with my money. If it was up to me, they wouldn't get a brass razoo. Safety net, my eye – it's more like a bloody hammock. Let's hear what you think – we're taking your calls now.'

Freckleton drove his Porsche 928 out of the car park, through the empty streets of Takapuna, and over the harbour bridge to Herne Bay. In sight of home, he activated the remote control to raise the garage door. Nothing happened. He pulled up in front of the garage, held the remote out the window, and tried again. It still didn't work. He swore, reversed, and parked on the street.

He got out of the car. Two men in dark boilersuits and ski masks got out of a station wagon parked over the road. They crossed the road towards him, unhurried but purposeful.

Freckleton was dizzy with fear. He gabbled, 'Who are you, what do you want?'

'You can call me Betty,' said the smaller of the pair suavely. 'And you can call him Al. We'd like you to come with us.'

'What for?' squeaked Freckleton.

'All will be revealed in good time.'

Al advanced, eyes animal-bright in the slits of his ski mask. He sank fingers like sharkhooks into the loose flesh of Freckleton's upper arm. He thrust Freckleton into the back seat of the station wagon and got in beside him. Betty slid behind the wheel and drove towards the city.

Freckleton tremulously broke the silence: 'Am I being kidnapped?'

The only response was the driver's amused snort. When Freckleton repeated the question, Al carefully gripped his right ear and wrenched violently. Freckleton heard a squishing sound, as if sinew and gristle were being pulped, and suffered a jolt of hideous pain which receded to a slow, hurtful throb. After that, he didn't dare speak or even assess the damage.

Betty parked in a side street by St Matthews-in-the-City. They escorted Freckleton, now thoroughly cowed, up the hill to Hobson Street. It was a clear, cold night, about five degrees. The inner city was silent and deserted, as if a neutron bomb had blotted out all life, leaving brick, mortar, and reflective glass intact. They came to a fenced-off building site. The wire-mesh fence was cut; Al wriggled through the gap then peeled back a section of fence for the others to follow. Cranes perched like prehistoric birds of prey on the unfinished high-rise which towered above them. Freckleton gazed up at it, shuddering.

'Now we climb,' Betty told him. 'I hope you're fitter than you look.'

They went up fifteen flights of concrete stairs. By the time they reached the top, Freckleton's face had popped sweat and he was gobbling air like a footballer in injury time.

'Show time,' said Betty, breathing easily. 'We've brought you here tonight, Mr Freckle, to give you a taste of your own medicine. Right now, this building's more or less the same height as that one right alongside. We've bridged the gap with a sturdy if somewhat narrow plank: all you have to do is walk across it.' His face split in what seemed to Freckleton a transparently sadistic grin. 'Seeing you're so anti-safety nets, we haven't provided one.'

Freckleton's legs almost buckled. He croaked: 'What is this – some sort of fucking sick joke?'

'Oh, it's no joke. Under this flippant exterior, I'm serious to a fault.'

'There's no fucking way you're getting me on that plank,' blurted Freckleton. 'I'm shit-scared of heights.'

Betty nodded. 'Well, it wouldn't be a cakewalk for a steeplejack – it's pitch black and there's a tricky breeze. Before you make up your mind though, you really ought to consider the alternative: if you won't do it, we'll simply shoot you. Look at it this way: if you plummet fifteen floors to a horrible death, you'll be remembered as a martyr for free speech; but if you make it, you'll really have something to talk about on the show.'

Freckleton implored him. 'Why are you doing this? What have I ever done to you?'

Betty shrugged. 'You're a hate-mongering demagogue, you're shallow as a birdbath, you're in love with the sound of your own voice, you play too much Billy Joel – take your pick. Well, what's it going to be?'

Al produced a semi-automatic pistol. He took a silencer from his breast pocket and screwed it on.

'It's up to you, Mr Freckle,' said Betty. 'Your fate is

entirely in your hands – just as you're always saying it should be.'

The talkback man stood rooted to the spot. A minute passed. Betty told Al, 'I'll do the honours.'

Al passed him the pistol. Freckleton forced himself to move, shuffling woozily to the edge of the building. The plank was ridiculously narrow and the neighbouring building seemed several postcodes away.

Betty said, 'Off you go then. Take my advice: don't look down and don't try anything fancy, like a pirouette – we're hard to impress.'

Freckleton extended his arms in a crucifixion pose and stepped onto the plank. He wobbled sickeningly but managed to keep his balance. He took another step. With his arms still extended, he lowered himself very slowly onto one knee, then gripped the plank with both hands. When he had both knees on the plank, he began to inch foward.

'I said walk, not crawl.' Betty's tone was mildly disapproving. He sauntered to the edge of the building, put his right heel against the plank, and shoved.

Freckleton hit the ground at 113 kph, which is just over half the maximum speed a falling body can reach – what physicists somewhat ghoulishly call terminal velocity. It was quite fast enough for Betty's purposes.

Construction workers discovered the body at 7.05 a.m.

The fact that Freckleton was a celebrity of sorts whose pugnacious glower adorned several billboards around town didn't facilitate the identification process. The examining pathologist described the corpse as compelling evidence that human beings aren't designed to jump off anything higher than a beanbag. When it came to nominating the actual cause of death, the pathologist found himself quite spoilt for choice. Eventually, he narrowed it down to the lacerated liver – the organ had split open like a well-read book – and the ruptured aorta. Then again, the almost instantaneous loss of 40 per cent of his blood hadn't done the poor bugger much good either.

Although the contents of the deceased's wallet were blood-soaked, his platinum American Express card scrubbed up well enough to permit a tentative ID. This was confirmed by dental records and Freckleton's GP who, over the years, had become more intimately acquainted with his patient's physique and physiology than he would have liked.

Thanks to its good police contacts, Radio Mainstream was first with the news of its star announcer's mysterious death. The station's Head of News assured staff that the Freckle would've wanted it that way.

At 10.20 the next morning, the 28-year-old television current affairs reporter Amanda Hayhoe left the St Mary's Bay villa she shared with her landlady.

Hayhoe liked the area: as people always said, it had character. She'd decided that having character meant it had more cafés, restaurants, and weirdos per head than most parts of town. She liked the house, the rent was reasonable, and her landlady/flatmate was okay to live with most of the time. The pluses, therefore, outweighed the minuses, of which there were two.

The first drawback was that she got little, if any, sleep when her flatmate's boyfriend was in town. He was a 44-year-old married man from Henley-on-Thames who flew 747s for British Airways. The second was the amount of emotional support she had to provide whenever he flew away. The flatmate would get it into her head that he'd be rostered on to another route, somewhere like Johannesburg or Budapest, and she'd never see him again. For a couple of nights, she'd go on sobbing jags which took several hours of Hayhoe's undivided attention and general jollying along to bring under control.

Hayhoe had come to find these performances irksome, especially when her reward for providing a shoulder to cry on was mascara smudges and lipstick smears on her Rosaria Hall shirt. She felt that, seeing the pilot had been loving and leaving for a couple of years now, her landlady, who was, after all, thirty-five and a practising psychoanalyst, really should have come to terms with it.

What's more, when the psychoanalyst was bingeing on self-pity, it never seemed to cross her mind that in the ten months they'd flatted together, the most exciting thing which had happened in Hayhoe's bedroom was her radio alarm suddenly and inexplicably picking up a rugby league commentary from Papua New Guinea.

Hayhoe was late for an appointment. That wasn't the end of the world but she had a hangover which felt like it very well could be.

As she walked to her car parked down the street, she tried to remember when she'd last had an alcohol-free day. The recollection prompted a curious half-smile and a rueful shake of the head: she'd stayed off it for a week last summer after waking up one Sunday in an Epsom motel next to the wife of one of Auckland's wealthiest men. Hayhoe was wondering which question to ask first when Mrs Moneybags saved her the trouble by declaring that Amanda hadn't thrown up or snored or hogged the blankets or made a drama of declining her invitation to a spot of amateur lesbianism.

Whether it was the hangover or the motel flashback, Hayhoe had driven her four-year-old Honda Civic up the hill to Jervois Road and through Ponsonby village before she noticed the white envelope tucked under the windscreen wiper. She pulled over and got out of the car. The envelope was sealed but not addressed. It contained a single sheet of paper with a message handwritten in block capitals:

COMMUNIQUÉ NUMBER ONE

The Aotearoa People's Army has dealt decisively with the reactionary broadcaster Freckleton.

Freckleton has methodically vilified progressive forces and sought to incite hatred towards those who reject and resist laissez-faire multinational capitalism. He has actively promoted a fascist line against the poor, the disenfranchised, minority groups, and those in the vanguard of the struggle for Maori liberation and sovereignty.

Freckleton did not act in isolation: the volume of extreme right-wing propaganda in both the mass media and the socio-political arena has increased significantly in recent months, signalling the mobilisation of reactionary elements. The Aotearoa People's Army was not prepared to allow this process to go unchecked.

The crypto-fascists in the government–big business axis and their mouthpieces in the media should heed this warning. If they choose to ignore it, they should not be surprised when the Aotearoa People's Army administers further direct revolutionary justice.

Amanda Hayhoe had to read it three times before the full implications sank in. When they did, she said, 'Fuck a priest,' which wasn't an expression she used lightly or often, and resumed her journey. Her hangover seemed to have disappeared.

TWO

At three o'clock that afternoon, a meeting began in a glass-walled, venetian-blinded ground floor office in Television New Zealand's state-of-the-art studios on the corner of Victoria and Nelson Streets. The only item on the agenda was the apparent outbreak of urban terrorism, a blight from which New Zealand had been thought to be immune because of its isolation and the phlegmatic, some would say passionless, disposition of its inhabitants.

Taking part were the network's head of news and current affairs, the producer of the six o'clock national news, the wholesome mixed double who presented the news and who were called, behind their backs, 'Ken and Barbie' and 'the Blands', a producer from 'The Holmes Show', the reporter Ainsley Tarr, a network lawyer, and Amanda Hayhoe. Earlier, the lawyer and Hayhoe had gone to Auckland Central Police Station, where he'd handed over the original of the Aotearoa People's Army communiqué and she'd been fingerprinted.

The news producer opened the meeting. 'Okay, we've just heard from the cops that they're holding a press conference at five to release the text of the communiqué. They'll say they've never heard of this outfit, they're not ruling out a hoax, and all the usual shit – enquiries are proceeding, blah, blah. What that means is we don't have an exclusive but we do have an edge, due to the fact that the terrorists chose to announce themselves via our very own Amanda Hayhoe.'

Mr Bland glanced uncertainly at Hayhoe. 'Are you – is she doing the story?'

The head of news and current affairs said, 'No, it's business as usual: Ainsley's covering the story; you'll do a live cross to Amanda in the newsroom and run through it with her.'

Hayhoe and Tarr exchanged fleeting, insincere smiles. Ainsley had been to make-up before the meeting: she didn't miss a trick.

Amanda couldn't have cared less about not doing the story for news. Two minutes air-time maybe, three max, most of it cops and politicians grinding out waffle and 'no comments'. Forget it. She had a bigger fish to fry: an in-depth story for her current affairs program, 'Sixty Minutes'.

'How are we going so far?' asked the head of news and current affairs.

'The Wellington bureau's jacking up comment from the PM and the leader of the opposition,' said the producer. 'They're bound to be pretty guarded so we're trawling the backbenches for someone who'll say it's the end of civilisation as we know it...'

The woman from 'Holmes' said, 'How about Chas Gundry, media slut extraordinaire?'

'Yeah,' enthused the producer, 'he's absolutely fucking rabid. Point a camera at him and he foams at the mouth.'

'And who'll speak for our brown brethren?' asked the head of news and current affairs.

Ainsley Tarr breathed, 'I'm on to it, Phil.' According to the network's market research, her husky delivery activated erectile tissue from North Cape to the Bluff. 'Whetu Porima's agreed to front.'

'What's he going to say?'

Tarr flipped open her notebook. 'Whatever they are, the Aotearoa People's Army aren't *tangata whenua*; Maori don't need anyone else to fight their battles for them; none of the leading radicals have ever advocated violence against individuals. Off the record, it couldn't have happened to a nicer guy.'

'Yeah, fine Ainsley, but don't give Porima a soft ride, eh? Put it on him that the inflammatory shit he and his mates are always coming out with might've given these guys the idea.'

Tarr numbed him: 'Phil, have you ever known me to give a soft ride?' Complete with slow-motion, heavy-lidded smile.

Holy creeping shit, thought Hayhoe, *that was an official announcement*. She scanned the table. The head of news and current affairs dropped his eyes to his blank notepad; Tarr met her glance with an unfathomable smile and a fractional lift of her right eyebrow; the others wore studiously blank expressions.

After that, Hayhoe didn't take much interest in the discussion. Instead, she thought about Ainsley Tarr: twenty-two, just out of the Canterbury University journalism school, and zeroing in on media stardom with the pre-programmed implacability of a cruise missile.

It helped that she was sexy: soap-star looks and that super-vamp voice. A cameraman had told Hayhoe that talking camera angles with Ainsley was better than phone sex.

The camera loved her, no doubt about that. And Ainsley loved it right back with a lack of inhibition which sometimes made Hayhoe envious but usually made her change channels. It was like watching a dirty movie: it wasn't so much what they were doing that bothered you, it was the fact they seemed so proud of themselves.

A secretary knocked and poked her head in. 'Amanda, there's a Detective Sergeant Ihaka to see you…'

'Ihaka.' The producer pulled a face. 'He'll make your day.'

'Is there anything I should know?'

'He's got a chip on his shoulder the size of a satellite dish.' He paused for effect. 'And he particularly hates the media.'

Hayhoe's first impression was that the producer's thumbnail sketch might have erred on the side of generosity.

Ihaka was a Maori in his mid-thirties, about 180 cm tall, wide as a bathtub. He had a Popeye jaw, a greedy mouth, and a flat, sprawling nose. After that, things improved marginally: his eyes were large and brown, with long, dark lashes, and would have been attractive if they'd contained a glimmer of warmth. He looked tough, cynical, not very nice.

He certainly wasn't one of your devious, roundabout interrogators. As soon as she'd sat down, he demanded, 'How come they made you the messenger girl?'

She shrugged. 'No idea.'

'You're a journo, aren't you? Surely to Christ you've thought about it.'

That was true enough. 'Well, I guess, basically, they wanted a journalist to make sure it got publicised...'

Ihaka rolled his eyes, murmured, 'No shit?'

'And when you're on TV, people you don't know from Adam know you – or at least your face.'

'And the rest – these jerk-offs know where you live and what car you drive.'

Hayhoe flapped her hands, a bit rattled. 'I don't know, maybe they followed me home from work or saw me out somewhere and followed me.'

'See, you have thought about it. I need a list of places you've been in the last couple of months, especially anywhere you go regularly. Anything unusual happened lately? Anyone hassled you, stared at you, watched you get into your car, hung around outside your place?'

'Not that I've noticed – you get used to the odd person gawking at you. After a while, it doesn't really register.'

Ihaka grumbled – it wasn't what he wanted to hear. 'Freckleton sucked it on Monday night. Why'd they wait a day to stick the note on your car?'

Hayhoe had to think about it. 'Maybe they tried on Monday night – my car and I were otherwise engaged.'

'Doing what?'

'I had dinner at a friend's place. I drank too much wine so I stayed over, responsible citizen that I am.'

'What's his name?'

'Whose?'

Ihaka raised his eyebrows. 'Your friend.'

'Deirdre – funny name for a bloke, don't you think?'

Only two hats had been tossed into the ring when nominations for the position of coach of the Auckland rugby team closed that afternoon.

One belonged to a hulking, pock-marked, bull-necked 48-year-old builder named Barney Tingle. Tingle had a brick-red complexion and eyes like trampled grapes, perhaps because he had Scotch for morning tea and at increasingly regular intervals thereafter. Curiously, almost three decades of excess had done little to undermine his impressive physique.

Since giving up the game at thirty-seven, Tingle had coached several club teams, with mixed results. His bulk, gruffness, and the chilling reputation for brutality he'd acquired during his playing days meant that, as a rule, his teams were far more frightened of him than the opposition and competed accordingly. Tingle was, however, handicapped by the growing consensus that it was high time the tyrant coach was consigned to the dustbin of history.

Clyde Early, the other candidate, was rather more palatable. He was a trim, telegenic 39-year-old whose promising playing career had been aborted by injury. He immediately took up coaching, with spectacular success. At twenty-seven, he'd gone to France and taken an obscure fourth-division club into the first division and the sports pages. That had brought him to the attention of a rugby-mad northern Italian multimillionaire whose sponsorship of his local club was the only thing it had going for it. The tycoon hired Early to make his feeble team a force to be reckoned with. It took him five handsomely rewarded years.

After ten years in Europe, and having turned down an opportunity to coach the Italian national side, Early came home. He settled in Auckland, invested his considerable savings in property, blue-chip stocks, and a highly profitable hardware retailing franchise, and embarked on the third and final phase of his carefully planned coaching career.

The first step – winning the Auckland club championship – had been safely negotiated. Step two was to be appointed Auckland coach. That, in turn, would be the springboard to the goal he'd set his sights on seventeen years ago as he sat in a hospital bed absent-mindedly caressing the livid scars on his right knee: to coach the All Blacks.

Publicly, Early down-played his ambitions. In private, he was quite specific about both his destination and timetable. No-one who'd heard him on the subject doubted that he'd arrive on schedule.

When he'd finished with Amanda Hayhoe, Ihaka went across town to the university. He had an appointment with Dr Ralph Skeet, a history lecturer who'd read a lot of books about terrorism, was toying with the idea of writing one himself, and was therefore what the media called 'a recognised expert' on the subject.

Dr Skeet was aged between thirty and fifty and had gone to a lot of trouble to look the part of the mad professor: he had frizzy, grey-black hair, a moustache like a burst cushion, and pinkish, demented eyes behind red-framed spectacles. He wore cowboy boots, black jeans, a blue denim shirt, and a tie which looked as if it had been used to clean up after a seasick Italian.

He had a poster of a B-1 bomber on the wall behind his desk. The caption said: 'US Bomber Command – Nuke 'Em Till They Glow.'

They shook hands. Ihaka said, 'Nice poster; I bet it gets a few people going.'

'You're not wrong there, bud,' replied Skeet. He had a surprisingly deep voice and a strong American accent. 'Matter of fact, it offends the shit out of some folks. I figure, fuck 'em if they can't take a joke.'

'Fair enough.' Ihaka handed him a copy of the Aotearoa People's Army communiqué: 'See what you make of it.'

Skeet seemed to like it. He giggled as he read it and looked up at Ihaka with a wide grin: 'Don't you love it?'

Ihaka stared.

'Oh man, it's a classic – the jargon, the rhetoric, the euphemisms. I mean, how about "dealt decisively with", when what you really mean is, we threw the sucker off a fifteen-storey building? It's beautiful.'

Ihaka dripped sarcasm. 'Did I miss something?'

'Chill, baby,' said Skeet blithely.

Ihaka could remember a woman calling him baby, but seeing it was tacked on to a threat to behead him with a breadknife, he'd assumed she was being ironic. He'd never had a man call him baby, ironically or otherwise; it took him a few seconds to get over the shock.

'I'm looking at it from an academic perspective,' Skeet continued, apparently unaware of the stir he'd caused. 'Personally, I think anyone who believes politics is worth shedding blood over should be lobotomised. But hey, are you guys totally convinced that whatsisname, Freckleton, was shoved as opposed to, maybe he took a jump and this is some sick fuck's idea of a joke?'

'That's always a possibility but we're working on the basis he was shoved. It looks like someone fucked around with his garage-door remote so he couldn't drive straight in. Why? Doesn't it ring true?'

'Most urban terrorists, in the western world anyway, have been young, university-educated zealots from middle-class backgrounds. They talk about the class struggle like we talk about movies; they see themselves as intellectuals but all they are is Exhibit A for the proposition that a little knowledge is a dangerous thing.' Skeet tossed the communiqué on to his desk. 'I've seen carbon copies of this from a dozen different outfits in Europe and the States. I sure as hell never thought I'd see the Kiwi version.'

'Could they be students?'

Skeet scratched his head. 'That's the profile, but shit, that kind of New Left campus radicalism's as passé as The Monkees. The kids today are into working their tickets, period; all they ever jump up and down about is money – grants and fees. Put your average Rotarian in Levis and Doc Martens and he'd fit right in.'

'What about the name?'

'Names are a big deal for these guys – it's like their corporate logo, their brand. They're into names that make catchy acronyms: IRA, ETA, PLO.' He shrugged. 'APA – voilà. "People" is meant to give them legitimacy – this is who we're fighting for – and the military touch is standard too. Deep down, most of them are Che Guevara wannabees – what they really want is to look cool on posters in brainy chicks' bedrooms.'

'Obvious question: does Aotearoa make you think Maori?'

'I guess so, but Jesus, half my honky colleagues use it as a matter of course.'

'Do you take the threat of more where that came from seriously?'

Skeet took off his glasses and squinted at Ihaka. 'If this is for real, then I'd say the chances are pretty good. You're the cop, you tell me. But isn't the way it works, the first one's the hard one, after that it just gets easier? I guess it's the same whether you're strangling a little old lady for her pension or striking a blow for the oppressed masses.'

THREE

The September issue of *New Nation* which came out that Friday had a cover story testing the claim of some publicity-seeking think-tank that New Zealand was poised to become the Switzerland of the South Pacific.

The businesspeople and economists surveyed fell into three broad camps: those who agreed; those who felt it could happen, providing the democratic process was suspended for two or three decades; and those who assumed it was some kind of practical joke. There was also a story which failed to deliver on its promise to explain what the America's Cup would mean for Auckland, a fairly fawning profile of Clyde Early, the would-be coach, headlined 'Early To Rise?', and the regular features and columns.

The issue departed from the usual formula in one respect. As a rule, the editor Jackson Pike used his editorials to flag the strongest or most controversial stories and/or to stroke the ego of whichever staff writer was agitating for a pay rise that month. This time, however, Pike had unburdened himself of some novel, if not eccentric, thoughts on the subject of capital punishment.

It was headed 'A Modest Proposal?'

Recently, I saw a murder victim's father interviewed on television. Asked what he thought of the twenty-year prison sentence given his daughter's killer, he replied, 'We should bring back the death penalty; scum like that don't deserve to live.'

I wondered how many New Zealanders would agree with him.

A lot, I suspect. Anyone who's discussed crime and punishment in a public bar, a trendy restaurant, or a boardroom has heard numerous variations on the theme of 'string the bastards up'.

But no matter how strong the sentiment in favour, there's next to no chance of capital punishment being reintroduced. Servants, compulsory military service, and the six o'clock swill are all more likely to make a comeback. The fix is in, the establishment has decided capital punishment is not for us, and that's the end of it.

But despite being unfashionable, capital punishment is, if you'll pardon the expression, an idea which refuses to die.

Perhaps it's time to explore the middle ground between death row on the one hand and a system many see as soft on perpetrators of horrific crimes on the other.

In the same interview, the victim's father claimed he'd be prepared to look the murderer straight in the eye and 'press the button'. Well, why not? If the system isn't prepared to do the job, why not throw it open to the victim's nearest and dearest?

This is my modest proposal: if the accused is found guilty of murder and the judge considers that the crime warrants the maximum penalty, the victim's immediate family or next-of-kin should decide what form the punishment takes: life imprisonment or death. But if they chose the death penalty, they'd have to do the business themselves – pull the lever, administer the lethal injection, form a firing squad.

This would have several benefits: victims' families would no longer feel let down by a system too detached to feel and express their pain; the element of participation would restore public interest in the legal process; and the punishment would once more be seen to fit the crime, without the disquieting overtones of state execution.

And we'd also find out if we really are a nation of hangmen.

It was a curious piece which caused some headshaking among the magazine's staff. Eventually, a sub-editor asked Pike exactly what he was trying to say.

Pike was short with boyish features, a combination which often led people to underestimate his age and toughness. He examined the sub-editor through narrowed eyes. 'Doesn't the headline give you a clue?'

The sub opened the magazine: '"A Modest Proposal?"' He shook his head. 'Sorry, don't get it.'

'Have you heard of Jonathan Swift?'

The sub shook his head again.

'He wrote *Gulliver's Travels*; surely you've heard of that?'

'Oh yeah.' The sub forced a weak grin. 'Have to admit, I've never actually got round to reading it.'

'Course not,' snapped Pike. 'There isn't a serial killer in it. Swift wrote an essay called 'A Modest Proposal', about poverty in Ireland. He suggested the solution was for the Irish to breed like mad, fatten up their babies, and sell them to the English as delicacies.'

'Jesus.'

Pike could see the sub-editor had no idea what he was talking about. 'I'm glad we've had this little chat,' he said with a thin smile and walked away.

The sub reported the conversation to a colleague.

'It doesn't surprise me,' said the colleague. 'Pike's been very strange lately. If he was still married, I'd say he was having an affair.'

It took Leo Strange most of the day to track his man down. He finally found him just before six, in the upstairs bar of The Globe.

Brandon Mules was sitting by himself at a corner table, reading the racing section; there was one decent mouthful or three sips left in his beer glass. Strange suspected he was making it last.

When Mules heard the chair being pulled out, he lowered his newspaper and ran a hostile eye over the inoffensive-looking middle-aged man who'd sat down opposite him. Satisfied he didn't owe the man money and therefore had no reason to be civil, he raised the newspaper and said firmly, 'Feel free to fuck off.'

A minute passed. Having heard nothing to indicate that his invitation had been acted upon, Mules lowered the paper again. He was almost two metres tall and weighed close to 120 kilograms and was used to people fucking off with alacrity when he suggested it, so there was a trace of curiosity in his glare.

'Didn't I just tell you to fuck off?'

'Well, more or less,' said Strange with the conciliatory half-smile of a man who didn't want to get into a debate over semantics. 'You look like you could do with a refill; allow me.'

Mules stared at him for a few seconds, then shrugged and went back to his paper. 'Double Jack, ice, and a splash of Coke,' he said from behind the racing section.

'Tell that poof barman just a splash or else he'll drown the bastard.'

Strange fetched Mules' bourbon and a single-malt whisky for himself. He sat down and raised his glass: 'Your very good health.'

Mules said, 'Chin fucking chin,' swallowed half his drink, went back to the racing pages.

Strange took a careful sip of his single-malt. 'My sources tell me you're not as dim as you sometimes appear, Mr Mules. I hope they haven't let me down.'

Mules sighed. He folded the racing section and dropped it on the floor.

Whoever he was, this bloke wasn't one of those all-time losers who hang around pubs hoping someone will take pity on them. He was in his fifties, balding, with placid, shrewd grey eyes. Now that Mules had a good look, he saw prosperity in the pink, smooth features, the comfortable plumpness, and the expensive, understated clothes: single-breasted dark pinstripe suit, white shirt with discreet gold cufflinks, navy-blue polka-dot silk tie, and oyster-white raincoat which had fallen open to reveal a Burberry label.

'Okay,' said Mules. 'I'll play the game: who the fuck are you and what the fuck do you want?'

'Leo Strange is my name. I have a proposition for you, one I think you'll find attractive. It involves significant financial reward – and the opportunity to get even with Clyde Early.'

Brandon Mules was an ex-rugby player. In 1982, when he was twenty-three, he was being tipped for big things by a few pundits; unfortunately, the new Auckland coach wasn't one of them. At the start of that season, he'd taken Mules aside and given him a concise, scathing and perceptive evaluation of his ability and prospects. With that door slammed in his face, Mules had followed the lira trail to Italy, where New Zealand players were in hot demand and the game's amateurism regulations were paid the sort of nonchalant lip-service the French pay their marriage vows.

In September 1988, Mules was about to start his second season with a struggling small-town club located two hours' drive north of Venice. It usually took a club a couple of seasons to realise that he wasn't half as formidable as he looked. Then the new coach arrived. Within an hour of parking his brand-new BMW 325i outside the club's headquarters, Clyde Early had summoned Mules to his office and sacked him.

Mules said what about his contract? Early said he didn't give a rat's arse about contracts.

Mules spluttered: 'You haven't seen me play yet so how the hell can you sack me?'

'I saw you at home,' said Early dismissively. 'Once a sheila, always a sheila.'

Mules had tried going over Early's head to the club's director, a nephew of the tycoon who bankrolled the whole show. The director was an obliging young man; Mules expected he'd be easily bullied. But before Mules could build up a head of steam, the director made Latin gestures of the fatalistic variety and asked what could he do. His uncle had given Early a free hand. Mules demanded that his contract be paid out. The director opened a folder on his desk. It contained bills and expenses which Mules, without authorisation, had charged to the club: massive phone bills, petrol accounts, even bar and restaurant tabs.

The director went through the bills, digressing to compare notes on various restaurants before suggesting that, under the circumstances, perhaps they should just call it quits.

When Mules began to make vague threats, the director's habitual smile slowly shrank until it had disappeared altogether, like a ripple fading from the surface of a pond.

'You have a saying in English, no? When in Rome, you do like the Romans. This is Italy, my friend, but you are not Italian. You should think about that before you make trouble.'

Mules did think about it. He concluded that it could mean various things, ranging from being hassled by the tax people to starting his car one nippy morning and having his ballbag blown over the Dolomites. He decided not to rock the boat.

Mules had always claimed he'd up and left Italy simply because he'd had enough of the place, so he asked, 'Get even with Clyde Early? What the fuck for?'

The question seemed to surprise Strange. 'For dumping you from that club in Italy, of course.'

'What gave you that idea? I'd just had a gutful of the dagos.'

Strange placed both hands on the table. 'Mr Mules, we're wasting time. I do my homework: Early sacked you; he threw you out like last week's milk. Why pretend otherwise?'

Mules shrugged and finished his drink. 'It was ages ago; who gives a shit?'

'If you don't, I shouldn't have thought anyone would,' said Strange, whose unflappable, omniscient manner was getting on Mules' nerves. 'If you do, I'm offering you a chance to get your own back – and, as I say, earn good money while you're at it.'

'What sort of money are we talking about?'

'I'll pay you ten thousand dollars, half in advance, for an assignment which shouldn't take more than a couple of weeks and which you can do in your spare time. If it transpires that more time is needed, we'll come to an arrangement based on the initial fee.'

Mules grossed $3500 a month working night shifts as a security guard. He nodded warily. 'What do I have to do? Kill his wife and kids and the cocker spaniel?'

A pained expression appeared on Strange's face. 'Good Lord no, nothing of the sort.' He leaned forward, lowering his voice. 'I understand Mr Early's playing up – not seeing enough of his wife but seeing far too much of someone else's. I want you to find out if that's so and, if it is, to get proof of it.'

'How the hell would I do that?'

'I'll give you the woman's name. You're to observe her, record her meetings with Early and, if possible, photograph them together.'

'Why don't I just spy on Early?'

'He knows you, she doesn't; this way there's less risk of being spotted. Are you interested?'

'You got the money on you?'

'The advance? Yes, it's in here.' Strange patted a tan leather satchel beside his chair.

When Mules nodded agreement, Strange took a small leather-bound notebook and a fountain pen from inside his suit. He wrote in the notebook, tore off the page, and handed it to Mules. He'd written: MRS MAURICE TROUSDALE.

Mules shot him a sharp look. 'Trousdale's loaded, isn't he?'

'I'm led to believe he's worth in the order of $250 million.'

Mules slipped the piece of paper into his jacket pocket. 'There are a couple of things I'd like to know.'

Strange nodded. 'I assumed there would be.'

'If I get what you want, what are you going to do with it?'

Strange tapped a thumbnail against his teeth as he pretended to weigh up whether or not to answer the question. 'I suppose you're entitled to know. I'd simply point out to Mr Early that with something like that bubbling away in the background, it wouldn't be a good time for him to be in the spotlight – as he undoubtedly would be if he became the Auckland coach, for instance.'

Mules' mouth fell open. 'You mean you want to stop Early getting the coach's job? What the fucking hell for?'

Strange pursed his lips in an expression of polite regret. 'I'm afraid I'm not at liberty to reveal that. Suffice to say, Mr Early would like to become the Auckland coach; I'd prefer that he didn't.'

Mules sat back scratching his jaw, which was blue-black and looked as hard as a horseshoe; like a lot about him, it was a case of appearances being deceptive. He stared at Strange, who held his gaze until he became distracted by the thick black fuzz on the back of Mules' hand.

Eventually Mules said, 'Well, you've certainly come to the right bloke – I mean, you'd have to hunt high and low to find anyone who'd get more fun out of fucking things up for Early than me. But say what you like about the prick, he can coach; the other bloke belongs in a zoo. So I'm confused about a couple of things: the first is, why someone like you would go to all this trouble to help a suckback like Barney Tingle. The second is you, Mr Leo Strange – if that's who you really are. I bet you couldn't tell the difference between a rugby ball and King Kong's left testicle. So how about you tell me what's really going on here?'

Strange finished his drink. 'You can look me up in the Wellington phone book, under Strange and Associates. You know what and you know how much; that's all you need to know and it's certainly all I intend to tell you. So for the last time: do you want the job or not?'

'Shit yeah, I'll do it.'

Strange said, 'Good,' with a short, satisfied nod. He picked up his satchel. 'Shall we find ourselves somewhere a little more private?'

As Strange led the way downstairs, Mules asked, 'What do Strange and Associates do?'

Strange smiled primly over his shoulder. 'I suppose you could call me a facilitator; that's as good a description as any.'

FOUR

The phone call which changed Meredith Fife-Crossley's life came at 7.19 a.m. on Christmas Eve 1993, a Friday.

Fife-Crossley, who was known as Rusty because of her eye-catching red-brown hair, had been dreaming of the time she and her sister Milly had netted a small trout from a stream on Fife Station, the fifty-thousand-acre family property in McKenzie Country. They'd run all the way back to the house with it, uphill across three paddocks.

The housekeeper had cleaned the trout, fried it and served it with new potatoes no bigger than golf balls and runner beans. Their parents had gone to Geraldine for the day and, at the last moment, Milly had a flutter of remorse over the trout and opted for reheated shepherd's pie, so Meredith had it all to herself. Whenever she remembered that meal, she wondered why none of the trout she'd had since tasted half as good. She also wondered what had happened to Milly's conscience.

That was 1976, the year before Meredith went to boarding school and got her nickname. She was twelve years old and happier than she'd ever been since.

Fife-Crossley resented being jerked from that enormous sunlit kitchen, with its stone floor and mingled smells of roast meat and baked bread, back to her south-facing shoebox of a flat off Parnell Rise. She snatched up the bedside phone and complained about it.

The caller was Caspar Quedley, a public-relations hot-shot who'd once made a women's magazine's list of New Zealand's ten most eligible bachelors. Quedley liked to claim that he was the only heterosexual on the list, which wasn't quite true.

He and Fife-Crossley had been lovers for a time, a surprisingly long time given that both of them suffered from low boredom thresholds in their relationships. When the affair ended without emotional damage on either side, they'd pledged to remain friends. They'd managed to do so, despite their practice of spending the night together every now and again for old times' sake.

He asked, 'Are you alone?'

A good question. 'Hang on.'

She propped herself up on one elbow and took stock: the other half of the double bed was empty and bore no sign of recent occupation.

'It would appear so.'

'So where did you strike out last night?'

'The French Café. I went with a crowd. Actually, I did toy with the idea of dragging one home...'

'Don't tell me he baulked?'

'Well, things were going fine until he put tomato sauce on his confit duck leg. As you know, Caspar, I'm nothing if not broad-minded. I mean, I've done it with a Pakistani – granted, he went to Eton and Oxford and was an international cricketer; I've done it with a negro, a West Indian to be precise, who also played cricket...'

'I didn't know you had a thing about cricket players?'

'I'd admit to a slight weakness for cricketers although, paradoxically, only foreign ones.'

'And particularly those of the dusky, loose-limbed, hung-like-a-wildebeest persuasion?'

'That does seem to help. Now Caspar, much as I enjoy talking about big black dicks before breakfast, I'd appreciate you getting to the point. I was sound asleep when the phone rang, dreaming of better days.'

'Lydia Trousdale croaked last night; I just heard it on the radio.'

'How terribly sad. But seeing I've never met the woman, I fail to see why you had to wake me up to tell me.'

'With Lydia out of the way, her son and sole heir, Maurice, aka the Troll, is now up for grabs.'

'What are you talking about?'

'Come on, Rusty, get with it. The main reason Maurice has never married is that every girl he took home for the once-over got the thumbs-down from the old hag. Trousers, to his credit, always managed to foil her match-making with passive resistance. The point is, he's now free to marry whoever he likes – and if dribble is a reliable indicator, he likes you.'

'Caspar, that's a vile suggestion, even by your standards – Maurice Trousdale wouldn't win a beauty contest in a leper colony.'

'He wouldn't get past the first round but that's hardly the issue. How many lepers of your acquaintance are worth two hundred million bucks?'

Fife-Crossley rolled onto her back and stared thoughtfully at the ceiling. She'd never had much time for the school of thought which maintains that looks aren't everything, but hey, it was a woman's prerogative to change her mind.

Rusty's great-great-grandfather Jock Fife established one of the first of the great South Canterbury hill stations in the up-land valleys of the Two Thumbs Range, east of Lake Tekapo. His son transformed the stone cottage Jock built on the property into an impressive fifteen-room homestead. The house and station remained intact and in the Fife-Crossley family until late 1984 when Milly, who was three-and-a-half years older than her sister, came back from Europe with her fiancé.

Her husband, as he quickly became, was an English stockbroker. His family claimed lineage from George Villiers, a courtier noted for his dancing, to whom King James I, the Scottish homosexual, gave a dukedom for services to pillow-biting. Because Mrs Fife-Crossley was a snob and was bored with her high-country existence, she championed the son-in-law's suggestion that the family should sell up, invest the money on the buoyant stock exchange, and move to Christchurch to lead more interesting lives.

She got her way. Things went pretty much as the son-in-law had predicted until June 1987: Mr and Mrs Fife-Crossley and their younger daughter returned from a week's skiing at Mount Hutt to discover that Milly and her husband had liquidated the family's $2.5 million share portfolio, transferred the money to a bank account in the Cayman Islands, and caught a plane to Los

Angeles. Where they and the money went after that was anyone's guess.

There'd been only one confirmed sighting of them since: on television, in a close-up of the crowd at the 1989 Wimbledon Ladies' Final. After they'd watched the replay several times, the Fife-Crossleys agreed that at least some of the family fortune had gone on plastic surgery – rhinoplasty for her, a chin-tuck for him. Opinions differed on whether it was money well spent.

In 1992, a friend of Rusty's returned from the USA adamant that she'd seen the brother-in-law coming out of a Pizza Hut in Fort Lauderdale, Florida. The friend said he'd had a red bandana on his head and a diamond stud in his left ear and was chatting up a pair of schoolies in cut-off jeans and bikini tops. When she'd approached him, he'd hustled the girls into a Honda Prelude and driven off.

Rusty doubted it. The Lolita syndrome had the ring of truth and, at a pinch, she could believe the red bandana and the diamond stud. But the Japanese car was stretching things, and as for the idea of her brother-in-law going to Pizza Hut, that was too much to swallow.

The Fife-Crossleys were forced to sell their five-bedroom home in leafy Fendalton, with its grass tennis court and swimming pool, and move into a two-bedroom townhouse in scruffy Sydenham. Rusty was twenty-four and had never had a proper job. When she asked her mother what she should do, her mother looked at her a little sadly and said, 'My dear, why don't you do what girls like you have always done? Marry money.'

It took a while but she managed it. Eight months after Lydia Trousdale choked to death on a Spanish olive, her son Maurice married Meredith 'Rusty' Fife-Crossley on the manicured lawn of Greywater, the Trousdale family home perched on the cliff above Mission Bay.

After the ceremony, a couple of male guests took their flutes of Krug '83 down to the edge of the cliff to smoke cigarettes and enjoy the magnificent view of Rangitoto Island and the Hauraki Gulf before the light faded.

'You know,' said one, 'I really don't know whether to envy Maurice or feel sorry for him. He's got the best address in Auckland, he's worth a fortune, he's never had to do a stroke of work in his life, and he never will. On the other side of the coin, he's the ugliest white man in the eastern suburbs, he's got the personality of an ottoman, and now he's married to Rusty.'

'Yeah, I know what you mean,' said the other. 'Someone was just saying that Rusty wanted to invite every bloke she's ever shagged but they couldn't find a marquee big enough.'

At 10.45 on Sunday morning, 27 August, the electronically controlled gates of Greywater swung open and a British-racing-green Mercedes E220 cabriolet swept out. It was a perfect late-winter's day: still, bright, and warm enough to encourage people with cabriolets to put the tops down.

All Leo Strange had been able to tell Brandon Mules about Mrs Trousdale was that the lady was a youngish, attractive redhead with something of a reputation. He hadn't elaborated on that point, the implication being that women earn reputations for one thing and one thing only. Mules was parked thirty metres up the street from Greywater; when he saw that the driver of the Mercedes was a woman with auburn hair, he started his Ford Laser and followed her down to Mission Bay and into the waterfront car park.

The woman, whom Mules assumed, correctly, was Mrs Trousdale, crossed Tamaki Drive and sat down at a café's pavement table. Mules watched her from the car park for a couple of minutes, then followed suit. He sat behind her, at a table just inside the open double-doors, so he could study her at leisure while she'd have to twist around and look over her right shoulder to see him.

Lustrous chestnut hair fell to her shoulders; the fringe swooped over one eye and curled around her jawline. She had a sharp little nose faintly dusted with freckles, and a wide, well-defined, slightly pouting mouth accentuated by crimson lipstick. She was slim, neither short nor tall, and wore black leggings and a thick, loose-fitting cream turtle-neck sweater which reached the tops of her thighs. When she arched her back and stretched, Mules saw the tight swell of her breasts under the sweater.

As if she'd sensed that she was being watched, she took off her sunglasses, draped an arm over the back of her chair, and looked around. Her gaze swept the café, not pausing for an instant on Mules or the other customers. The way her green eyes slid indifferently over him convinced Mules, not that he needed much convincing, that he was dealing with a 24-carat, nose-in-the-air rich bitch.

He'd seen plenty like her during his stint in Italy, in the smart shops and cafés, promenading along the canals of Venice or in the squares of Treviso. He'd based many a lurid fantasy on the premise that, behind their disdainful exteriors, those elegant creatures were on the prowl for uncouth beefcake such as himself to satisfy their yen for rough trade. The fact that, in six years, not one of them so much as asked him for a light didn't deter Mules from similar thoughts vis-à-vis Mrs Trousdale.

She was checking her Patek Philippe watch yet again when her mobile phone rang. After a brief conversation which didn't seem to please her, she ordered a caffe latte. She took a cloth-bound book the size of a fat paperback from her handbag and began to write in it.

Once it had dawned on Mules that Mrs Trousdale was updating her diary, it didn't take him long to grasp the implications and work out his next move. Leo Strange's sources had been as reliable as ever: Mules wasn't as dim as he sometimes appeared.

Since the break-up of his second marriage, the editor Jackson Pike had lived alone in a rented townhouse in Grange Road, Mt Eden.

At getting on for eleven o'clock that Sunday night, Pike was about to switch off his word processor and treat himself to a nightcap and half an hour of *Madame Butterfly*, courtesy of Von Karajan, Pavarotti and the Vienna Philharmonic, when he heard a noise downstairs. Fearing that he might have inadvertently programmed the dishwasher to irrigate inner West Auckland, he hurried to investigate.

At the foot of the stairs, he was confronted by a figure in a ski mask and dark boilersuit who pointed a pistol at

his Adam's apple and said, 'Trick or treat?' Pike was
trying to think of a reply when a third party rabbit-
punched him behind the right ear and he fell over
unconscious.

For a few awful moments after he came to, Pike
thought he'd gone blind. He felt fabric against his face
and realised that he had a hood over his head. He also
had a gag in his mouth and his hands were tied behind
his back. All he could do was roll back and forward, and
even then only a little way because he was in some kind
of container.

After what seemed like an hour but was actually a
quarter of that, Pike heard car doors quietly open and
close and an engine start.

He was moving. He was in the boot of a car.

The car stopped. They hadn't gone far, ten kilometres,
if that. The boot was opened, he was hauled out and set
on his feet. Strong hands gripped him; a voice said,
'Walk.'

They went from road to shingle path to soft, uneven
ground, kicking up dead leaves and crunching twigs.
Pike's mind raced on the spot, spitting out panic, like a
news wire ten minutes after someone took a shot at the
President.

'Stop.' The hood came off.

*Trees. Not dense bush, more like woods. Silence, no
lights. Where the hell are we? The Waitakeres? Too far.
Two of them in ski masks and boilersuits. Holy Jesus
God, is that a silencer?*

The one with the pistol said, 'Shall we ungag him?
Why not? Al, see to it he doesn't make a fuss.'

Al came behind him. He slipped his left arm under Pike's and wrapped his hand around the back of his neck. He clamped his right hand over Pike's jaw, the thumb and fingers digging into his cheeks. Al's hands seemed inhumanly powerful, as if he could squeeze Pike's head until his eyes popped like champagne corks.

The gunman said, 'Let me introduce overselves: we represent the Aotearoa People's Army – you may have heard of us. We've had our eye on you for some time, Mr Pike, and I'm afraid that editorial was the last straw.'

'Christ, that wasn't meant to be taken literally,' gasped Pike, working his jaw laboriously in Al's iron grip.

'"A Modest Proposal?" Yes, I wondered if you were modelling yourself on Dean Swift. A little presumptuous of you, if I may say so.'

The shock lifted: Pike had a moment of terrible clarity. He went to scream.

Al felt Pike's chest heave as he filled his lungs.

Pike heard a sound like a thousand bullwhips cracking in unison and the bank of screens in his head went to black forever.

FIVE

Amanda Hayhoe left for work on a Monday morning feeling rested, clear-headed, and a little smug. She'd had a very quiet weekend.

When she spotted the envelope under her windscreen wiper, she thought about it for a few seconds, then went back to the house and got the rubber gloves from under the kitchen sink: Sadie the Cleaning Lady meets Nancy Drew, girl detective.

She took the envelope inside. It was plain white and unaddressed, like the one from the Aotearoa People's Army. She dithered over whether to open it or ring the police; eventually she reminded herself that she was a journalist, not a cop. Besides, for all she knew, it might be a marriage proposal from her near-neighbour, the Sultan of Brunei.

So she carefully slit the envelope open with a short-bladed knife and removed the note with her landlady's eyebrow tweezers. As she read it, her eyes widened and her left hand went slowly to her open mouth.

She rang Auckland Central and was put through to Detective Sergeant Ihaka.

'You thought of something?' His voice didn't throb with expectation.

'No, it's not that. I got another letter this morning.'

'From them?'

'Yes, from them.'

'You opened it.' It wasn't a question; a disapproving silence followed.

She gabbled into the vacuum: 'I was going to ring you first, then I thought, What if it's got nothing to do with the APA? I'd just've wasted your time. I was pretty careful – I used washing-up gloves and eyebrow tweezers so there shouldn't –'

'Ms Hayhoe.'

'Yes?'

'Who's this week's human sacrifice?'

'Jackson Pike.'

'Who's he?'

'The editor of *New Nation* magazine. He's probably the best-known print media journalist in the country.'

'Well, if he wasn't before, he sure as shit will be now,' said Ihaka with breezy callousness. 'What do they say?'

'I'll read it. It's headed Communiqué Number Two. "Last week, the Aotearoa People's Army carried out revolutionary punitive action against the reactionary broadcaster, Freckleton. We issued an unequivocal warning to the crypto-fascists in the government–big business axis and their media mouthpieces that we would undertake similar action against those who persist with extreme right-wing propaganda intended to mobilise reactionary elements.

' "In his magazine, J. Pike has been openly hostile towards progressive causes. In particular, he has promoted an imperialist and racist line on the struggle for Maori liberation, sovereignty, and the return of lands, forests and fisheries to their rightful owners and guardians.

' "In his most recent editorial, Pike signalled his intent to campaign for the reintroduction of the death penalty. While he purported to be concerned with violent crime, it is axiomatic that judicial execution is a weapon used by authoritarian regimes to eliminate so-called enemies of the state – i.e., radical oppositionist forces. Transparently, Pike aimed to fuel this campaign – and camouflage its true purpose – by whipping up hysteria over supposed lenient sentencing.

' "Accordingly, the Aotearoa People's Army, acting on behalf of the masses, has administered revolutionary justice. No-one should doubt our seriousness or our resolve to undertake similar action. Those who continue to ignore our warnings will have only themselves to blame for the consequences." That's it.'

'Same as last time – stuck under your windscreen wiper?'

'Yep. Same sort of stationery, same printing in capital letters.'

'They don't say what they've actually done with him?'

'No. So nothing's...happened?'

'There's no fresh meat in the morgue if that's what you're trying to say. Are you at home?'

'Yes.'

'Sit tight. I'll send someone to pick up the mail.'

About the time that Hayhoe was alerting the producer of the six o'clock news, Brandon Mules was getting Strange and Associates' phone number from directory service.

He rang it and got a recorded message: 'You have reached the Wellington office of Strange and Associates. All our staff are occupied at present so please leave a message after the beep. If you wish to send a fax, press Start after the beep.'

Mules waited a few minutes and tried again, with the same result. He rang every three or four minutes for half an hour but Leo Strange's brutally overworked staff didn't have time to answer the phone.

Mules left home. He stopped in at a post office to check Strange and Associates' address in a Wellington telephone directory. It didn't come as a big surprise that it was a post-office box number, nor that there wasn't a private listing for L. Strange.

He got back in his car and drove east to resume surveillance of Mrs Trousdale.

Mules guessed he was in for a day in the life of a lady of leisure: coffee and lunch with the big-hair, year-round-tan set, then hit the boutiques to try on more outfits than they've got in drag-queen heaven. And if Strange's dirt was on the money, somewhere along the line she might take time out for a bounce on the mattress trampoline with Clyde Early.

It wasn't quite like that.

It was mid-morning and raining hard when Mrs Trousdale steered the green Mercedes out of Greywater. She passed Mules' Laser without a sideways glance and followed the previous day's route down to Tamaki Drive. She went into a delicatessen then drove up St Heliers Road, through Tamaki and Panmure, and across the Panmure Bridge to Pakuranga Heights. She parked outside a centre for intellectually handicapped children and went in.

The rain eased and finally stopped; patches of blue sky appeared; a pale sun came out but Mrs Trousdale didn't. Mules read the paper, listened to the radio, smoked a couple of cigarettes.

At one o'clock, Mrs Trousdale and another woman came out hand-in-hand with two small children who were well wrapped up against the weather. They got into the Mercedes and went back across Panmure Bridge, through Ellerslie to Cornwall Park where they went for a walk, made friends with a few sheep, and had lunch on a park bench.

Fifty metres away, Mules cursed himself for not bringing something to eat. He tried to take his mind off food by working out the quartet's relationship: the kids belonged to the other woman but Christ knew where Coppertop fitted in – unless ferrying them around was her good deed for the month.

After an hour in the park, she returned them to the centre, then headed back over the bridge. This time, she turned left into Mt Wellington Road and got on the motorway. She came off at the Market Road exit and went down Remuera Road towards Newmarket. Okay, time to thrash the plastic. But at the top of the hill where Remuera Road descends to hit Broadway, she swung off the road and pulled up outside a church hall.

Mules snarled, 'What the fuck's she up to now?' and looked around for a park.

It took him twenty minutes to get one in sight of the Mercedes. He'd just switched off when Mrs Trousdale and an almost elderly woman came out of the church hall carrying covered trays. The Mercedes being a two-door, there was a bit of a performance over getting the trays onto the back seat. Then she jumped in and took off.

She went through Newmarket and up Khyber Pass to Newton, where she stopped outside a shabby old wooden bungalow. It might've fitted the first-home buyer's formula of the worst house in the neighbourhood's best street, but whoever dreamt that up probably didn't have Newton in mind.

Mules watched her take in a tray. *I don't believe this; first the mongols, now fucking meals-on-wheels. I thought she was meant to be the town bike, not Florence fucking Nightingale.*

She made drops at equally unsalubrious residences in Eden Terrace and Grafton before crossing back to the right side of the tracks for another call, in a quiet street overlooking Orakei Basin.

As she got out of the car, the rain fell like a silver curtain. She slung her handbag over her shoulder and reached into the car for an umbrella. She unfurled it but when she went to get a tray from the back seat, it all got too awkward. She put down the umbrella, tossed her handbag into the car, pulled out the tray, grabbed the brolly, kicked the door shut, and ran for it. Mules was idling back at the corner; when she disappeared up a long drive, he knew he'd never have a better chance.

The other visits had taken five to ten minutes. Shit, it'd be the highlight of a bedridden old fart's week; no way they'd let her dump the grub and fuck off without a bit of a yarn, even if she had left her car unlocked.

He cruised up alongside the Mercedes and double-parked. It took him seventy-five seconds to get out of his car and into hers, grab the diary from her handbag and a leftover sandwich from the brown paper bag on the passenger seat, get back in his car, and zoom.

Without checking the filling, he took a bite of the sandwich. He gagged: smoked salmon with alfalfa and cream cheese. No fucking wonder it was left over; even mongols wouldn't eat that shit.

He tossed it going down Greenlane Road and dropped in for a party pack at the KFC on the corner of Dominion and Balmoral.

Dudley Garlick, the Anglican Dean of Auckland, was forty-five when he first felt the dull ache of what turned out to be loneliness. Because it had never occured to him to consider any domestic arrangement other than self-contained bachelorhood, it took him a while to diagnose his condition. At first, he'd wondered if it foreshadowed a loss of faith.

Identifying the problem was one thing; solving it was another matter altogether. There were, for instance, several maiden ladies among his flock who appeared to nurse fond and, he suspected, maternal feelings towards him. For his part, he was surprisingly unintimidated at the thought of embarking on a relationship with a member of the fair sex after a twenty-year hiatus.

But after some careful thought, he decided that it wouldn't work. It wasn't that he recoiled from the intimacy of marriage. After all, if it actually got to the point of conjugals, it would more than likely transpire that in the kingdom of the blind, the one-eyed man – i.e. himself – was king. No, the sticking point was that while he accepted that marriage required some suppression of the idiosyncratic self in the interests of co-existence, he knew that he'd suited himself in too many respects for too long not to begrudge infringements on his autonomy.

So after a good deal of meditation, and having urged the Lord to throw in His two cents' worth, the Reverend Garlick decided to get a dog; a golden labrador, to be precise.

Martin – named after Martin Scorsese, whose film about the crucifixion had impressed Garlick – was a sweet-natured animal with a quite phenomenal appetite. The dog owners among his parishioners warned him that unless he rationed Martin's tucker with an iron hand and exercised him regularly, the pooch would bloat before his very eyes.

Garlick, himself capable of shifting industrial quantities of food and drink and no fan of activities requiring physical effort, took little notice. A fat, jolly dog for a fat, jolly man, was his attitude: he and Martin would exemplify the serenity conferred by a well-nourished, reflective existence.

So it came as a rude shock to the cleric when, a mere forty in doggy years and resembling a baby hippo in a fur coat, Martin simply lay down and died. After hoovering two kilos of gravy beef with his usual blinding speed and bestowing a final, loving look on his master, he'd flopped down in a patch of sunlight, never to stir again.

Garlick got another golden lab when he moved into the deanery. This time, he vowed to do it by the book. There would be no repeat of the indulgent regime which brought about poor Martin's premature demise.

Thus, every evening, whatever the weather, Emma – after Emma Peel, the character in 'The Avengers' played by Diana Rigg and the object of roughly 90 per cent of the carnal thoughts Garlick had permitted himself since taking holy orders (the other ten per cent being evenly shared among Mary Tyler Moore, anonymous lingerie models, and stilleto heels) – and the dean could be found taking their constitutional in Auckland Domain.

It was cold, with a moist, blustery wind, and the light was fading fast when they set off at five-fifteen that Monday evening. They entered the Domain off St Stephen's Avenue and marched up the rise to the War Memorial Museum. Coming down the slope towards Stanley Street, Emma, who was as wolfishly scrawny and tirelessly curious as Martin had been obese and complacent, began straining at the leash, tugging Garlick towards the woods on the lower, northern side of the Domain, below the road.

This was normal behaviour. On summer evenings, Garlick often took Emma into the woods, sometimes even let her off the leash so she could plunge madly into the undergrowth. *Not tonight, my girl; this isn't a night for the woods.* The rain was driving flat on the wind, spitting icily in under Garlick's umbrella; darkness was closing in. He had an overpowering urge to get back to the deanery, build a blazing fire, and get outside several brandies-and-soda.

But Emma was pulling like a mad thing. Faced with having his right shoulder wrenched from its socket, Garlick gave in. They crossed the road and followed a track in amongst the trees. The dean hauled grimly on the leash to prevent Emma forcing him to break into a gallop and muttered profanely as he skidded on wet leaves and planted his brogues in sucking mud.

Suddenly Emma surged forward, ripping the leash from his grasp, and bounded off the track into the light undergrowth. Garlick swore horribly and blundered in pursuit. It was mercifully short-lived: less than thirty metres off the track, Emma had found whatever it was that had provoked her mutiny and was giving it her full attention.

When Garlick reached the scene, she'd embarked on an exploratory chew of what proved to be the Timberland boat shoe on the dead Jackson Pike's left foot.

SIX

Same old scene, thought Tito Ihaka.

Blue lights flashing for no particular reason; traffic jam – cop cars, unmarked grunt machines, a dog-handler's van, the morgue-mobile; people standing around doing bugger-all except pulling a bit of overtime; radio babble sound-track.

They say the violent crime rate goes up with the mercury; there are even stats to prove it. A hot afternoon, a guy has five or six beers too many, gets one of those mean, thumping headaches, works himself up till any fucking thing's going to set him off – man, he's looking for it. So some guy he's never seen before walks into the bar and winks at his chick, maybe just gives her a little sideways smile. Whack! Stick a broken-off pool cue in his neck.

The night before, Sir Lancelot probably slapped her till her fillings rattled for changing channels on him.

They can say what they bloody well like but it doesn't get any worse than this: going out on a wet night, about seven degrees before the wind chill kicks in, to look into a dead man's face. Right on dinnertime, too.

He got out of the car, pulling on a hooded tracksuit top. A uniformed constable pointed the way with his torch beam.

Ihaka took the magazine with him, the one with the article under Jackson Pike's picture by-line that the Aotearoa People's Army had objected to. Not that he'd need it. He knew in his bones that the dead white male in the trees was Pike, just as he'd known the APA wasn't kidding the moment he'd set foot in Pike's place.

Nothing you could put your finger on: no kicked-in doors, no blood on the rug, no flesh in the waste disposal. Just something in the air he'd felt a hundred times, each time a little stronger than before: bad vibes, bad karma, bad medicine. Whatever you called it, it meant the same: someone's time had come early; someone's life just stalled on the tracks and the shit-train ran right over them.

Ihaka went along the path, towards the lights in the trees. He met Detective Constable Johan Van Roon coming the other way.

'Over there, Sarge.' Van Roon pointed right, into the undergrowth.

'What's the story?'

'The doc thinks it's a broken neck but wants to get him on the slab for a good look. The bloke who found him was walking his dog, so what with its scent and the rain, our dogs are running round in circles, disappearing up each other's arse.'

'Who found him?'

'A bloke called Dudley Garlick. I think we can rule him out – he's a priest.' Van Roon jerked his head. 'A big cheese at the cathedral over in St Stephen's Avenue. A couple of the crew are up there now.'

'Okay, let's have a gander.'

A couple of cops and a police pathologist were in a huddle no more than three metres from the dead man's feet. Dirty-joke guffaws floated: it didn't take long before you could look at a corpse and only see paperwork.

Flashback: his first, a hippie type in a dump over in New Lynn. The guy had gobbled bad acid and decided cutting his head off with a breadknife would be a trip. He'd got a fair way too, a lot further than you'd think. There was enough blood to float a rubber duck. A cop and a police photographer sat on the sofa, smoking cigarettes and arguing about the Moscow Olympics.

The cop, a sergeant, beckoned Ihaka. 'Hey, it's the big Maori boy. What do you reckon, fella? Keep politics out of sport, right?'

He noticed Ihaka changing colour and looking everywhere but at the mess on the floor. 'Yeah, didn't this deadshit do a number on himself? Jeez, we all cut ourselves shaving now and again but that's fucking ridiculous.'

Laugh? He nearly puked.

Ihaka said loudly, 'I hear there's been a murder round here – anyone seen the victim?'

The huddle broke up. Ihaka ignored the muttered greetings and squatted beside the dead man. It was Pike all right; his head lolled like a broken flower.

Ihaka headed back to his car thinking, *Fuck me, now they're killing each other over magazine articles.*

He segued to his 22-year-old niece. It wasn't that long ago she was as normal as a kid with a Meccano set on her teeth could be. She used to follow him around like a puppy: Uncle Tito was Superman with a suntan. Even after she turned pretty and got an attitude she wasn't a bad kid under the poses. Now she wore a hard face and raved about burning forests and blowing up dams and necklacing Uncle Toms.

The other night, he'd asked her if being a cop made him an Uncle Tom. Her voice said, *Not necessarily*, but her expression said, *What do you think?*

His sister shook her head, bewildered. Their mother said softly, 'Something bad's coming, Tito; I can feel it, like a storm out at sea.'

It's your lumbago, Ma.

A man answered the first time Brandon Mules rang Greywater. He asked for Bob and was told, a little huffily, that there was no Bob there and to kindly check the number.

He rang back a few minutes later. This time she answered – just 'hello', but it was enough. He'd heard her in the café and it wasn't a voice you forgot in a hurry: cool, confident, posh – yeah, and sexy.

'Mrs Trousdale, yes or no: are you alone?'

'I'm sorry, I...'

Stupid bitch. 'Is there anyone else there with you?'

'Well, yes.'

'Okay, this is a wrong number – I asked for Bob. I'll ring again in exactly five minutes – ten to eight, right? Get yourself next to a phone, somewhere private.'

Mules rang at ten to eight on the dot.

She picked up after one ring: 'Who is this?'

'Never mind that. Are you alone?'

'Yes, I'm upstairs but what…'

'Mrs Trousdale, are you missing something?'

'No. Should I be?'

'You checked your handbag since you did your bread-for-the-poor act this afternoon?'

'Would you mind telling me what this is about?'

'I wouldn't mind at all; in fact, I'd be bloody delighted. I've got your diary.'

'My diary?'

The penny hadn't dropped. *Get ready, baby; you're about to spoil your frillies.*

'Yeah, your diary. You know, that book you write it all down in, every little thing that happens? What Maurice got you for your birthday; how you just about broke your neck skiing; how one of your boyfriends porked you on an office desk while the blokes he was meant to be having a meeting with twiddled their thumbs next door. Ring a bell?'

Silence.

'You there, Mrs Trousdale?'

'Are you saying you've got my diary? My private diary?'

'Well shit, if this isn't private, I'd love to read one that was.'

'How did you get it?'

The indignation in her voice made Mules smile; he'd half-expected hysterics.

'What does it matter? The point is, I've got it. If you don't believe me, I'll read you some. Hang on, let me find a juicy bit. Here we go: Queen's Birthday – remember it?

Maurice was in Sydney; Clyde bullshitted his missus that he had a business appointment and scooted back to town, leaving her and the kids at Taupo. Jesus, don't tell me you've forgotten already? This should jog your memory. Quote: "Sometimes I amaze myself. For three weeks, I've hardly thought of anything else then, finally, we're in bed, Clyde's pounding away like a man possessed, and what am I thinking? M's coming home tomorrow and I mustn't forget to change the sheets! *Zut alors!* C went at it hammer and tongs – he's no maestro but a frisky lad and fit as a fiddle. To put it crudely, he fucked the daylights out of me." Unquote. Good old Clyde, eh? Wouldn't have thought he had it in him. Okay, what else have we got here? Oh yeah...' Mules sniggered nastily. 'The weekend of the 25th and 26th of February. Bugger me, you do get up to some far-out –'

'That's enough,' she said in a low, hard voice. 'I'm convinced.'

'Glad to hear it.'

'When can I expect it to be returned?'

Mules chuckled. 'Nice try, Mrs Trousdale; full credit for positive thinking. I can see why you'd want it back though – shit, this thing's worth its weight in gold.'

'Oh, I'm beginning to get the picture,' she said flatly. 'You want money – is that it?'

'Give the lady a stuffed toy.'

'How much?'

'Now that's the sort of attitude I like – no pissing around, just get straight to the point. Well, the way I look at it, your husband's worth two-hundred-and-fifty million bucks, so what's a lousy half a million more or less? That's just loose change.'

'You're a fool, whoever you are,' she said contemptuously. 'Who do you think my husband is – Scrooge McDuck? Do you think he rolls around in a pile of gold coins every morning? For a start, there's hardly any cash: it's all tied up in trusts and investments. Secondly, it's looked after by an army of accountants and lawyers who might just notice if I sold off half a million dollars worth of Fletcher's shares. And I somehow doubt they'd believe me if I said I'd spent it on having my colours done.'

Mules growled, 'Who the fuck are you calling a fool? It's your fucking diary, lady, your fucking problem. I couldn't give a shit if you have to sell your nice green convertible or the family hierlooms – or your arse, come to that. And while you're making up your mind, think about this: if you don't cough up, it won't be just you in the gun, it'll be your playmates as well. I bet you didn't tell them you were keeping a record.'

'I'll need time.'

'You've got to the end of the week. You'll be hearing from me.' He hung up.

Rusty Trousdale sat on the edge of the bed with her head in her hands. Hearing her husband coming up the stairs, she scuttled into her ensuite and closed the door behind her.

He called, 'Who was on the phone?'

'Vicky. I took her and the kids to Cornwall Park today. She just rang to say thanks.'

'Are you almost ready? I'm a touch peckish.'

There's a surprise. 'Just putting on my face – I'll be down in five.'

She sat in front of the mirror dabbing on make-up, her mind whirring. She had to consult someone who wouldn't be judgemental and who could give her sound advice. Luckily, she knew such a person: not only was Caspar Quedley unshockable, he also happened to be something of an authority on blackmail.

Detective Inspector Finbar McGrail looked up from the September issue of *New Nation* when Ihaka walked into his office. Although he'd been at work for thirteen hours, McGrail was his usual clean-cut, buttoned-down self: the subdued maroon tie was still tightly Windsor-knotted and his two-shaves-a-day complexion shone pinkly.

'Nice night for a murder, Sergeant,' he said in an Ulster brogue which the fifteen years and 20 000 kilometres separating him from Belfast hadn't modified. Ihaka had grown used to it, if not fond of it. 'You'd think the bugger didn't have a tongue,' was his widely quoted description of McGrail's accent.

'Yep, it's nights like this make it all worthwhile.' Ihaka nodded at the magazine. 'You reading Pike's article? Bloody good idea, I thought.'

McGrail massaged the dark rings under his eyes. 'The proposition has a certain appeal although I'm not sure Mr Pike was being altogether serious.'

'It's a piss-take, right?'

'Not a particularly subtle one either but it still seems to've gone over our terrorists' heads.' McGrail tapped a copy of the APA communiqué. 'I don't suppose that should surprise us: fanatics aren't renowned for their sense of humour.'

Look who's talking: Mr Fun himself.

'What can you report, Sergeant?'

'Not a lot, sir. Nothing so far from Pike's place: Forensic's still over there but it doesn't look promising. We know he was home last night – someone from his work rang him there around nine. The joint looks normal – no signs of forced entry or struggle. It's like he just up and left without turning off the computer, the lights or the central heating. I'd say the front door was unlocked and they just walked in. The bed's still made up so it probably happened between nine and, say, midnight. Zilch from the neighbours: nice quiet street, mainly families – Sunday night, they stay in and have an early one. We're still doorknocking but. Meanwhile, back at the Domain, the rain's made a nice fucking mess of things. What about the communiqué?'

McGrail's thin-lipped mouth turned down at the corners. 'Same story as last time – it's a cheap brand of stationery, there's a ton of it in circulation. Same writing; our resident expert seems to think this block-letter style isn't the writer's usual hand.' He shook his head dolefully. 'Experts – what would we do without them? No fingerprints, not even the TV woman's. Speaking of whom, is surveillance underway?'

Ihaka looked at his watch. 'Started an hour ago.'

McGrail put his hands behind his head and leaned back in the swivel chair, looking at the ceiling. It meant he was collecting his thoughts before delivering unwelcome news.

'I had a call from the commissioner a short while ago.' McGrail had a particularly arid tone he adopted when referring to his organisational superiors and intellectual inferiors. 'He'd had a call from the minister and was merely passing on the message. The gist of it was that we can't go on losing media identities like this. Apparently, Pike wasn't just another scribbler.'

'I'd say he was the best-known print journo in the country,' said Ihaka, as if he'd researched the matter thoroughly.

McGrail's eyebrows twitched with surprise. 'You're in good company, Sergeant: the minister – via the commissioner – said more or less the same. Anyway, the upshot is, Wellington's decided we need some help. They're sending us an expert.'

Ihaka groaned, 'Oh, shit no. Who?'

'An SIS man who specialises in counter-terrorism. I didn't bother to ask in which terrorist hotbeds he earned this reputation – the Commissioner doesn't care for what he calls negative nitpicking.'

'A counter-terrorism specialist, eh? You must've come across a few of them in Ireland?'

'You mean Ulster,' said McGrail firmly.

Ihaka was briefly tempted to be flippant but thought better of it. 'Sorry, Ulster.'

'Yes, I did.'

'What were they like?'

'They were...' McGrail hesitated, choosing his words.

'Cunts?' offered Ihaka helpfully.

McGrail nodded slowly. 'Yes, I suppose that's as good a term as any. And rather stupid ones at that.'

SEVEN

Maurice Trousdale's favourite things in life were French cuisine, Italian cuisine, South Australian red wine, his wife's smooth, responsive body, and his pearl-grey Bentley Mulsanne Turbo. In that order.

Most mornings, he took the Bentley for a spin. It was as good a way as any of filling in time between breakfast and lunch, after which his blood-alcohol count was usually too high for carefree motoring. And while experience had taught him that it was both pointless and dangerous to make assumptions about when he was likely to be granted access to his wife's body, she was seldom at her most playful – or most obliging – early in the day.

As soon as the Bentley glided out of Greywater that Tuesday morning, Rusty Trousdale set about contacting Caspar Quedley. That wasn't entirely straightforward since, to all intents and purposes, he'd disappeared off the face of the earth.

The decline and fall of Caspar Quedley was triggered by a story in the January 1994 issue of *New Nation* magazine. It revealed that as a pupil at Auckland's exclu-sive Prince Albert College, Quedley had blackmailed the school chaplain over his masochistic infatuation with a choirboy. A few weeks later, the chaplain drove his car into a brick wall. It also emerged that Quedley had unleashed a notorious standover man in an attempt to stop the reporter airing his dirty laundry.

Quedley had prospered and made himself influential in a shadowy, behind-the-scenes way by running what amounted to a political and corporate intelligence service, in tandem with his public relations consultancy. He had the ears and, frequently, the undivided attention of some of the most powerful people in the land through his judicious dissemination of the rumour, gossip and information he accumulated from his network of contacts spanning the business, political, and media worlds.

By close of business on the magazine's publication day, Quedley had taken calls from representatives of the prime minister, the leader of the opposition, and the heads of several major companies. The message from all of them was short and sour: henceforth, Quedley was as *non grata* as a *persona* could be.

By mid-January, as the nation drifted back to work after the Christmas break, the vultures were circling. With the media's habitual relish for kicking a man when he's down, a TV current-affairs program did a bludgeoning follow-up of the *New Nation* story. Cornered by a reporter and cameraman, a haunted-looking Quedley had expressed the hope that his clients would bear with him in this difficult time. They didn't.

By February, Quedley Communications (Counsel, Strategy, Crisis Management) had closed its doors. Quedley sold his Lexus and put his Mission Bay townhouse and Coromandel hideaway on the market. Then he simply disappeared.

In May, Rusty Fife-Crossley received a postcard. Quedley wrote: 'Greetings from beyond the pale. How goes the Troll hunt? Answer on a postcard to Private Bag, Rotorua. CQ.'

She wrote back to inform him of her betrothal and beg him to attend the wedding.

Six weeks later he replied thus:

Dear Rusty,

Congratulations. I hope it makes you very happy although I wouldn't put the house on it – not that I have one to put. If that strikes you as a bit rich after my Cupid act, what the hell? This is no time for you to start giving a toss what others think.

I won't be at the wedding. Much as I appreciate the invite, Trousers would find me as welcome as an outbreak of genital warts. Besides, I'm planning to lay low for a while; as Captain Oates said, I may be some time. If you want or need to get in touch, write care of my lawyer, Paddy Tickford, at Trubshaw Trimble.

Yours in disgrace,

Caspar

When Rusty returned from Mauritius, she wrote Quedley a chatty letter describing, in perhaps unnecessary detail, the wedding, the honeymoon, and her new life as Mrs Maurice Trousdale.

The reply, post-marked Tauranga, was snappy: 'It sounds divine but you left out the most interesting bit – how often does the little toad expect you to spread 'em?'

Somewhat miffed and mindful of her husband's fear and loathing of Quedley, she'd allowed the correspondence to lapse.

Rusty rang Trubshaw Trimble. She introduced herself to Tickford and explained that she needed to see Quedley.

The lawyer put her on hold. Two minutes later: 'Well, you are on the list, Mrs Trousdale – one of the select few – but could you tell me why you want to see Caspar? His instructions were quite clear – emergencies only.'

'I can't give you the details but trust me: it's an emergency.'

'For who?'

'For me.'

'Surely you've got others you could call upon?'

She took a deep breath. 'Mr Tickford, Caspar is the only person I know who just might be able to solve my problem; he's also the only person I'd even discuss it with.'

'Well, I wish you luck, Mrs Trousdale. But I think I should warn you: speaking as one who's had a bit to do with him since his fall from grace, I wouldn't want to be relying on him.'

'Why not?'

'Because I don't think my trials and tribulations concern him in the slightest – and right now, I'm probably the best friend he's got.'

Maybe so, but I bet he's never worn a pair of your undies to a meeting with Rupert Murdoch.

'I'll risk it,' she said. 'I've got nothing to lose.'

Tickford gave her the address. Quedley was in Cambridge; she could be there in a couple of hours. She didn't ring ahead in case he told her not to bother coming.

66

At twenty minutes past midday, Rusty pulled up behind a filthy Land Rover parked outside a white weatherboard cottage in a short street four blocks back from the main road through Cambridge. She imagined that in spring, with the sun shining, the flowers coming into bloom, and leaves on the trees, it could be a picture of small-town, slightly olde worlde charm. But at the fag-end of a wet winter, with a cold wind shaking skeletal branches, it felt more like the last, drab, sad stop on a terminal decline. She shivered and shrugged into her black leather coat, pulling the belt tight.

She walked up the crazy-pavement path to the front door and pressed the bell. A gaunt, shaggy refugee wearing a navy-blue fisherman's pullover and old corduroy pants opened the door. They examined one another for a few seconds.

Finally she said, 'I'm in deep shit, Caspar.'

Quedley looked into the middle distance. 'You're just in time for luncheon. It's *specialité de la maison* – baked beans on toast.'

Amanda Hayhoe sat at a table in the Red Dog café in Ponsonby Road spooning down caffe latte and reviewing the recent phone conversation with her producer.

The way he'd gone on about Pike's murder making it a whole new ballgame and what a nightmare unsolved crime gigs were, she'd got it into her head that he was going to can the story – or give it to someone else. 'The punters like happy endings, Amanda, they like things cut and dried. You could spend a month on this story and not know any more about the APA than we do now. Alternatively, the cops could have someone behind bars and we'd get sub judiced.'

Minor tantrum time: 'Phil, don't even think about taking me off it. I just can't believe you're getting cold feet over the biggest story –'

'Who said anything about taking you off it? I happen to have budgets and schedules to worry about and I just want to make sure we end up with something to show for this, all right? I want you to put together some stuff on Pike so if we come up light on the APA, we can re-angle it to Jackson Pike, Media Martyr.'

So now Hayhoe was waiting for Justin Hinshelwood, a *New Nation* staff writer she vaguely knew and was relying on to shed some light on the late, self-effacing Mr Pike.

Hinshelwood showed up. He was around thirty, tall and gangly with designer spectacles and dressed for the wilds of Ponsonby in a green anorak, plaid shirt over a grey t-shirt, jeans, and sturdy boots. After allowing a decent period for lamentations, Hayhoe asked him to fill her in on Pike.

'Pike was driven, workaholic.' Hinshelwood talked like he wrote. 'He didn't do small talk or socialise with the troops. He didn't confide – like, we only twigged that his marriage had folded because he started putting in even longer hours.'

Hayhoe sighed. 'What were his interests outside work?'

'You tell me. Far as we could see, there was no outside work. I know he was into classical music only because I bumped into him in Marbeck's one night. Come to think of it, his performance pretty well summed him up: I asked what he'd bought, and the way he carried on, you'd think I'd asked to see his will. The bottom line on Pike is this: knew how to get a magazine out but not someone you'd choose to be marooned on a desert island with.'

'He sounds a bit paranoid?'

Hinshelwood took the cue: 'Get this: he wouldn't use the hard disk on his office word processor. He worked on floppies and took them home because someone once tapped into his machine and went through his files.'

'What did they find?'

'Big brother was watching us – that's what they found. He kept tabs on everyone: how much time we took over a story, how much rewriting it needed, how many letters of praise or complaints it got.'

'So he was hands-on?'

'Yeah, but less so lately. He came back from holiday with the bit between his teeth about something and spent a lot of time on it. Typical Pike, he didn't tell anyone what it was.' Hinshelwood snapped his fingers. 'I'll tell you who you should talk to – if he's still alive: Garth Grimes. You know who I mean?'

Hayhoe lied, 'The name rings a bell.'

'He was sort of like Pike's mentor – they worked together on the old *Standard*. Pike went to see him every month, come hell or high water. Some people reckoned Pike hadn't had an original idea in his life: he got them all from Grimes. Our in-house joke was that the day Grimes died – he's about a hundred and ten – was the day to send out your CV because the mag would go straight down the tubes.'

'Did you believe that?'

Hinshelwood finally showed some emotion: shame flitted across his face. 'I guess all of us did at some stage – shit, you know what journos are like.'

Rusty Trousdale sipped her mug of supermarket-brand tea and assessed what ruin and neglect had done to the handsomest man she knew.

Quedley had aged ten years, gone from looking five years younger than he really was – early forties – to five years older. The hair had a lot to do with it. It had lost its dark gloss and the loose curls, now flecked with grey, fanned out in a disorderly tangle, like wild brambles. The beard, almost white at the chin and temples and bushy as a tramp's, wasn't a good look, while the loss of half a dozen kilos which hadn't been doing any harm gave him the bony, wasted appearance of the seriously decadent or seriously diseased. Eventually she realised who he reminded her of: one of those ageing rock stars, lined and leathery beneath their grizzled, lifeless mops, who criss-cross the globe on never-ending farewell tours.

After she'd reached this bleak conclusion, she asked, 'Why, Caspar?'

'Why what?'

Her gesture took in Cambridge, the beard, and the baked beans. 'Why any of it?'

Quedley shrugged indifferently. 'What did you expect me to do – run for parliament?'

'Well no, but I didn't expect you to stop shaving and become a recluse.'

'Nor did I.'

'What's that meant to mean?'

'I didn't plan it. The idea was to drop out of sight for a while, do penance, let the fuss die down, then slip back into town and start again. But...' he paused and looked at the ceiling 'I've found that self-denial can be addictive.' He smiled sardonically. 'Think of it as anorexia of the soul.'

She absorbed the explanation with a few confused blinks. 'Are you working?'

He shook his head. 'I'm officially unemployed. Every now and again I have to apply for a job – assistant store manager maybe, or some sort of clerk. I even get a haircut so I can't be accused of making myself unemployable. But they keep turning me down; apparently, I'm over-qualified.'

'You're on the dole?'

'Why shouldn't I be? I've paid enough sodding tax over the years.'

'I didn't mean it that way, you goose. How on earth do you manage?'

'It's not that hard,' he said mildly, 'once you've renounced your vices.'

'So if you've given up everything that's bad for you, what on earth do you do with yourself?'

'The trick is to have lots of sleep – leaves less time to fill. Then there are the chores: the cleaning, the washing, the supermarket. I read, I jog by the river, I potter around in the garden, I watch a fuck of a lot of TV. And I wait.'

'What for?'

Quedley smiled distantly. 'For Godot, for motivation, for something to turn up. And here you are.'

'It doesn't sound like a lot of fun, Caspar.' She couldn't keep the pity out of her voice.

He looked at her with a steady, incurious gaze. 'It keeps me out of trouble – I'm not the one who needs help.'

'Touché.'

'What's up, Rusty?'

She heaved a long, expressive sigh. 'I'm being black-mailed.'

'Sex, of course.'

'Of course. Someone got hold of my diary.'

He closed his eyes, pinched the bridge of his nose with his left thumb and index finger, and said slowly, 'You daft little bitch.'

She nodded glumly. 'I know. I should've given it up when I got married.'

'How far back does the fucker go?'

'Oh, he's only got this year's, thank God.'

'Been a big year, has it?'

'I haven't been that bad,' she said defensively.

'Pig's arse. How many?'

She lowered her eyes. 'Three – but nothing happened with one.'

Quedley's eyes opened wide.

'We shared a bed but when it came to lights, camera, action, the young lady got stage fright.'

'Well, shit, that doesn't count.'

'I'm not so sure about that.' She blushed slightly. 'The Dear Diary version wasn't entirely accurate.'

He shook his head in disbelief.

Rusty hung her head. 'I didn't say we did it; I just sort of left it up in the air.'

'It's all spilt milk anyway. What does he want?'

'A mere half a million – by the end of the week.'

Quedley whistled.

'Exactly. He seems to be under the impression I can dash off a cheque and no-one will notice.'

'Any idea who it is?'

She shook her head.

'Who knows you keep a diary?'

'No-one.'

'If the worst comes to the worst, what'll the Troll do?'

'If you mean my beloved husband, I'm pretty sure he'd send me packing.'

'Come on, Rusty, he knew the score. You can't tell me he didn't expect you to play up now and again?'

She grimaced. 'The trouble is, he did. Before the wedding, we had a full and frank discussion, all very grown-up. Maurice said he was prepared to turn a blind eye to the occasional fling as long as I was discreet, but if I made him a laughing-stock, it'd be lawyers at ten paces.'

'Hmmm. I suppose he locked you into a bomb-proof prenuptial agreement?'

She nodded. 'You could hardly blame him for that. On the subject of laughing-stocks, I should mention that for the last few weeks, Maurice has been telling the world that we're trying for a bambino.'

'Jesu,' said Quedley reverently. 'You don't do things by halves, do you?'

'Caspar, what the hell am I going to do?'

'Stall for time, that's what,' he said decisively. 'You told the guy there was a problem getting the money?'

'Yes. He said he couldn't give a shit, it was my problem.'

'Course he did, but the point is, he's more interested in getting his hands on some loot than in wrecking your life. As long as he thinks you're going to come up with the goods – and not necessarily the full whack either – he'll hold fire. So you've got to string it out: you tell him you can get the money but it's going to take time – weeks, if not months. He'll make all sorts of threats, but at the end of the day he'll go along with it. That'll give us time to work out what to do next.'

'I'll have to tell the others, won't I?'

'Some would argue that you owe it to them to warn them what's going on. More to the point, you need to find out if the leak came from them.'

She moaned, 'Oh God, Caspar, I don't think I can face them.'

Quedley stared at her, genuinely surprised. 'I assumed you wanted me to do it. Isn't that why you came down here?'

EIGHT

The last Justin Hinshelwood had heard, Garth Grimes was still in the land of the living – occupying a choice patch of it in fact, right on Takapuna beach.

Amanda Hayhoe checked the phone book: there was a listing for G. Grimes in Minnehaha Avenue, Takapuna. She rang the number and asked the woman who answered if she could speak to Mr Grimes.

'I'm afraid not. He's had a terrible shock and he's rather under the weather. Perhaps you could try again next week...' She broke off; Hayhoe heard her say, 'I don't know who it is, Dad.'

Grimes' daughter came back on the line. 'Who's calling please and what's it regarding?'

'It's Amanda Hayhoe from TVNZ. I was hoping Mr Grimes could help me with a story I'm doing.'

There was another pause. The daughter sounded piqued when she spoke again. 'Could you try again tomorrow morning, about eleven?'

'I'll do that,' said Hayhoe hurriedly. She thanked the woman and hung up.

Next morning, Grimes himself answered. His voice was rich and mellow, not the reedy old codger's crackle she'd expected.

'It's Amanda Hayhoe, Mr Grimes. I rang yesterday.'

'Yes, I vaguely remember yesterday. And what you do at TVNZ, my dear?'

'I'm a reporter on 'Sixty Minutes'. It's sort of magazine-style current affairs.'

'I must admit I haven't seen it. I watch very little television these days – too many buffoons for my liking. They're even doing the weather.'

'We call them personalities.'

'Do you indeed? Are you a personality, Amanda? Have you had your picture in a women's magazine cradling your mulatto love-child called, let's see, Tiffany – or perhaps Amber?'

Hayhoe let go a low, bubbling laugh. 'If I had a love-child, which I don't, I certainly wouldn't call her Tiffany or Amber. They're the sort of names strippers call themselves.'

'I'll have to take your word for that; it's some time since I was on first-name terms with a stripper. Now then, to what do I owe the pleasure?'

'I was wondering if I could come and talk to you...'

'Oh?' The velvety voice took on a thin, high note of surprise. 'Oh really? Well, in that case you'd better tell me about yourself. So far we've established what you won't be calling your love-child, which is interesting insofar as it goes. I seem to remember an English lady cricketer with a double-barrelled name, Heyhoe-something-or-other. You don't play cricket, do you?'

'No.'

'Glad to hear it. Dodgy lot, women cricketers.'

Hayhoe felt she was starting to get the hang of it. 'Mr Grimes, don't tell me you think all sportswomen are hairy-legged dykes?'

'Good heavens, no. As a matter of fact, the last time I achieved anything remotely resembling an erection was watching women's tennis on the television. An Argentinian lass caused the most excitement.'

Bloody hell. Hayhoe stammered, 'Gabriela Sabatini?' only just managing to get the ball back over the net.

'I believe it was. What a splendid creature. Reminded me of a senorita I shacked up with down in Vera Cruz just after the war – that's the Second World War in case you're wondering. From memory, her features were somewhat coarser than Miss Sabatini's; on the other hand, given the way she plays tennis, I suspect my little Mex was the more adventurous spirit. There we are. Let's press on: how old are you?'

'Twenty-eight.'

'Yes, I'd have put you around there on the basis of that knowing undertone in your laugh. Are you pretty?'

'Isn't that in the eye of the beholder?'

'Come now, Amanda, I want a dispassionate assessment. I'm a very old man and I long ago reached the stage of pleasing myself in all things. There was a time when I'd no more talk about erections over the phone to a young lady I hadn't met than wear yellow braces. Now, you're obviously very nice and lots of fun, but if you're not pretty, I'm afraid we'll have to confine our relationship to the telephone. No offence intended; it's just that…well, I think that when one reaches my age, one's entitled to a certain amount of arbitrariness.'

'Well, I'm certainly no stunner but I might just scrape in as pretty if the bar wasn't set too high. What else would you like to know?'

Grimes was suddenly all business. 'What do you want to see me about?'

'It's uh…Jackson Pike.'

Silence. When Grimes eventually spoke, there wasn't a trace of banter in his voice: 'First of all, you should know that I was immensely fond of Jackson. I'm prepared to talk to you because his contribution to journalism should be acknowledged and better I do that than some back-biting mediocrity who wished him ill every step of the way. But I will not be party to a hatchet job – is that clear?'

Hayhoe was a little taken aback. 'That's not what we've got in mind at all. In fact, the piece will probably focus more on this Aotearoa People's Army…' Her voice trailed off as it occured to her that she might be digging herself into a different hole.

'Well, let's see how it goes, shall we?' Grimes' voice warmed up again: 'I have a feeling we're going to get along very well.'

They arranged a time. Afterwards, Hayhoe reflected that it was a bit like her first real kiss: it took her by surprise, but once she'd got over that, she found herself quite looking forward to the next step.

Tito Ihaka would've disliked the counter-terrorism expert Wayne Cramp at first sight but he didn't see any point in waiting.

His version of the golden rule was that people were shitheads until proven otherwise – that went double for people who were going to tell him how to do his job – so it wasn't as if he needed a reason to dislike the bloke.

Cramp gave him one anyway; in fact, he gave him several.

They met early on Wednesday afternoon in Detective Inspector Finbar McGrail's office.

Cramp was late thirties, half a head taller than Ihaka and almost as heavily built. He had a round, fleshy face with a beard light enough to qualify as designer stubble. He was losing hair and tried to disguise it with the chrome-domes' tablecloth: growing his hair long on one side and draping it over the scalp. Ihaka suspected he used hairspray to keep it in place.

The hair was one reason. Ihaka enjoyed mocking the bald as much as anyone, but, when all was said and done, it was just another physical defect, like buck teeth or knobbly knees. Your genes dealt you a hand: some guys came up trumps in the hair department and some didn't. No big deal; no-one's perfect, right? But to pretend you weren't bald via a wig or a ridiculous hairstyle said something about the sort of person you were – something along the lines of 'Call me Fuckweed.'

The clothes were another, specifically the chunky gold cufflinks and the waistcoat with a silver back, like the underbelly of a dead fish. Ihaka reckoned anyone under fifty who wore cufflinks and a waistcoat when they didn't have to was a wanker, simple as that. It wasn't as bad as having a personalised number plate or wearing sunglasses inside or wearing a baseball cap backwards after your balls have dropped or putting some inane shit on your answer-phone – but it was pretty fucking close.

They shook hands. Cramp closed his grip a fraction early, catching Ihaka's fingers rather than the palm of his hand. He might've looked like a head waiter but he had a powerful grip. Ihaka couldn't return the pressure and had to stand there looking unconcerned while Cramp mashed his fingers.

That was the third.

McGrail said, 'Mr Cramp has a theory about the APA.'

Ihaka slumped into a chair. 'If it involves aliens, I've heard it.'

Cramp plonked a meaty buttock on the corner of McGrail's desk and set off in a deep, confident voice: 'I think the key is to focus on the political – as opposed to the criminal – nature of these killings. We should be asking: who has the motivation for terrorism? Who has the underground organisation and the hard core of fanatics you need to conduct a terrorist campaign? Who's indicated that they're prepared to resort to terrorism? You and I both know there's only one group out there who gets a tick on all three: the extreme Maori nationalists. Their objective – New Zealand under Maori rule – demands a strategy of what ideologues call the armed struggle, simply because it's not going to happen any other way.'

McGrail looked at Ihaka. 'Sergeant?'

'Well yeah, I guess they'd have to be on the list but why would they target the media? Christ, they love publicity; they depend on it. And how fucking underground can you be when you're on TV every week?' He pointed his chin at Cramp. 'I bet you blokes know where most of them are twenty-four hours a day.'

Cramp leaned forward, upping the intensity. 'What we're seeing here, Sergeant, is a textbook case of a transition from a political campaign to stir things up and put pressure on the government, to a terrorist campaign to sap the community's will. These transitions occur when extremists conclude that the political campaign either won't deliver the goods or will take too long about it. At that point, the hard men take over. They're not interested in winning hearts and minds; their strategy is to intimidate society into submission. For a while now, we've been predicting the emergence of a hard-line pro-violence faction among the Maori radicals, something like the Provisional IRA; I believe that's what we're seeing now. As for targeting the media, well, frankly, we don't think the media is the target. Our theory is that Freckleton and Pike were just practice runs. The real target is always the power structure: politicians, civil servants, businessmen, judges – and the security forces. That's us.'

Ihaka ended the silence which followed. 'Well, you know what they say: opinions are like arseholes; everybody's got one.'

Cramp stared at Ihaka, working his jaw. He turned to McGrail. 'Looks like I got here just in time, Inspector. I'll skip the rest of amateur hour if you don't mind. I haven't had lunch yet.'

Amateur hour? That made four.

He headed for the door. Ihaka said over his shoulder, 'Wayne, if you hit the canteen in that gear, the boys'll think you're going to do magic tricks.'

Cramp exited, shutting the door with a bang which drew an irritated, slow-motion blink from McGrail. He tidied some papers which had been disturbed by Cramp's rump. Without looking at Ihaka, he said, 'Pretty predictable so far, eh Sergeant?'

Clyde Early worked out of an office at the back of his Mr Fixit Hardware franchise in the Birkenhead shopping centre. He was set to call it a day when he remembered there was someone waiting to see him. The guy wouldn't tell his secretary what it was about, just that it had nothing to do with hardware or rugby.

That was three-quarters of an hour ago. Early got up from behind his desk and opened his office door. A man he didn't know sat in the small waiting area. The visitor glanced up from his paperback. He didn't seem impatient or expectant; just neutral.

Early said, 'You wanted to see me?'

The man nodded. 'If it's convenient. I won't keep you long.'

'Sure.' Early stepped back from the doorway. 'Come on in. Sorry to keep you waiting – it's been one of those days.'

'No problem.' The man closed a slim, dog-eared Penguin with an old-fashioned cover. 'I had my book.'

Early saw it was by Jean-Paul Sartre, whoever he was. He asked, 'Good read?' just for something to say.

The man frowned at the book, as if he were marshalling the strands of a powerful critique. 'No, it's a load of crap really.' He extended his right hand. 'Caspar Quedley.'

That morning, Quedley had spent an hour and $55 getting pruned by one of Parnell's trendier hairdressers.

He was wearing a navy-blue cashmere overcoat over a dark, roomy double-breasted suit, white Oxford-weave shirt, and blue silk tie. Early, who'd become moderately fashion-conscious during his time in Europe, guessed the suit was Ermenegildo Zegna.

With his slightly emaciated appearance and sober, expensive clothes, Quedley cut an elegant and, Early couldn't help thinking, faintly sinister figure. Early ushered him into his office, sat behind his desk, and waited for the pitch, which he expected to be smooth.

Quedley took his time. He sat down, had a cursory glance around the office, and a long, careful look at Early. He concluded that Early was probably smart, but not necessarily bright in the high-IQ sense, tougher and more worldly than his regular-guy looks would suggest, and as hungry as a barracuda.

Whatever his other attributes, Early wasn't overly patient. He made a show of looking at his watch. 'I don't mean to be rude but it's been a long day and I was looking forward to some time with the kids.'

Quedley smiled politely. 'Of course, I was forgetting you're a family man. I'll get straight to the point: I'm here as a go-between, on behalf of our mutual acquaintance, Mrs Rusty Trousdale.'

Early's eyes narrowed and he shifted on his seat. 'I know Mrs Trousdale,' he said guardedly, 'but what does she need you for? She could've just picked up the phone.'

Quedley had wondered how he'd feel once things got underway. He was a little surprised to find that he was enjoying himself. He brushed a speck of fluff off the arm of his overcoat and tried to look sombre. 'It's a bit embarrassing I'm afraid. Rusty just didn't feel up to it.'

He paused. Early leaned across his desk, eyes wide open. 'Up to what?'

Quedley shook his head ruefully. 'You'll have to bear with me, I'm out of practice. Up to telling you that she's being blackmailed over your relationship.'

Early was starting to look quite unfriendly. He leaned back in his chair and snapped, 'What fucking relationship?'

'Yep, that's the one.' Quedley permitted himself a lop-sided half-smile. 'You see, the bugger of it is, it doesn't matter a hell of a lot whether you two had a relationship or not. What matters is that Rusty said so in her diary – at some length. I'm talking dates, places, who did what to whom, how often, and from which direction. The blackmailer's got the diary.'

Early paled but maintained his cold stare. He said, 'And you're here to do what exactly?' coming down hard on the last two words.

'A couple of things: firstly, to warn you what's happening; secondly, to ask if it's possible that you let on about Rusty to anyone? Maybe without even being aware of it at the time?'

'What do you think?'

Quedley shrugged. 'Well, you'll appreciate I had to ask. Maybe the blackmailer got lucky but it doesn't look that way to me. He could've walked off with the contents of her handbag – a few hundred bucks, a chequebook, and a full set of credit cards. Instead, he just took the diary, which kind of suggests that's what he came for. Which in turn kind of suggests that he had a pretty good idea what was in it. Now you might be an exception, Mr Early, but in my experience, a secret is something you tell one other person.'

Early shook his head emphatically. 'Absolutely no way. So what now?'

Quedley shrugged again. 'I'll see what the others have to say.'

'Which others?'

'Rusty's other partners in sin.'

'Jesus Christ, how many of them are there?'

'Two.' Quedley paused before adding blandly, 'I'm sure you were her favourite though.'

NINE

At eight o'clock the next morning, Thursday, Rusty Trousdale left her husband to his breakfast – grapefruit juice, fresh mango, scrambled eggs with smoked salmon, chocolate brioche, two double espressos – and went upstairs. She locked herself in her bathroom, ran the bath, and used her mobile phone to ring the motel where Caspar Quedley was staying. She was anxious to know how he'd fared with Clyde Early.

So-so, was the answer. 'He didn't shoot the messenger but the thought might've crossed his mind. He says he hasn't told anyone.'

'Damn. Not to mention fuck. One down, two to go.'

'Not necessarily.'

'*Excuse moi?* Don't you believe him?'

'I don't know him. Would he own up if he'd blabbed? You tell me.'

'Under the circumstances, I'd bloody well hope so.'

'Ask him yourself – you'll be hearing from him before long.'

An hour and twenty minutes later, in fact.

Rusty went into damage control: 'God, Clyde, I'm absolutely mortified about this. I know I should've come myself but –'

'Forget it,' said Early impatiently. 'Where'd you find that guy anyway?'

'Caspar? He's an old buddy. He used to be quite a mover and shaker around town – knew everybody who's anybody – until he came a cropper. He's had some first-hand experience of blackmail.'

'Oh yeah? From which side of the fence?'

Rusty tittered. *Aren't we perceptive today?*

'So how the hell are you going to handle it?'

'Basically, stall for as long as possible. He wants a ridiculous amount of money. I tried to tell him I can't just dip into the Trousdale fortune, not that it cut any ice. I'll just keep putting him off and hope that he gets fed up and goes away – and in the meantime, try to find out who he is.'

Early was disbelieving. 'That's the plan?'

'Clyde, if you have a better one, feel free to let me in on it.'

'Well, Christ, what if it doesn't work? What if he won't go away?'

'Then I suppose the choices are: call his bluff; offer him whatever I can scrape together; confess all to Maurice and throw myself on his mercy; or go to the police. Or some combination of the above.'

'Shit.'

'Tell me about it.'

'You've got no idea who it is?'

'Not the foggiest,' she said flatly. 'Actually, something did occur to me as I tossed and turned last night: it almost sounded as if he knew you.'

'Why, what'd he say?'

'Well, he read a bit out of the diary – you and I sharing a tender moment. Naturally, you get a glowing mention, and he said something like he didn't think you had it in you.'

'That doesn't mean a thing – he's probably seen me on TV or something.'

'Maybe. It was the way he said it though.'

'If you think about it, it's a damn sight more likely he knows you – I mean, how else would he've known about the frigging diary?' Early's voice subsided to an accusatory monotone: 'Quedley said there were others.'

'Did he now?' she said coolly. 'That was thoughtful of him. Let me put your ego at rest: they both pre-date you and with one of them, nothing even happened.'

Early sniffed as if he found that hard to believe. He said, 'Keep me posted, eh?' and hung up.

Miss you too, darling.

She'd just put the phone down when it rang again. The blackmailer said, 'You got the money yet?'

'It's not the end of the week.'

'What's a day or two between friends? Well, have you?'

'No, and I won't be getting it in a hurry either. Remember, I warned you it wouldn't be easy? Well, it's proving even harder than I thought. I'll need a lot more time.'

'Don't give me this shit – I told you: how you get it's your problem –'

'Look, I'm just explaining the situation: it's going to take weeks to get that sort of –'

Mules grated: 'You've got a week, you hear me? That's it: no excuses, no extensions. Either I get the dough next Thursday or the party's over, lady.'

It was true, to the extent such claims ever are, that Caspar Quedley knew everybody who was anybody. Obviously, he knew some a lot better than others.

Serge Le Droff, who qualified as a somebody because he displayed most of the symptoms of serious wealth, was one of the others. Quedley had met him once, at a cocktail party a few years ago. All he remembered was that Le Droff wasn't fazed by all the attention paid to his companion, a languid New Caledonian beauty who didn't look away when Quedley made eye contact.

When Le Droff's name appeared in the press, which wasn't often, it was usually with a tag to the effect of 'publicity-shy millionaire'. He ran a package-holiday company from the ground floor of a downtown high-rise and lived in the penthouse apartment, twenty floors up.

Quedley parked in the Customs Street car park and walked around the block to Quay Street. He went into the Eurotours sales office where one of the counter staff directed him to the corporate office on the nineteenth floor.

The lift opened onto a reception area dominated by a monolithic marble-topped desk. To the left of it was a badge-operated security door; to the right, a couple of plush sofas and a low coffee table overlooked by a huge picture from the chimp with spray-can school of painting.

The receptionist's smile dimmed when Quedley said he'd like to see Le Droff. She asked, 'Do you have an appointment?' knowing the answer. He told her he was representing Mrs Maurice Trousdale on a personal matter.

The receptionist told him to take a seat. She picked up the phone and murmured into it. Ten minutes went by. The phone rang; she listened for a few seconds then escorted Quedley through the security door into an unoccupied meeting room with a view of the harbour and North Shore. He was staring out the window without seeing very much when someone joined him.

It wasn't Le Droff, nor the blow-dried personal assistant Quedley had half-expected. It was an erect, vigorous-looking, broad-shouldered man of fifty-odd. He had thick wavy silver hair swept back from a low forehead, a ruddy complexion, flat, peaked ears, cobalt-blue eyes, eyebrows which curled upwards like budding horns, and a toilet-brush moustache several shades darker than his hair. His wide mouth was curved in a permanent half-smile and the whole face seemed to come to a point in a sharp, upturned nose above protruding front teeth.

There was so much happening on the man's face that it took Quedley a few moments to see the big picture.

Fuckfire, it's Rin Tin Tin in a three-piece suit.

'Now then, old chap, what can we do you for?' He might've looked like a German shepherd but the accent was upper-crust English.

'You're not Serge Le Droff.' Quedley tried not to make it sound too much like criticism.

'Well done. Close observation leading to a sound conclusion.' Rin Tin Tin pulled a chair out from the small table and sat down, crossing his legs. His shoes were black leather, size thirteen or fourteen, polished to a sheen, and ideal for kicking to death anything smaller than a Shetland pony. 'Take a pew.'

Quedley did as he was told. The man took a card from his breast pocket and dropped it on the table. It identified him as Colonel Wyatt Bloodsaw, head of security for the Le Droff Group of Companies.

'Colonel – what of?'

Bloodsaw barked, 'Thirteenth Parachute Regiment, British Army,' as if he was giving his name, rank and serial number. 'Packed in soldiering years ago but it seems to carry some weight in my lark.'

Quedley raised his eyebrows. 'This might be a silly question but why does Le Droff need a head of security? I thought he was a travel agent.'

'He'd be frightfully chuffed to hear himself described that way,' replied Bloodsaw cheerfully. 'In point of fact, LDG's a varied and far-flung empire; take it from me, old son, I earn my modest keep.' He strummed his bristly moustache. 'One of my tasks is running the rule over bods we don't know who come calling for reasons we don't understand.'

'We being…?'

Bloodsaw bared his teeth in a ferocious grimace which Quedley took, from the look in his eyes, to be a grin. 'We being we.'

Quedley nodded. 'Can I take it I won't be granted an audience with the bwana?'

'Affirmative.'

'It's personal. Extremely personal in fact.'

Bloodsaw's blue eyes twinkled merrily.

Quedley shrugged. 'Okay. I'm here on behalf of Mrs Maurice Trousdale. A few days ago, her diary was stolen. It contained references of a, let's say, intimate nature, to Le Droff. Whoever's got the diary is trying to blackmail her and she's concerned that Le Droff might get dragged into it. She wanted to warn him; she'd also like to know if he's discussed their relationship with a third party.'

Bloodsaw dropped his chin and studied Quedley from beneath his devilish eyebrows. 'Delicate situation, what?'

'Very.'

'So you've popped in to alert the boss that his name could be...bandied around?'

Quedley nodded.

'Well, that's damned decent of you, old boy, but I doubt the boss'll lose much sleep over it. You see, he's what used to be called a bachelor gay: footloose and fancy-free, no strings attached. Chaps like that are bound to roger other chaps' wives every now and again – law of averages, what? Get my drift?'

Quedley smiled. 'He must be popular at the tennis club.'

Bloodsaw snorted explosively. 'Not one for clubs, the boss; not one for giving much of a fig what people think either.'

'Lucky him. What about whether he told anyone?'

'Stand easy. We'll sort that out, toot sweet.'

Bloodsaw grabbed the phone on the desk and jabbed buttons: 'Bloodsaw...I'm downstairs with brother Quedley...apparently the lady kept a diary which has fallen into hostile hands...hmmm, dispatched him to sound the alarm.' He released an abrupt, jarring laugh. 'I told him that, almost those precise words...he wants to know if you told anyone...what? What?...Oh, I say.' Bloodsaw laughed again and slam-dunked the handset.

'The boss says one thing a gentleman never, ever does is kiss and tell.'

'Is that right? Some would say another thing a gentleman should never do is someone else's wife.'

Bloodsaw let fly with another machine-gun laugh. 'Shrewd thrust, old boy, shrewd thrust. However, in these matters one must draw a distinction between your bachelor gay, who occasionally happens to find himself at close quarters with a married lady, and your cad, who goes out of his way to seduce same.'

He sprang to his feet, signalling that the discussion was over.

'Did he have anything else to say?' asked Quedley.

'He was vaguely curious to know how many other chaps you're calling on.'

'Someone else asked me that,' said Quedley pleasantly, 'but he wouldn't pretend to be a gentleman.'

Chas Gundry MP was proud of the fact that he'd topped the parliamentary press gallery's Arsehole Index three years in a row.

But then perversity was Gundry's trademark. Nothing illustrated that better than his oft-quoted pronouncement that his American pit bull terrier, Sam, had been the major influence on his personal and political creed. Sam had lived to a good age despite the efforts of Gundry's neighbours, local council officials, and the postal service to have him destroyed in the interests of public safety. When Sam finally passed away, he was replaced in Gundry's affections by the pick of the last litter he'd sired: a chip off the old block which the MP, to the amusement of no-one but himself, named Son of Sam.

Gundry was an ex-used-car salesman and repo man who'd been swept into parliament in the National Party's 1990 landslide. But with the first mixed-member proportional representation election approaching, and facing formidable obstacles in the form of disadvantageous boundary changes and party chiefs who couldn't wait to see the back of him, Gundry had decided to set up his own party.

The Queen and Country Party had two basic aims. The first was to ensure that the British monarch remained New Zealand's head of state. While Gundry sincerely believed that an English grandmother with an unfortunate taste in hats was all that stood between New Zealand and anarchy, the stance was also based on the hard-headed political calculation that a combination of diehard monarchists, recent British immigrants, and morons who ticked the wrong box would lift Queen and Country above the five per cent of the vote threshold which guaranteed parliamentary representation. That would enable the party to achieve its other, undeclared aim: to prolong Gundry's political career until he was eligible for an MP's pension.

The trouble was, other MPs were adopting similar strategies and the populist right was becoming a crowded corner of the political landscape. Gundry believed it was time for him to take ownership, as the fancypants consultants liked to say, of another emotive, gut-level issue.

He found it that Thursday at the Wellington Club. Over lunch, an SIS officer gave him a deep background briefing on the Aotearoa People's Army. By the time the port and cheese arrived, it had all fallen into place. Later that afternoon, on the floor of the house, Gundry indulged in some forthright speculation about the APA's membership and motives.

His speech would've rung a few bells with Detective Inspector Finbar McGrail and Detective Sergeant Tito Ihaka since it stuck closely to the line pushed by Wayne Cramp. This wasn't a coincidence: Gundry's briefing had come from Cramp's immediate superior, who'd decided it was time to take the initiative in the shadow war against the enemy within.

Late that afternoon, Gundry flew to Auckland to deliver a speech to an anti-republic meeting and spend the weekend in his electorate. At the airport he bumped into another MP, who suggested, without seeming too concerned about it, that Gundry's speech might have whistled him straight to the top of the APA's hit-list.

'Do I look worried?' Gundry jerked a thumb at a tall, athletic-looking young man who stood nearby, scrutinising passers-by through narrowed eyes. 'See that bloke? One of the top men from the Protective Services Unit. And he's just the back-up – if those cunts come after me, I'll send him round with a hose and bucket to clean up after Son of Sam's finished with them.'

TEN

At 4.57 that afternoon, twenty-seven minutes late, Amanda Hayhoe knocked on the door of Garth Grimes' slightly shabby weatherboard bungalow perched on a little crag above Takapuna beach.

The woman who opened the door was well into middle age. Going by her serviceable hairstyle, sensible clothes, and general air of flustered irritation, she believed in acting her age.

She gave Hayhoe a dubious once-over. 'You're the reporter, are you?'

'Yes.'

'I was beginning to think you weren't coming.'

'Sorry I'm late – there was an accident on the bridge.'

It obviously wasn't the first time the woman had heard the harbour bridge blamed. 'People never seem to allow enough time for the bridge,' she sniffed. 'Not that it matters; I decided not to wake Dad until you'd arrived.'

She led Hayhoe into a living room lit by pale late-afternoon sun streaming in through sliding glass doors.

'Before I get Dad up, can I ask you please not to get him excited?' Grimes' daughter wrung her hands anxiously, a gesture at odds with her head-librarian demeanour. 'He's almost ninety-five, you know; he mightn't show it – he's very good at that – but I can assure you, Jackson's death knocked him for six.'

Hayhoe was out on the wooden deck admiring the view and wondering if there was some kind of inverse relationship between the father's defiance of the ageing process and the daughter's surrender to it when the glass doors slid open. Garth Grimes shuffled out to the deck, supporting himself on a walking stick and his daughter's shoulder.

Grimes mightn't have acted his age but he certainly looked it. He was stooped and shrunken; a few strands of fine white hair swayed above a nut-brown scalp and his spectacularly mottled face hung in folds like a blood-hound's. Behind half-moon spectacles, dark eyes glistened in yellowing eyeballs, like black olives floating in melted butter. They were the eyes of a man who'd seen everything there is to see and been shocked by too little of it.

He had on pleated grey flannel trousers with cuffs, brown leather brogues, and a green checked woollen jacket over a washed-out heavy cotton shirt which was done up to the throat. The buttons for the button-down collar were missing and the collars curled like dead leaves.

Hayhoe suspected that every visible item of Grimes' attire was as old as she was and would support the argument that, in the long run, it pays to buy quality.

Grimes let go of his daughter's shoulder to extend a dessicated, almost transparent hand. 'Amanda, my dear,' he purred, 'welcome. What a pleasure, all the more so for being unexpected.'

Grimes insisted they sit outside. He reclined on a padded deck chair; Hayhoe sat at the outdoor table. He introduced his daughter, then politely but firmly dismissed her. She hovered, reluctant to depart.

'Now off you go, Veronica,' he said. 'That husband of yours will be home shortly and you know how he performs when he feels you're dancing attendance on me at his expense. I'm sure Amanda can look after me.'

The daughter left. Grimes confided: 'Don't be alarmed, my dear – you won't have to undress me or lower me onto the potty. I can fend for myself passably well but I don't like to rub it in. Veronica and her booby of a husband have coveted this site for years and I suspect they regard it as monstrously inconsiderate of me to continue to dodge the Grim Reaper. I keep telling them I'm ready when he is but they don't believe me.' He paused to examine her. 'You're a most attractive young woman – why on earth were you coy about it?'

She shrugged, forcing a weak smile.

Grimes tapped the deck with his stick. 'I wouldn't care to be classified as one of those insufferable old bores who forever offer unwanted advice but let me just say this: journalism is no trade for the modest; if you undersell yourself, you'll be overtaken by those whose sole ability is self-promotion. What line is your young man in? Something more lucrative than journalism, I trust?'

Hayhoe changed position on the wooden bench. 'I'm unattached at the moment; have been for a couple of years, actually.'

Grimes' sparse eyebrows jumped. 'A couple of years? Great Scott, you must've been gallivanting like Lillie Langtry to need a break of that duration.'

'Nothing of the sort,' she said indignantly. 'I just had a...messy experience.'

'No self-respecting journalist should be deflected by enigmatic responses. Please explain.'

Hayhoe sighed. 'If I do, can we talk about Jackson Pike?'

Grimes lit a cigarette. 'Perhaps,' he said airily. 'Before you embark on your lurid narrative, why don't you mix us a gin and tonic?'

Hayhoe made the drinks and took them outside.

She made a half-hearted plea: 'Look, there's nothing special about it – in fact, just the opposite. I bet you've heard it a hundred times before.'

Grimes, whose collapsed face now shone with curiosity or perhaps even excitement, was implacable. 'I've heard everything a hundred times before.'

She took a deep breath. 'I was a late starter in journalism: I used to work for an investment bank in Wellington. To cut a long story short, I ended up getting involved with one of the directors.'

'Ended up getting involved?' Grimes feigned uncertainty. 'I'm not sure exactly what that means. Can you be more precise?'

Hayhoe made a face at him. 'You can needle me as much as you like, Mr Grimes, but I'm not going into the sordid details. I wasn't some naive little convent girl in a tartan skirt with buckles on her shoes, if that's what you think I was implying.'

'No, I can't quite see you in that light.' Grimes looked pleased with himself.

Dirty old goat.

'He was twelve years older than me and married with a couple of kids. He told me he'd leave his wife and I sort of believed him. At the time, I think he sort of believed it himself.'

She asked herself why she was telling her only deep, dark secret to a grubby-minded museum piece she'd known for all of half an hour. *Not even Mum knows this stuff.*

'One night he went home, packed a suitcase, and told his wife he was leaving. As I heard it later, she didn't bat an eyelid; just said if that's what he wanted, fine, but could he collect little Johnny from his tennis lesson first? When he got back with the kid, both sets of parents were there waiting for him. They talked him out of it; I don't think it took them that long. Next day, he stayed at home and his wife came into the office to ask the MD if it was now company policy to hire home-wrecking sluts. His answer was to give me fifteen minutes to clear my desk and vacate the premises. The end.'

Grimes went, 'Hmmm. And now you've decided you can't be trusted around men?'

Hayhoe couldn't help laughing. 'I prefer to think of it as being choosy.'

'Well, bear in mind what they say about falling off a horse. You subbed that story with a heavy hand, my dear; one day, when we've got to know one another better, you must tell me the unadulterated version.' He heaved himself to his feet. 'It's getting a little chilly for these old bones – let's go in.'

They went inside. She made him another gin and tonic. He took two greedy mouthfuls, lit a cigarette, leaned back on the sofa, closed his eyes, and spoke fluently and fondly for twenty minutes about his late protégé, Jackson Pike.

She asked, 'When did you last speak to him?'

'A month or so ago. He rang up in a foul mood to say he couldn't come over for lunch because they'd had a break-in at the office.'

'What was stolen?'

'Next to nothing, which is why I didn't take it too seriously. Jackson was riled because the intruders had fiddled around with the computers; I made a flippant comment on a Luddite theme which, understandably, he didn't find vastly amusing. It wasn't a long conversation.'

'So you actually hadn't seen him for a while?'

'No. Jackson had a couple of months in Europe this winter – his first proper holiday for Lord knows how long. The last time I saw him would've been early May, just before he went'.

'A guy on the magazine told me he came back from holiday hyped up about something. Would you know what it was?'

'No. The only mention of his trip was to thank me for suggesting a visit to D'Arcy Potterton; he said it was well worthwhile.' Grimes' eyes lit up. 'Now there's an idea – I'll tell you my Potterton story.'

'Is that the writer who died not long ago?'

'By sad coincidence, yes. He wouldn't mean much to your generation but twenty-five years ago, Potterton was the young literary lion. He took himself off to France in a fit of pique, supposedly to live among more civilised folk. I suggested that since Jackson would be in the vicinity, he should drop in on him. I did in '79 and no-one had talked to him since. Jackson was lukewarm so I told him about my visit. Now then, let's have dinner and I'll tell you.'

Hayhoe protested, in vain. It was all there, ready to go, courtesy of Veronica: just a matter of setting the table, dishing up, and pulling the cork out of a bottle of wine – French, he thought, under the circumstances.

They sat at a little table in front of the sliding glass door. Over Veronica's carbonnade of beef accompanied by a green salad, Côtes du Rhone, and the whisper of high tide thirty metres below, Grimes told his story about the dead writer, D'Arcy Potterton.

'I lived abroad for over thirty years,' he began, 'all over the place, so I was never much of a one for junkets. Then in '79, on the brink of retirement, the French tourism people invited me on a gastronomic mini-tour. Well, even the most jaded old hack – which I was – wouldn't knock that back. Someone at the paper suggested tracking Potterton down. It was a few years since he'd brought out that God-awful book portraying us as a nation of fascist yokels and it seemed worth finding out if he still felt that way. I tottered round to his publisher and wheedled Potterton's address and phone number out of him.

'I gave him a ring from Bordeaux. He was wary at first but came around. I think what swayed him was discovering how old I was – people have this extraordinary notion that old age confers benevolence. Anyway, I got the go-ahead and drove down – he lived just outside a village called Levignac, about half an hour from Toulouse. I wasn't expecting the red-carpet treatment so I had lunch on the way and got there mid-afternoon.

'I must say, he'd set himself up rather nicely: in a grey stone villa on a hilltop, looking down a little valley with woods on one side and meadows on the other and a stream winding along the valley floor. Behind the house was a large lawn with flowerbeds and lots of fruit trees – mainly cherry, I seem to remember. He even had a couple of fields with a few cattle and some fat geese which the old boy next door looked after for him. It was springtime and we sat out in the garden drinking pastis; I couldn't help thinking that perhaps he'd had the right idea after all.

'He was forty-odd, not a bad-looking fellow; too much hair, as they all had in those days. He was perfectly civil, gave me a quick tour, and then, as I say, we sat outside with our pastis and our Gitanes. Now here was the funny thing: as soon as he decently could, he began pumping me for news from home. What was the state of play in politics? What was the gossip in the book world? Then he got on his high horse and raged about Piggy Muldoon, how he was leading the country to rack and ruin and if he got half a chance, he'd stand intellectuals and trade unionists up against the wall. On and on in this vein – he was a tremendous lefty of course – until I got bored and told him he was talking through his hat.

'Things rather petered out after that. He suddenly announced he had work to do and he'd see me to my car. We walked to the front of the house in strained silence just as a little Renault came up the drive. A most attractive woman got out, whom Potterton introduced as Madame Dubois, a neighbour. I said hello and goodbye, she gave me a haughty nod, and I went on my way rejoicing.'

Grimes broke off to make a mini-assault on his meal. Then he pushed his plate aside, refilled his glass, and continued. 'I drove away thinking three things. The first was that, despite what he'd said in his book, Potterton hadn't cut his emotional ties with New Zealand; the second was that the people in my daughter's French textbooks were always called Dubois; and third, it was a bit odd that he'd addressed his neighbour in English.

'By now it was getting on for six o'clock. I'd had a couple of pastis on top of several glasses of wine at lunch and wasn't up to driving back to Bordeaux so I went down to the village and checked into a little inn. I had a nap and got up about ten with a fair appetite. It was a Monday night and *le patron* was about to close the restaurant but after some argy-bargy and the inevitable bribe, he agreed to cook something for me. He perked up when I ordered the best bottle on the wine list and invited him to join me and we got talking – by that stage I was starting to get the lingo back. Naturally, he wanted to know what had brought me to Levignac and I told him about Potterton.

' "*Ah, l'écrivain*," he exclaimed. "*Il mange souvent ici. Un moment, un moment*," and he scuttled off and rummaged behind the bar. He came back with a Polaroid of a group dining in the restaurant – you know the sort of thing: everyone toasting the camera and grinning like apes. There was friend Potterton and next to him the Dubois woman. I pointed to her and said, "*Madame Dubois, n'est-ce pas? J'ai rencontré cette dame cet après-midi chez Monsieur Potterton*." You understand?'

'You said you'd met her that afternoon at Potterton's place?'

'Not just a pretty face, eh?' mocked Grimes. 'Well, *le patron* waggled his head most vigorously at this. "*Ah non, monsieur, pas Madame Dubois; c'est Madame Potterton, la femme de monsieur l'écrivain.*"

'There'd been no mention of a wife in the files so I asked him if Madame P was a local lass. There was much semaphore and expostulating and, "*Pas du tout monsieur, Madame est Nouvelle Zélandaise; elle est venue ici avec son mari il y a quatre ans.*" So Potterton's wife was a Kiwi and had been there with him all along. By now, the Frog was in full flow, jabbering away about what a romantic couple they were, so in love, always holding hands and whispering sweet nothings. I, meanwhile, was wondering why the blazes Potterton had fibbed about it – clearly with her approval.'

Grimes glanced at Hayhoe: she was perched on the edge of her chair, eyes wide, nibbling her lower lip. He smiled a private smile.

'I told *le patron* I'd be off first thing in the morning and fixed up the bill. I got up at five; there wasn't a soul about. On the way out, I slipped into the restaurant and commandeered the Polaroid. When I got back here, I dropped in on the publisher to report how it had gone. I casually produced the Polaroid and pointed to the mystery woman. "She's rather nice," I said. "Do you happen to know who she is?"'

'"That's Belinda," he said, "D'Arcy's sister. Last I heard she was living in London. I'm glad to see they're getting on so well these days; they used to be very offhand with one another."'

Hayhoe stared at Grimes. He leaned back in his chair as if exhausted but lights danced in his black eyes.

She said slowly, 'Spell it out for me, Mr Grimes.'

Grimes' loose mouth twisted sardonically. 'Well, it would appear that Potterton didn't go into self-imposed exile because his towering genius wasn't sufficiently appreciated or because he feared the fascists would bump him off come the putsch. He cleared off to the other side of the world so he could peg sister Belinda to his heart's content.'

ELEVEN

When the cops at Auckland Central had covered sport, sex, and whichever aspect of the job was particularly shitting them off that day, they sometimes got on to the relationship between Detective Inspector Finbar McGrail and Detective Sergeant Tito Ihaka.

They were an odd couple, just about any way you looked at it.

McGrail was built like a bullfighter, Ihaka like a bull; McGrail ran marathons, Ihaka had been known to drive to his letterbox; McGrail was pernickety, Ihaka was a slob's slob; McGrail didn't drink, Ihaka could put away a six-pack waiting for a home-delivered pizza; McGrail played chess, Ihaka played poker; McGrail was religious, Ihaka was profane. In a nutshell, McGrail took life very seriously while Ihaka didn't give a rat's arse.

Even so, it hadn't proved all that easy to come up with a nickname which did justice to their double act. 'Laurel and Hardy' was too predictable; 'Abbott and Costello' didn't stick because hardly anyone knew who the fuck Abbott and Costello were; 'Holmes and Watson' was too highbrow, and 'The Captain and Tenille' was rejected as too dangerous after Ihaka made a reasonably serious attempt to run over the guy who'd thought of it. In the end, they'd gone for 'Jake and the Fat Man', even though the nitpickers argued that, in the TV show, the Fat Man was the boss.

The big question was: what did they really think of each other? There were guys who 'knew for a fact' that, deep-down, they hated each other's guts and guys who claimed the opposite. A story did the rounds that McGrail only put up with Ihaka because the Fat Man 'had' something on him. Oh yeah? said the sceptics; what, did he forget to wash his hands after a crap?

Occasionally, there was talk of blow-ups and falling-outs. Like now: those in the know reckoned McGrail had a shitload riding on the APA investigation and was already taking political heat over Ihaka's bolshie attitude towards Wayne Cramp, the SIS man.

Ihaka had heard the rumours so he wasn't too thrilled when, on his way out that night, he poked his head into McGrail's office and found him in conference with Cramp.

McGrail waved him in. 'We were discussing this after-noon's events in parliament. Chas Gundry had quite a lot to say about the investigation – much along the lines of Mr Cramp's theory.'

Ihaka leaned against the wall. 'Gundry, eh?' He looked at Cramp, deadpan. 'Great minds think alike.'

McGrail took the cue before Cramp could think of a comeback: 'That's being too kind to Gundry. I can't imagine him working it out all by himself. I suspect someone's been putting ideas in his head. You wouldn't have a theory on who that might be, Mr Cramp?'

Cramp did his best to look surprised. 'It hadn't occured to me, Inspector.' Pause. 'Oh, I get it – you think we primed him?'

McGrail smiled thinly. 'Well, I must admit, I did wonder. Then I asked myself, why on earth would the SIS think it was a good idea? I suppose a bureaucrat with an agenda might want to get it on to the front page but for those of us at the sharp end, it'll just make an already difficult job even harder.'

Cramp, defensively: 'Why's that?'

'In Belfast I saw what happens when murder investigations become political footballs.' McGrail's voice took on a harder edge. 'I can do without rent-a-mob camped outside and civil liberties nuisances bleating every time we interview someone with a brown face. I can certainly do without blowhards in parliament muddying the waters and badgering the minister for information I'd prefer to keep under wraps. If you do come across anyone who might've put ideas in Gundry's head, perhaps you'd be good enough to pass the message on.'

McGrail and Cramp locked eyes for a few seconds. The SIS man shrugged nonchalantly and glanced away.

McGrail opened a manila folder. 'We've had an update on Pike's autopsy report: in layman's terms, his neck was snapped like kindling. The perpetrator is either very strong or knows some nasty tricks.'

'Gang members, maybe?' said Cramp. 'Some of them would qualify on both counts and we know the radicals have been recruiting in the gangs.'

'Gang guys don't dick around like this,' said Ihaka with weary irritation. 'This sort of tricky shit isn't their style.'

Cramp said, 'We obviously move in different circles, Sergeant. I wouldn't have thought there was anything very tricky about shoving people off high buildings or breaking their necks. Anyway, I'm not suggesting this is a gang operation, just that they could be being used as muscle. We're more interested in some of the activists who went to Libya a few years ago, courtesy of Colonel Gaddafi. You're probably not aware of this but the Libyans have these training camps out in the desert – they're finishing schools for international terrorists.'

'I thought those guys went to Libya for some bullshit anti-imperialism conference,' said Ihaka.

Cramp smiled, shaking his head as if bemused by Ihaka's naiveté. 'Sergeant, attending conferences is standard cover for indoctrination and training trips to places like Libya and Cuba, like it used to be for going behind the Iron Curtain. Just for a change, why don't you tell us what you think instead of trying to pick holes in everything I say?'

'I don't have a theory,' said Ihaka slowly, 'because there's not enough to hang one on. But my gut instinct tells me this isn't a Maori thing.'

Cramp laid on the sarcasm: 'Oh, so it's your gut telling you, is it? Well, you'll have to make allowances for me: I was trained to use my brain.'

'I wouldn't take the Sergeant's gut too lightly, if I were you,' murmured McGrail. 'It's got rather a good track record.'

The 'Repulse the Republic' meeting began at eight o'clock sharp that night in the distinctly unimperial surroundings of the Mt Roskill War Memorial Hall in May Road.

Chas Gundry MP had an audience of thirty-three, twenty-seven of whom were old enough to vote; they included his bodyguard and a reporter from a Jesus 'n' muzak radio station.

Gundry delivered his usual rant, portraying life in the average republic as a maelstrom of revolving-door governments, corruption, hyper-inflation, and uncollected rubbish. He closed with the quip that, under a republic, they'd probably still have a queen as head of state. Not many in the audience got it.

Afterwards, he had a cup of tea and a Girl Guide biscuit and worked the room. He was quickly cornered by four recent arrivals from Britain who whined at him in bewildering accents until his head started to pound. It wasn't until after nine-thirty that he managed to lie his way out of the hall. It had been a long, stressful day; now it was time to relax and unwind.

Gundry and his bodyguard ate in an Italian restaurant in Dominion Road. Sergeant Kerry Keene, known as Kay, was a shy, strapping 29-year-old who'd been seconded to the VIP Protective Services Unit from the Christchurch police.

As they waited for the bill, Gundry studied Keene carefully. 'You married, Kay?'

'No sir.'

'Me neither, thank Christ. Tried it once; never again. You got a girlfriend?'

'Yeah.' Keene sighed. 'Trouble is, she's in Christchurch – I only get to see her once a month.'

'Son, in that case, you owe it to yourself to get out and about, have a bit of fun. You'll go blind otherwise.'

The policeman's habitual frown deepened. 'What've you got in mind, sir?'

'There's this place, sort of members only – you can't get in unless they know you. But once you're in,' Gundry whistled and winked, 'it's on for young and old, if you know what I mean.'

Keene's eyebrows collided on the bridge of his nose. 'Sir, are you talking about a brothel?'

Gundry sat up, scraping his chair loudly. He glanced around the restaurant, then hunched forward, elbows on the table. 'Jesus, Kay, keep it down, if you don't mind. And give me some credit: I'm an MP, you're a cop – I'd hardly be suggesting we bowl into the nearest knock-shop, would I? This joint's a completely different kettle of fish – it's what you'd call an exclusive private club. The bloke who put me on to it's got a knighthood, that's how classy it is.'

'It sounds interesting, Mr Gundry, but I don't think so. My job is to keep an eye on you, not have a good time.'

Gundry smirked. 'You can forget about keeping an eye on me, pal – I know some blokes don't mind an audience but it puts me right off my stroke.'

Keene went slightly pink and looked away.

'You're absolutely sure now? It'd be my shout – well, in a manner of speaking. Shit, every public servant deserves at least one root on the taxpayer.'

Keene declined, reflecting that when he'd volunteered for a stint in the VIP Protective Services Unit, he'd expected to be putting his body on the line for a nobler cause than the preservation of Chas Gundry.

They left the restaurant. Gundry drove round the back of Mt Eden Prison, through Newmarket, out towards Parnell. He turned right off St Stephens Avenue into Brighton Road. Halfway down the hill into Hobson Bay, he stopped outside a low-rise apartment block.

'This is it: last chance, son – you coming in?'

'I'll pass, thanks all the same.'

Gundry shrugged. 'Suit yourself. Listen, no harm in being discreet: I've got personalised number plates so why don't you park round the corner, in that side street?' He looked at his watch; it was 10.57. 'I'll be an hour or so.'

At fifteen minutes past midnight, Gundry exited the apartment block. He strolled down Brighton Road and rounded the corner. A dulling but not unpleasant weight of fatigue settled on him: he'd had two large vodkas-and-tonic, a bubble bath, a cursory and unremedial massage, and the most elaborate handjob of his extensive experience.

His Holden Commodore with the number plate PIT BULL and the reassuringly solid figure behind the steering wheel was parked twenty-five metres up the street. The MP gave a snappy American-style salute which was acknowledged with a circumspect wave.

Gundry felt an urgent need to urinate. He looked up and down the street: there was no-one around and only a couple of chinks of light peeped through drawn curtains. He turned his back to the car and flopped it.

As a teenager, Gundry had been known as 'Power-hose' because he could piss over the goalposts' crossbar. His favourite trick was to go into the school toilets with a couple of cronies and deposit a golden shower on the unfortunate youth snoozing, dumping or jerking off behind the cubicle door. He could still achieve impressive muzzle velocity, especially with a full bladder. Between his urine drumming on the footpath and his *sotto voce* rendition of 'There Is A Rose In Spanish Harlem', he didn't hear the man creep up behind him and prod something cold and hard into the nape of his neck.

Not that he knew it was a man until a quiet male voice said, 'Finish your piddle, shake your slug three times, put it away, put your hands up, and turn around slowly.'

When he turned around, he saw that the man was wearing a dark boilersuit and ski mask and the cold, hard thing was a silencer screwed onto a semi-automatic pistol.

The man tapped the silencer against Gundry's front teeth. 'The party's at your place, right Chas?'

Caught literally and figuratively with his fly open, Gundry was slow to grasp the implications of being in a deserted side street after midnight with a pistol poked in his face. It was only when a second man in a ski mask and dark boilersuit got out of his Commodore that the full horror of his predicament struck him: he was in deep shit, deep enough to drown in.

The accomplice disappeared into the night. The gunman told Gundry to get in behind the wheel and slid into the back seat.

With as much bravado as he could muster, Gundry demanded: 'Who the hell are you?'

'You can call me Betty.'

Betty? What the shit? 'Are you in the APA?'

'Anything's possible.'

'Where's Kay?'

'Would Kay be the minder?'

'Yeah, what...'

'In that case, he's in the boot.'

'Jesus, what did you do to him?'

'Not much. A bodyguard called Kay? Still, who am I to talk?'

Gundry twisted around to ask Betty exactly what he wanted. Before he'd got very far, Betty jabbed him stiffly on the nose with the silencer and snapped, 'Shut up and drive. We're going to your place.'

'I've had a few drinks,' said Gundry shakily. 'I'd be over the limit.'

'Don't worry your little head about it – if we see a cop, I'll blow you away before he can breathalyse you.'

Gundry started the car. He went down Gladstone Road, left into Quay Street, and through downtown, past the wharves. The city had pretty well closed up for the night. He kept fifteen kilometres under the limit until Betty rapped him on the ear with the gun and told him to speed up.

Going along Fanshawe Street towards the harbour bridge, Gundry noticed the van in his rear-vision mirror. It followed them over the bridge and along the northern motorway to the Tristram Avenue exit. It was about there it finally dawned on Gundry that he had Betty's offsider on his tail, not the Seventh Cavalry. From the motorway exit to the turn-off from the Albany Highway into Upper Harbour Drive, they passed two cars: one had no headlights and the other was having trouble straddling the white line.

Eighteen months previously, Gundry had reluctantly come to accept that a headline such as 'MP's Pit Bull Gnaws Triplets' could do terminal damage to his career. The solution was to decamp from suburban Glenfield and relocate to a brand-new kit home on a large, fenced-off block in semi-rural Greenhithe. His nearest neighbours were forty metres away in one direction, twice that in the other.

They got there. Betty told him to put the car in the garage. Gundry used the remote control to raise the door and drove in. It was a two-car garage with direct access to the house. As they got out of the car, the van pulled in and parked beside the Commodore.

Betty closed the garage. He walked over to the door into the house and rattled the handle. From inside came a long, vibrating rumble, like distant thunder.

'My, he sounds nasty,' said Betty. 'What's his name?'

Gundry had been counting on an unsuspecting Betty opening the door and getting torpedoed in the groin by a 25-kilogram ball of muscle with a bite like a bear trap, propelled by the mindless fury of a blood-crazed hammerhead. He hung his head, silently cursing himself for ever having bragged to the media about his pit bulls.

'I asked you a question.'

'Son of Sam,' mumbled Gundry.

'Cute. Al, would you get the minder out of the boot?'

Al hauled out Keene who was hooded with his hands taped together behind his back.

Betty asked, 'How mean is Son of Sam?'

Gundry shrugged.

'Put it this way: does he attack intruders on sight?'

'It depends,' lied Gundry. 'If he felt threatened, he might.'

Betty told Keene, 'Whatever you do, Kay, don't threaten the wee fellow.'

Gundry babbled, 'Jesus wept, what are you going to do?'

'I'm not very good with dogs,' said Betty silkily. 'Maybe they sense that I'm nervous – that's how it works, isn't it? We'll send Kay in first, to make friends with him.'

'Fucking hell, man, you can't do that, not with his hands...'

Al shut him up with a backhander across the mouth. As Gundry reeled, Keene pivoted on his left leg and karate-kicked Betty hard in the stomach; he doubled up, making a puking noise. Keene kicked out again, clipping his shoulder. Al picked up Gundry and heaved him at Keene as he launched another kick. They crashed together. Gundry bounced off, scrabbling at the garage door to stay upright; Keene lost his balance and went over. He thrashed blindly on the floor until Al subdued him with a boot in the head.

They dragged Keene to the door. Betty opened it just wide enough for Al to shove the policeman through, then yanked it shut.

There was another throbbing growl which swelled and sharpened into a blood-curdling snarl.

Keene's kung-fu hadn't disturbed Betty's urbane cool. 'They don't call them man's best friend for nothing.'

Thumps and bumps; Son of Sam's wild snarl rose and fell like the angry whine of a chainsaw. Eventually, it faded to a low hum.

Gundry swayed like a drunk, hands pressed to his face. Betty chided, 'Didn't you teach him it's rude to speak with his mouth full?'

Quiet inside. Betty told Gundry, 'Okay, your turn.'

Gundry was weeping; his voice trembled. 'You fucking evil cunt.'

Betty protested, 'He's not my dog. Now get in there and see if he wants dessert.'

Full of dread, Gundry pushed the door open. Son of Sam, his brindle face smeared with blood, quivered a moment, then relaxed. Keene lay awkwardly on his side, his head turned away. The hood was half torn off and blood bubbled from his throat. Ripped flesh gaped behind a shredded trouser leg.

Gundry dropped to his knees. Son of Sam padded forward to lick his master's tear-streaked face. When Al stepped through the door, the dog looked up at him. His lashless, almond eyes were placid and incurious, as if mauling Keene had drained his berserk energy.

Very slowly, Al extended his arm, aiming the stainless steel Smith & Wesson 10-mm semi-automatic which Keene hadn't had time to draw from his shoulder holster when they'd got the jump on him in the Parnell side street.

Popular usage notwithstanding, people – or, for that matter, dogs – seldom have their heads blown off by a single gunshot. In Son of Sam's case, what was left on his powerful shoulders when the smoke cleared was so inconsequential that only a pedant would have quibbled with the expression.

When Son of Sam's head exploded ten centimetres from his right ear, Gundry uttered a demented screech and rolled into a foetal position, eyes screwed shut and hands clamped over his ears.

He opened his eyes to find Betty kneeling beside him. 'Come on, Mr Queen and Country; time to go to work.'

Gundry's mouth moved but no sounds emerged.

'We're going to have a *hangi*.'

Gundry still mouthed silently.

'You know what a *hangi* is, don't you? I thought you had them all the time.'

That got a dazed nod.

'Guess what we're going to cook?'

The MP whimpered.

'You.'

TWELVE

Leo Strange, the facilitator, was early for his meeting with Brandon Mules.

Strange made a habit of being early. It was part and parcel of his policy of doing things at his own pace, which was nice and easy. He'd worked out long ago that, since getting from A to B rarely went exactly according to plan, life was a choice between a stroll and a scuttle, between having to fill in time and having to hurry, between boredom or stress. Being temperamentally suited to hanging around and physically unsuited to hurrying, Strange always allowed more than enough time to get from A to B.

Besides, being early had its rewards. It was amazing the scraps of information you could pick up lurking around a reception area, by cocking an ear to the receptionist's phone conversations perhaps, or by taking your time over signing in and having a quick flick through the visitors' book, or by noticing where the couriers were coming from and going to. Spend fifteen or twenty minutes in a company's reception area with your eyes and ears open and you could glean information about its operations that its competitors would pay good money for. And often did.

And when meetings were on neutral ground, the early bird could get a feel for the lie of the land and nab the best position. That might be the spot with the best view of proceedings or the one nearest the exit.

They were just little things but Strange had built a career on little things: pile up enough little things and they make a big thing. A little thing could also give you the edge and in the grey areas where Strange worked, it was all about having the edge.

Thus Strange arrived in the upstairs bar of The Globe at 1.50 p.m. for his two o'clock progress review meeting with Mules. He had on a single-breasted navy-blue wool suit with a white shirt and striped club tie and carried the tan leather satchel in his right hand and the oyster-white Burberry draped over his left arm. He bought a Campari and soda and sat with his back to the wall at the far corner table, where he could see everyone in the bar.

When he was satisfied that no-one in the bar was sufficiently sober, alert or curious to take any notice of him and Mules, Strange got out his airmail copy of *The Spectator* and began to read. At 2.15, he put down the magazine and checked his watch; looking a little vexed, he got another Campari and soda and went back to his seat and his magazine.

At 2.32, Mules walked into the bar. Ignoring the barman's offer of service, he sauntered over to the corner table and looked down on Strange from his almost-two-metres with a lazy and not especially respectful grin. Strange glanced up from his magazine just long enough to suggest he get himself a drink, then carried on reading.

Mules pulled out a chair and sat down. 'No double Jack today, Leo?'

Strange glanced up again, this time with a brief, patronising half-smile; the intentional rudeness was completely wasted on Mules. After he'd read for another minute or so, Strange put away the magazine and fixed Mules with a cold look. 'You're on the payroll now, Mr Mules. I paid you five thousand last week, in case you've forgotten. That enables you to buy your own drinks – and entitles me to punctuality.'

Mules responded with a casual toss of the head, dismissing the reprimand like a boxer slipping a punch. 'I got held up.' After a significant pause, he tagged on, 'Sorry,' in an ironic tone and with another mocking grin, just in case Strange thought he really meant it.

Strange frowned. 'Well? What progress can you report?'

'Not a fucking sausage,' said Mules blithely. 'I thought the Trousdale piece was meant to be a full-on nympho? Well, shit, I haven't seen any sign of it – just the bloody opposite, in fact. She's a do-gooder. She takes retards to the park; she does meals on wheels, for fuck's sake. You sure you got this right?'

Strange's well-upholstered poise wobbled; his forehead creased and his normally still grey eyes bulged anxiously. 'I'm quite sure; the information came from an impeccable source. You mean she hasn't met up with Early at all?'

Mules snorted, 'The little snake hasn't been sighted. I think I'll have one after all.'

When Mules came back with a beer, Strange was distractedly plucking his lower lip. 'You've got absolutely nothing to show for a week's work then?' he griped.

Mules bristled. 'Hang on, mate, don't you go pointing the finger at me. I did what you said, followed the bitch all over town. It's not my fault Early hasn't slapped one up her.' He shrugged. 'Maybe she's had the painters in.'

Strange's mouth twitched with distaste. 'So you followed her every day and didn't see a single thing worth mentioning?'

Mules gave it some thought. 'She went out of town one day – Tuesday it would've been.'

'Where to?' asked Strange hopefully.

'Wouldn't know; I stuck with her as far as the end of the motorway…'

'Dammit, man, why didn't you keep after her? That's what you're being paid for. She might've been on her way to meet Early somewhere.'

Mules took his time finishing his beer. 'You want to know why I didn't stick with her?' He had the cocky air of a man about to turn the tables. 'Well, you see, I've got a nine-year-old Laser and she's got a hot Merc with a couple of hundred grand's worth of poke – she'd have blown me off as soon as we hit the open road. So what I did was come back and ring Early at his junk barn in Birkenhead, said I was someone else; when he answered, I hung up. It seemed to me if Early was in Birkenhead and she was south of the Bombay Hills, wherever the fuck she was heading, it wasn't for the end of his wang.'

Having put Strange on the back foot, Mules followed up: 'You know, I got your outfit's number from directory and gave you a ring. All I got was a recorded message. I must've tried ten times, same thing each time. What's the fucking story, Leo?'

Strange couldn't help blinking with surprise. 'I'm semi-retired,' he said eventually. 'I do project work for a few clients who know how to contact me when the need arises. I didn't think it'd be necessary in this instance. Given the complete lack of progress, it was even less necessary than I'd expected.'

'Just thought I'd ask.' Mules stood up. 'See you next week then – same time, same place? Let's hope the root rats pull finger, eh?'

Mules winked at Strange and walked out of the bar. If he'd looked back, he would've seen Strange staring gloomily into his Campari and soda.

Strange was taking stock. He'd underestimated his man: he'd assumed that because Mules was short of money and lazy and lacked character, he'd be more than happy with ten grand. Instead, Mules had gone looking for an angle and had obviously found one.

It could've been worse: if Mules was smarter, he wouldn't have let on.

A little later that Friday afternoon, Clyde Early emerged from his office at the back of the Mr Fixit Hardware store in Birkenhead to tell his secretary, Judith, that he was off the air until further notice. As if to emphasise his anti-social mood, he shut the door behind him more forcefully than was good for the door or Judith's nerves.

Early sat down at his desk, reached for a pristine A4 lined notepad and one of the high-tech Japanese ballpens he favoured, and applied his methodical mind to the challenge of avoiding humiliation, divorce, and years of child-support maintenance.

He was past the stage of being angry that his exhilarating sexual adventure with Rusty Trousdale had

mutated into a ticking timebomb. He was even past
seething with frustration at not being able to do anything
about it.

There had to be something he could do, even if it was
just kiss his arse goodbye.

*Quedley reckoned the blackmailer took the diary
because he knew Rusty had been playing around. That
made sense but how did he find out in the first place?
Chances are she let it slip – or one of the other boyfriends did. But maybe she and I weren't as clever or as
careful as we thought; maybe somewhere along the line,
we gave the game away.*

Early made a list of the people who were present the
night they'd met. It was in late April, at a dinner party
hosted by a senior executive of a large company which
put a lot of sponsorship money into rugby. There were
the host and hostess, the Earlys, the Trousdales, and a
director of the company's advertising agency and his
girlfriend.

*Maybe one of them caught a vibe and gossiped about
it afterwards?*

Only if they had the sort of social radar that could
pick up a nipple hardening under three layers of clothing
across the room. Apart from some cautious eye contact
over pre-dinner drinks, he and Rusty had behaved like
strangers usually do at dinner parties: they'd politely
ignored each other.

Late in the evening, he'd overheard her enthusing
about her favourite new coffee place, Café Columbus in
High Street, where she often went for a mid-morning
latte or post-lunch macchiato. Early began dropping in
there regularly. On the seventh day, his ship came in. He

was nursing an espresso when she slid onto the next high stool murmuring, in a voice which gave him goose-bumps, 'Who's a clever boy then?'

Early tore the sheet off the notepad and dropped it in his wastepaper basket. They weren't sprung at the dinner party nor at Café Columbus, where they'd skirted around what was on their minds until she finished her coffee and said she had to run. She breezed out; he sat there wondering whether to go after her. Then he saw the mobile-phone number she'd scribbled on the paper napkin.

Which brings us to locations and communications.

After that time in Café Columbus, they didn't meet in bars or cafés or restaurants or anywhere there was a chance of bumping into people who knew them. The assignations took place at Greywater when her husband was overseas, and right there, in his office, outside trading hours – on Sundays or at night. When they used his office, they'd rendezvous in the car park under Aotea Square, drive to Birkenhead in his car, park in the basement, and come up the internal stairway.

They always communicated by digital mobile phones so the calls couldn't be answered by others or eaves-dropped on an extension. Let it ring four times: if it wasn't answered, flag it away and try again later…Early froze as his mind, now in overdrive, seized on a fragment of dim memory. *What about the day you forgot your mobile?*

He jumped up and paced around his desk.

Shit, that's right. It was the Thursday before Queen's Birthday weekend: Trousdale decided to go to Sydney on the spur of the moment and Rusty had to catch me before I left work so I could invent a reason to come back from the lake early.

He sprawled on the sofa and closed his eyes, squeezing his memory. The phone rang: 'It's a Miss Rust from the accountants – she says it's urgent.' It took him a few seconds to twig – what the hell's she playing at? Then he heard the delicious, low giggle and didn't care. He said, 'Hello,' his mouth suddenly dry. She said, 'You goose, you left your mobile at home, didn't you? I just tried to ring you on it. God, when I got "Jane Early speaking", I just about drove off the road. Listen, Maurice's off to Sydney till Tuesday so the coast's clear at long last if you can swing it...'

Early rewound his mental tape. The phone rings. Judith says, 'It's a Miss Rust from the acountants...' – EXCEPT IT'S NOT JUDITH.

He lunged for his diary and pawed through it. She'd written 'Judith on holiday!' across the top of the page for Thursday, 1 June. She'd taken some time off and they'd got a temp in.

Sweet bleeding Jesus, it was the temp – the bitch must've listened in.

He grabbed the phone. 'Judith, could you dig out the file for that temp who filled in for you over Queen's Birthday?'

When Chas Gundry MP failed to show up at Glenfield College on Friday morning to talk politics with the sixth formers, they heaved a collective sigh of relief and went back to daydreaming about a world without acne. The teacher who'd organised the session was disgusted but not overly surprised. It merely bore out his – and most teachers' – opinion that politicians don't give a toss about education. He didn't bother wasting breath on an indignant phone call to the MP's electorate office.

When Gundry didn't make a midday meeting with a publisher in Takapuna to discuss his idea for a book provisionally titled *The Joy of Pit Bulls*, the senior editor thanked God, which she was later to regret, and went shopping. The firm's publishing committee had given the idea short shrift and she'd been steeling herself for a scene. Dealing with authors every day, she got plenty of exposure to egomaniacs and drama queens but a guy who went gooey-eyed over pit bulls was something else.

When Gundry didn't appear at the North Shore Golf Club for the Glenfield Small Business Association's monthly lunch, the small businesspeople just got drunker than usual, faster than usual. The lunch was Gundry's last engagement for the day: he'd set aside the afternoon for discussing the economic outlook with the small businesspeople until he fell over or they shut the bar.

About four o'clock, when the lunchers graduated from throwing cheese to throwing chairs, punches, and finally bottles, some of which weren't even empty, the police were called to what was officially classified as an affray.

One of the constables dispatched to the golf club happened to be going out with a teacher at Glenfield College. In the course of their lunchtime phone conversation, she'd mentioned Gundry's no-show.

When the constable reported in, he asked the desk sergeant if it was normal for an MP to just not turn up for engagements which his electorate secretary had confirmed the previous day. The sergeant didn't think so; he looked up Gundry's address and told the constable to swing past and check the place out, seeing he was in the vicinity. The sergeant then called the MP's local office and spoke to his electorate secretary, who was both baffled and concerned by the no-shows.

Shortly before five-thirty, the constable reported no-one home at Gundry's place; the sergeant told him to hang around. The electorate secretary, a 64-year-old semi-retired bookkeeper, picked up a key to the MP's house from his cleaning lady and drove out there. He unlocked the front door and went inside. The constable, mindful of procedure, waited to be asked in. He didn't have to wait long: the invitation came in the form of a gargling scream which scrambled sparrows from branches and powerlines within a 75-metre radius.

In the entrance hall the constable came across a man who appeared to be dead, a dog which couldn't have been any deader if a tactical nuclear device had gone off in its kennel, and a semi-retired bookkeeper who wasn't going to be the odd one out for much longer, judging by the way he was clutching his chest and spraying milky-white spittle from bloodless lips.

It was dark when the APA delegation from Auckland Central – Detective Sergeant Tito Ihaka, Detective Constable Johan Van Roon, and the SIS man Wayne Cramp – arrived at Gundry's house. A detective sergeant from Takapuna was standing on the front lawn, smoking grimly.

'What's the go, Pete?' said Ihaka. 'I thought murder was against the law this side of the bridge?'

Pete shook his head. 'You wouldn't fucking believe it, mate.'

'What?'

'We got a dog with its head splattered all over the shop – and a dead cop.'

Ihaka's eyes darkened and his face set like stone.

'Sergeant Kerry Keene out of Christchurch, according to his ID; seconded to the PSU.'

'Gundry's bodyguard.'

Pete nodded. 'You know the worst part? It looks like the fucking dog did him.'

'What about Gundry?'

Pete shook his head. 'No sign of him – we haven't done a proper search yet. We found a pistol though.'

'They left a gun?' Ihaka couldn't believe it. 'Give us a look.'

Pete led them inside. Ihaka took in the scene in one bleak sweep. He nodded to the white-coat crew. 'It just gets worse, eh boys?'

Subdued assent.

The pistol was in a tagged plastic bag on the hall table. Ihaka peered at it. 'That's a pretty serious unit.' He glanced over his shoulder at Cramp, who was mesmerised by the carnage. 'Hey Wayne, you know what this is?'

Cramp tore his eyes away and came over. He was pale and his fingers shook as he loosened his tie. He looked at the pistol, swallowing hard. 'Smith & Wesson ten-millimetre – the FBI use them. Your department brought in a batch last year; I heard they'd been issued – unofficially – to the PSU.'

Ihaka said, 'Fuck.' He walked through the house, ending up in the kitchen at the rear. A constable was stationed at the back door.

'You had a look out the back?'

'Just a quick squizz, Sarge.'

Ihaka borrowed his torch and went outside. The block sloped away out of the torch's range. Ihaka advanced, swinging the beam of light from side to side. Gundry's backyard was designed for the lawnmower: flowerbeds along both fences and a few well-spaced shrubs.

Ihaka got his first whiff of it as he heard the back door open. He muttered, 'Jesus,' and quickened his pace. The smell got worse. It was like bad, burnt grease and filled his mouth with a foul aftertaste. He'd smelt it before, at car crashes and house fires: it was the smell of human flesh cooking.

He went on down the slope. The back fence loomed in front of him when the torch beam fell on a low mound of earth. Steam rose from it. He saw a patch of white on the fence and shone the torch: it was an envelope. He was pulling on a plastic glove when Cramp arrived.

'Christ, what's that smell?'

'At a guess, the Honourable Member.'

Cramp goggled.

'See that?' Ihaka aimed the torch beam at the steaming mound of earth. 'That's a *hangi*.' He reached out to remove the envelope from the fence. 'I think we'll find the APA stuck Gundry in there and cooked the shit out of him. Say what you like about the fuckers, they don't do things the easy way.'

THIRTEEN

Around the time that the semi-retired bookkeeper was galvanising sparrows in Greenhithe and about two kilometres due south across Hellyers Creek, Clyde Early was confronting the temporary secretary.

Renee Adlington was a 46-year-old divorcee who'd been cute in a pert, snub-nosed way when she was twenty and would resemble a jowly Pekinese by the time she was sixty-five. Right now, she was somewhere in between.

Adlington's main interest in life was her family. Most days, she went to see her 82-year-old widowed mother at the old folks' home in Chatswood, which backed onto the Kauri Point naval armament depot. Her mother was reasonably compos but a little unsteady on her pins, which necessitated leaving the door open when she went to the toilet in case she fell over and trapped herself in. Adlington wasn't sure whether it was old age or had gone on for years behind closed doors, but without fail, her mother would fart like a draughthorse before, during, and after her motions. Listening to the blasts, Adlington would sometimes reflect that, if the armament depot ever did blow up, she probably wouldn't even notice.

Then there was her brother, who visited Auckland now and again from his hideaway in the Marlborough Sounds. He was worldly and well-informed so she consulted him on everything from her mortgage arrangements to which wine should accompany the chicken chasseur she planned to serve when she entertained her new man-friend.

Finally, there were her daughter and grandson in Cockle Bay, which was on the other side of town and a bugger of a place to get to. She assumed that was why her son-in-law insisted on living there.

When the doorbell of her Birkdale townhouse rang, Adlington wondered if it was the new man-friend: he'd been threatening to drop in unannounced since they'd first met, almost a month ago, at a mature singles night at Alexandra Park Raceway.

She'd had to be talked into going. Her view was that mature singles nights were just meat markets for people who were old enough to know better; her girlfriend had countered that a healthy diet should include a certain amount of meat. When Adlington thought about it, she found herself wavering. Who said, 'One strike and you're out'? Why should men be off the agenda just because she was a grandmother who carried the baggage of a marriage which had curled up and died after nineteen years, having spent half its miserable existence on a life-support machine? She still had her looks – well, some of them, anyway. Her figure wasn't too bad – a bit on the full side maybe but that cut both ways: it wasn't as if Alexandra Park Raceway would be swarming with Brad Pitt lookalikes.

So she'd gone along, vowing to take things very slowly.

As it happened, she'd been there all of five minutes when the best-looking man in the room had introduced himself by saying, 'Hello darling, I'm Henry. I suppose a knee-trembler would be out of the question?' Completely thrown, she'd blurted that she wasn't that sort of woman. He'd asked the obvious question: what sort of woman was she then? The sort of woman who'd have to get to know a man properly before she'd consider…you know. And how long would that take – an hour, a week, a month, a year? A week was rushing things and he didn't seem the type who'd hang around for a year so she'd opted, hesitantly, for a month. Henry had nodded, as if weighing up options, then announced his verdict: while he wouldn't twiddle his thumbs for ten minutes for most of the old boilers there, he was prepared to do so in her case.

Henry was an experienced seducer of mature single women. Once he'd extracted the information that Adlington had been sexually inactive since the break-up of her marriage, he'd taken to spelling out, face-to-face and over the phone, what was in store for her when the month was up. These salacious spiels had the desired effects of eroding her inhibitions and, slowly but surely, arousing her anticipation.

'The fact is, when it comes to leg-over, most women need a bit of training,' Henry would say. 'Frankly, I can have a better time with a filthy video and a jar of coconut oil than the average dame at those singles nights; they haven't got any idea, most of them. You're different:

I picked you right from the off as a volcano just waiting to erupt. So we can skip the beginner's stuff. I'm going to throw you in at the deep end, gorgeous – we'll start with analingus.'

The word wasn't in Adlington's dictionary but you didn't need to be a professor of linguistics to get the gist. She'd felt queasy for the rest of the evening. By the following morning, though, she was once more tingling with the now familiar sensation of simmering excitement, spiced with a piquant touch of guilt over the sinfulness of it all. The coming week promised to be the longest of her adult life.

But it wasn't Henry at the door, it was Clyde Early. His expression suggested he was itching to do a number of unspeakable things to her but analingus wasn't among them. His hands were thrust deep into the pockets of a shin-length herringbone overcoat and he stared at her with all the benevolence of a vulture watching a lame horse hobbling through Death Valley.

'Mr Early? What brings you here?'

'I want to talk to you,' he said ominously.

'It's not really convenient right now – perhaps you could come back some other time?'

'Perhaps I could come back with the police.'

She took a short, involuntary step backwards. Early brushed past her and walked into the living room. Adlington rallied and went in hot pursuit. 'Who the hell do you think you are, barging into my home like this?'

Early shed his overcoat, which he'd bought in Milan and liked far too much to mothball even though it amounted to sartorial overkill for Auckland's mild, damp winters. 'Cut the crap – you know bloody well why I'm here.'

She flushed and stalked past him to the telephone on the kitchenette bench. 'I will not be spoken to like that in my own home. If you're not out of here in ten seconds, I'm calling the police.'

'Are you trying to tell me you don't know why I'm here?'

'I haven't got the faintest idea.'

He came closer, his eyes drilling into hers. 'When you temped for me before Queen's Birthday, you listened in on one of my phone calls, didn't you?'

Adlington's face went blank, then it went stupid. 'I...uh, I wouldn't do such a thing.'

Early grunted derisively. 'Do you know what the penalty for blackmail is, Mrs Adlington?'

'What? What's blackmail got to do with it?'

'The woman who rang me that Thursday, whose call you listened in on, is being blackmailed. I think – no, let me rephrase that – I know you're up to your neck in it.'

'This is ridiculous. For the last time, I'm asking you to leave...'

Early changed tack. 'Who'd you tell?'

'What?'

'Who did you tell that we were having an affair?'

Adlington's eyes darted and she gnawed her lower lip. 'You've got the wrong end of the stick, Mr Early,' she said without conviction. 'I'm sorry about whatever's happened but it's got nothing to do with me.'

Early gave a contemptuous shake of the head. He shrugged on his overcoat. 'You told somebody and he went and stole the lady's diary. Now he's blackmailing her. Maybe you're part of it, maybe not – I don't give a shit. Tell him to give the diary back and get lost. If it's not back by Monday morning, I'm going to the police.'

He threw her a final glare and walked out. Through a crack in the curtains, Adlington watched him get into his car and drive away. Then she crossed the living room, opened the door into the corridor, and called, 'You can come out now; he's gone.'

She sat in an armchair drumming her fingers impatiently until Leo Strange emerged. He didn't look quite his normal, unflappable self.

In a tone she rarely took with her big brother, she demanded, 'Well, Leo? I think you owe me an explanation.'

When Amanda Hayhoe walked into Vinnie's restaurant in Jervois Road at 8.08 p.m. and was directed to his table, Caspar Quedley was mildly surprised on two counts: he hadn't expected her to be as punctual or as attractive.

He'd missed her at TVNZ that morning and left a message saying he'd call again. The name rang a bell so Hayhoe looked up his file in the clippings library. The most recent story on him was eighteen months old but she assumed he still looked and behaved like a cad from central casting.

He rang back after lunch wanting a meeting.

'What for?'

'We need to talk. It's a tricky business; better to do it in person than over the phone.'

'Oh?' She waited for amplification; none came. 'When did you have in mind?'

'Tonight if possible; I'd be more than happy to buy you dinner.'

'Tell me, this chat we need to have: would it be professional or personal?'

'The latter; I haven't got a hot scoop for you if that's what you mean.'

'I gave up believing I was irresistible the day I started kindergarten but just in case this is a roundabout way of asking me out, you should know that I've already had an older-man experience. It was underwhelming, to put it politely.'

'It happens sometimes: men are like wine – some age better than others. Rest assured, my intentions are beyond reproach. To tell the truth, I'm not too sure I can even put a face to you. I must've seen you on the box but I get all you glam young women mixed up.'

'It works like this: the game-show bimbos pout, the weather airheads simper, and we current-affairs bitches do that odd sort of smug frown. It takes lots of practice.'

'That's a useful guide; I'd better write it down before I forget.'

'Look, I don't mean to be coy but couldn't you give me a tiny clue what this is about?'

'Let's just say it's important – for yourself and others.'

Hayhoe stopped fighting it. *Admit it, kid, you're intrigued.* 'Okay, I give in – I'll let you buy me dinner. Somewhere decent, I hope?'

'So do I – you choose.'

'I like Vinnie's in Herne Bay but we haven't got much show of getting in there...'

'I'll see what I can do. If you don't hear back from me, I'll meet you there. Eight o'clock okay?'

It was and she didn't hear back.

Hayhoe scarcely recognised Quedley from his file photo. When she got a closer look, she realised that the big change wasn't so much in what he'd gained – a beard and grey streaks in his hair – as what he'd lost: the livewire glow and that 'the joke's on you, sucker' look in his eyes. He looked older, slower, less potent, no longer bullet-proof. She wondered if he was wiser.

The restaurant was full. 'I'm impressed. How'd you manage it?'

He shrugged diffidently. 'I used to be a regular – either that or they felt sorry for me.'

A waiter went through the specials. Quedley asked for a jug of water, no lemon, no ice.

'I read up on you.' She watched for a reaction. 'You were notorious for a while.'

His low-voltage smile came and went. 'I gave it up.'

'Notoriety or public relations?'

'Both.'

'So what do you do now?'

'As in a job? Not a thing; I'm unemployed.'

Hayhoe had had a couple of drinks after work; she'd come prepared to joust. 'Gosh, yet another reason to feel sorry for you.'

That seemed to amuse him. 'It obviously didn't have that effect on you.'

The waiter came for their orders. Quedley still hadn't looked at the menu; he told Hayhoe to go ahead. She ordered salt-roasted chicken; he asked for the fish of the day, whatever it was, grilled and served plain, with a green salad. The waiter looked confused. Quedley handed him the unread menu. 'My apologies to the chef.'

The waiter offered wine. Quedley deferred to Hayhoe who said she wouldn't mind a glass of Chardonnay. He told the waiter to bring her a bottle; a good one.

'Aren't you having any?'

'I don't think so – I'm out of practice at alcohol, among other things. Besides, I've got to drive to Cambridge tonight.'

'What for?'

'I live there.'

Hayhoe wondered what was the big attraction in Cambridge but didn't bother asking; Quedley seemed to specialise in cryptic answers.

After the wine had been poured, Quedley said, 'I've kept you in suspense long enough: you know Rusty Trousdale?'

Her expression changed several times in as many seconds. 'We've met.'

'I'm here on her behalf – we go way back. I like Rusty a lot but there's no denying she's been an idiot.'

'She can afford to be, can't she?'

'Not this time. To begin at the beginning: she kept a diary in which you rate a mention.'

Alarm stirred in Hayhoe's eyes; her wine glass stopped in mid-voyage and returned to base. 'Did she tell you what happened?'

'She told me what didn't happen.'

Hayhoe relaxed and refocused on the wine. Quedley lowered his voice. 'Amanda, you declined an invitation to have sex with Rusty: that's a rare – possibly unique – distinction. It must've been a blow to her ego because she skated over the fact in the diary.'

Hayhoe's eyebrows rose in slow motion and stayed up. 'Come again?'

He tugged an ear lobe. 'Apparently, the way she described the encounter, anyone else reading it would probably get the wrong idea.'

Their meals arrived. As soon as the waiter had departed, she hissed, 'You mean she said we had it off?'

'I don't know that she went that far but she certainly didn't spell it out that you turned her down.'

'Is she mad or just on drugs? Why the hell did she do that?'

'Beats me. I asked her the same question.'

'What did she say?'

'Nothing very enlightening.' He refilled her wine glass. 'Your chicken's getting cold.'

She stared at him for a little longer then began to eat, chewing thoughtfully. He processed his greens without appearing to derive much enjoyment from it.

'There's more to it, isn't there?' she said. 'I mean, you're not buying me dinner just because your old bud implied she got her hand on my woolly.'

Quedley struggled to keep a straight face. 'Right. I'm buying you dinner because Rusty's got a problem which could become your problem: someone stole the diary and he's using it to blackmail her. You probably wouldn't be stunned to learn that yours isn't the only bedroom scene in which her husband is conspicuous by his absence. The blackmailer wants big bucks – which incidentally she hasn't got, it's all Trousdale's – or else. "Or else" could mean several things: he might be satisfied with wrecking her marriage; on the other hand, he might get really vindictive and send copies of the naughty bits to every media outlet in the country.'

Hayhoe's face fell. She said, 'Oh, that's just fucking peachy,' loud enough for the people at the next table to hear and lunged for the wine bottle. 'So when can I expect to be outed?'

'She'll stall as long as she can. I'm sure the blackmailer knew what was in the diary before he stole it which is why I'm going round asking Rusty's playthings whether they told anyone. You're my last call.'

She was nonplussed. 'I haven't told a soul; I mean, what was there to brag about?'

'I don't know,' he said meditatively. 'I reckon anyone who gets through a night with Rusty with virtue intact deserves congratulations.'

'I presume you didn't manage it?'

'I didn't even get close. Mind you, she was single in those days and I was…'

'You were what?'

'Different.'

'What's changed?'

'You mean apart from my whole life? Well, for starters, I've been celibate for the best part of two years.'

She refilled her glass and solemnly raised it. 'To the good ship *Celibacy* and all who sail in her.'

'Don't tell me you're celibate?'

'That's the way it seems to be panning out.'

'That's appalling.' He looked as if he meant it. 'Why?'

She shrugged. 'Whatever's come my way – Rusty, for example – just didn't feel right.'

'Maybe you're being a little picky?'

'Isn't that the pot calling the kettle white?'

'It's not the same; in my case, it was part of a...' He stared into space. 'A retreat from society.'

'Permanent?'

'I don't really know. Sometimes I toy with the idea of making a comeback.'

'To society or are we still on sex?'

Quedley's eyes lit up. He flashed a lopsided, self-deprecating grin, giving her a burst of the killer charm mentioned in some of the file stories. 'I hadn't really thought about sex. First, I'd have to find a woman who didn't feel sorry for me. I'm not proud but I draw the line at sympathy fucks.'

She giggled. 'What are you suggesting – that we join forces to kick the habit?'

Quedley realised that she'd gone from coolly sober to playfully drunk in a single bound, skipping tipsy altogether. 'I wouldn't dream of it,' he said carefully, 'not after what you said about older men.'

She inspected him through heavy-lidded, slightly glazed eyes. 'You looked a lot younger without the beard.'

FOURTEEN

I t was still dark when Leo Strange woke up. Rain was falling with the timeless rhythm of a waterfall, as it had been when he'd gone to bed and when he'd woken during the night. For a few minutes, he thought about what he had to do that morning. He wasn't looking forward to it but he'd studied it from every angle. If there was a better way, he hadn't found it.

He propped himself up, flicked on the bedside light, and checked his watch: 6.09. Only two kinds of people got up at 6.09 on a Saturday morning: those who didn't drink and those who'd got their nuts caught in the wringer. Strange, who'd puked on liquors most people have never heard of, threw back the covers and got out of bed.

He showered, shaved, and got dressed in corduroy trousers, a cream lambswool skivvy, brown brogues, and a green Harris tweed jacket with leather elbow patches: weekend wear for a man of substance – worthy, solid, respectable. Strange was none of those things but didn't see any point in advertising the fact.

He dawdled over breakfast, having a second cup of tea and a third slice of toast and marmalade. At 7.15, he put the newspaper aside. He rinsed his breakfast dishes and put them in the dishwasher, left a note for his sister, picked up his suitcase, satchel, and raincoat, and left the house. He got into the rented Ford Telstar and drove down Birkdale Road towards Birkenhead until he found a phone box.

A minute went by without his call being answered but Strange didn't hang up. He could visualise the scene at the other end of the line. He was connected to a white bakelite telephone which had done three decades' service in the Paris office, above the Banque Rothschild on Avenue George V, from which Madame Claude ran her legendary call-girl operation. Now it sat on a Macassar ebony-veneer half-moon desk designed by the celebrated French art deco *ensemblier* Emile-Jacques Ruhlman, and which had once belonged to the Maharajah of Indore. The desk was in the study of a magnificent house overlooking the Heretaunga golf course, just outside Wellington. There were no extensions on that number, and house guests, mainly beautiful, transient girls, knew better than to go into the study, let alone answer the white bakelite telephone.

On the eighty-fifth ring, the white phone was picked up.

'It's Strange.'

'What is?' It was a male voice and an unusual one, harsh yet with a breezy undertone. Strange thought it suited the speaker to a T.

He ignored the question. Strange hadn't responded to jokes – good, bad, or indifferent – involving his surname since the sixties when he still thought that if you laughed every time a woman said something she thought was amusing, eventually she'd let you into her pants.

'There's a problem with Operation Early Bird.'

'That's one of the things I like about you, Leo. Some people would've said, "We have a problem." Not you; you understand that if God had wanted me to have problems, he wouldn't have made me filthy rich. How bad is it? We talking hiccup or fuck-up?'

'There's certainly potential for the latter.'

'Should we abort?'

'I think that'd be prudent.'

'Well, that's a pity, Leo, a real pity. I thought we were on to something with this one; I could see it having all sorts of applications.'

'Yes, I know.'

'You got any other bright ideas?'

'I'll give it some thought.'

'Okay, I'll leave it with you. I know you don't need reminding, Leo, but seeing you're paying for the call, I'll do it anyway: no mess, no loose ends, nothing that might come back and put me off my game somewhere down the track. Show me a man with a loose end on his mind, Leo, and I'll show you a man who can't putt for shit.'

'I'll take care of it,' said Strange because there was no point in saying anything else. They hung up simultaneously.

Strange got back in the hire car. The conversation had gone just as he'd expected, right down to the golf talk. It'd be nice to have nothing more to worry about than playing to your handicap – as opposed to, say, confronting a huge, obnoxious roughneck and forcing him to drop his get-rich-quick scheme.

He heaved a careworn sigh and started the car.

It was coming up to eight o'clock when Strange parked in a narrow avenue in Kingsland, between the Northwestern motorway and New North Road. He'd been there before, the day the whole sorry saga began: the day he found Mules, gave him five grand, and turned him loose on the Trousdale woman.

Mules lived in a granny flat at the rear of a sprawling villa. Strange guessed it was a century old and built of kauri. Intricate fretwork decorated the eaves over-hanging the wide verandah but the walls, once white, were a watery grey and the green paint on the tin roof had turned bile-olive and started to peel. The front garden was semi-jungle and trees hunched over the house, branches pressing up to the windows like peeping Toms. It looked like the wicked witch's cottage from some dark, cautionary fairy tale.

It was raining again. Strange pulled on his raincoat and reached into the car for the collapsible umbrella in his satchel. Rummaging for it, he came up with his emergency pack of single-malt whisky miniatures. It was a little early in the day for whisky, even for someone as open-minded as Strange, but if this dog's breakfast didn't qualify as an emergency, what the hell would? He selected the Glenlivet and threw it back in two quick hits. He popped the umbrella and crossed the road, feeling the Scotch trickle warmly through him.

He took the path to the rear of the house. The low branches forced him to retract the umbrella just as it began to pelt down. The leather soles of his brogues failed to grip on the slippery concrete and he skidded, flailing his arms like a slapstick comedian.

The door to the flat had a solid wood border framing latticed panes of frosted glass. The pane nearest the door handle was missing: it had been neatly cut out, leaving a centimetre or so of glass all the way round the lattice. Maybe Mules had been broken into recently; the flat was a burglar's dream, invisible from the street and surrounded by trees.

When his knocking got no response, Strange bent over and peered through the hole. It looked like Mules had had a party.

He was tempted to forget the whole thing. Handling Mules was never going to be easy; if the brute had a mean hangover, it'd be near-impossible, and probably hazardous to boot. Strange reminded himself that he was a pro; he had a job to do. There was also the small matter of ensuring he wasn't implicated in blackmail. He knocked again and called through the hole. When that got no reaction, he tried the door. It was unlocked.

Mules' flat had clearly been the venue for some form of group activity, either a party or an all-in brawl. The cushions had been pulled off the two sofas, the coffee table kicked over, and the shelves behind the TV swiped clean, leaving records, CDs, magazines, and a few paperbacks strewn over the floor. Strange spotted *The Bridges of Madison County*; it would take more than one book to persuade him that Mules had a soft centre behind the scaly exterior.

More mayhem: the dining table and chairs were over-turned; around the corner, in the open kitchen, drawers had been yanked out and emptied onto the floor.

Strange registered the absence of party debris: no empty bottles, no butt-choked ashtrays, no lipstick-rimmed glasses, no cigarette burns, no stains, no miasma of smoke, beer, and body odour, no vomit curdling in the potplants. Maybe Mules was away and there'd been a break-in last night.

Airing-cupboard stuff littered the corridor. The bathroom and a closed door, obviously the toilet, were off the corridor to the right; the closed door down the end had to be the bedroom. Strange picked his way through towels and sheets. He knocked: no response. He opened the door.

The bedroom had been done over as well: drawers pulled out, clothes dumped, bedside table overturned, bed stripped, mattress half-pulled off the base.

Strange caught sight of himself in a mirror. With his thinning hair plastered to his scalp, he looked bedraggled and disoriented, like one of those lost souls who tramp the streets gesticulating convulsively and barking to themselves as they wander ever-deeper into their interior mazes. He stepped back onto a plastic coathanger. It splintered with a sharp crack. He yelped, 'Fucking fuck.'

Shaking hands, fraying nerves.

Let's get out of this dump. Might as well take a leak while I'm at it.

He opened the toilet door. Mules sat on the toilet, head thrown back, arms dangling by his sides, trousers around his ankles. A wooden handle stuck out of his chest and his blue polo shirt was soggy with blood. His face was frozen in a querulous expression, as if he'd died complaining that he couldn't even have a shit without a homicidal maniac barging in on him.

Strange released a long, horrified gurgle. He wrenched the door shut and blundered towards the exit. Then he thought of fingerprints and retraced his steps, wiping doorhandles. He closed the door to the flat gently and skedaddled to the car as fast as his bulk and the treacherous path would allow. For once, Leo Strange didn't mind hurrying.

He scrabbled in his satchel for a whisky miniature, emptied it in one gulp. He started the car and, forcing himself to keep calm, drove sedately away. He turned right into New North Road and headed west, towards the airport. The lure of his little A-frame house in the Marlborough Sounds had never been stronger.

By the time he was ten kilometres above the Tongariro National Park, Strange had worked out his plan. The first priority was to avoid whoever butchered Mules; the second was to stay out of jail. The rest could take care of itself.

When he got to Honeymoon Bay, he was going to lock the door, light a fire, and settle down with a bottle of Scotch and a Patrick O'Brian book. For about five years.

Amanda Hayhoe didn't sleep well that Friday night either. That was partly due to too much wine and partly because, like Strange, she'd gone to bed in an unsettled frame of mind.

Around nine, she surfaced from a fitful doze. As recollections of the night before flooded in, her neck flushed crimson. The flush deepened and spread like ink through blotting paper until her face had the velvety, purple-brown tan of a park-bench wino. She groaned and pulled the bedclothes over her head.

It was a few minutes before she was up to assessing the damage.

How awful was it on a scale of one to ten? Item: when Caspar Quedley rang, I implied he was really after my body. Item: I told him I wasn't interested in older men. Item: I had too much to drink and...and what? Let's face it: without actually saying so in words of two syllables or less, I invited him to take me home and fuck me till my ears popped.

And that wasn't the worst of it: instead of jumping at the chance, he bolted.

As they came out of the restaurant, he said, 'Well, thanks for coming. It was nice meeting you.'

Thanks for coming? Nice meeting you? I'm on a date with Forrest Gump.

'Can I drop you somewhere?'

That was more like it. 'Well, if you wouldn't mind. I did bring my car but seeing you've plied me with plonk,' – flirty look, suggestive smirk – 'I better leave it here and pick it up tomorrow. I'm only a couple of minutes away.'

But when they got to her place, Quedley didn't turn off the motor or even let go of the steering wheel, for that matter. Just a polite smile and: 'Maybe we can do this again some time?'

'I take it you don't want to come in for a Milo?'

Another smile, almost pensive this time. 'I think I'd better just hit the road.'

Seeing you didn't beg, cry or grope him, we'll call it an eight.

Hayhoe got moving: no point sitting around and moping. She scribbled a note to her landlady/flatmate, apologising for losing it when she walked in and the flatmate asked if she'd had a good time. Hayhoe couldn't remember what she'd said but it wasn't pretty.

She went into work and pulled D'Arcy Potterton's file from the clippings library. The wire story about his death, dated 18 July, was headed 'NZ Writer Killed In Hunting Accident':

D'Arcy Potterton, the New Zealand writer who turned his back on his country, was killed in a hunting accident near his home in the village of Levignac, south-west France, on Sunday. He was fifty-seven.

Police have released few details but it is understood that Potterton was shot by a hunter while walking in the Forêt de Bucon, a large forest which is a magnet for the region's many keen hunters. He is thought to have died instantly. The hunter who fired the fatal shot, a local man, has been interviewed by police but is unlikely to be charged.

Potterton left New Zealand vowing never to return after the 1975 'Dancing Cossacks' election which swept the National Party, led by the late Sir Robert Muldoon, back into power. He settled in France and became a full-time writer, combining reviews and criticism for various British and American publications with fiction.

His novels and short stories were translated into several languages and earned critical acclaim, particularly in his adopted homeland. In New Zealand, however, he is probably best remembered for his 1977 collection of essays *She'll be*

Reich, Mate, which scathingly criticised the New Zealand way of life and predicted a fascist dictatorship within a decade.

Belinda Potterton, the writer's sister, said her brother would be buried in Levignac as soon as the authorities released his body.

There were follow-up stories with quotes from friends and literary types, including his local publisher, who said Potterton was 'a poet and a radical conscience who refused to compromise himself either artistically or politically. New Zealand wasn't ready for D'Arcy Potterton and that was – and is – our loss.'

Hayhoe, who'd hit the wall halfway through one of his novels and given the rest of his oeuvre a wide berth, decided she wasn't going to feel unworthy on the say-so of an overwrought publisher.

There was also an excruciatingly precious obituary by Dr Daniel Davenport, associate professor of English at Auckland University: 'driven to confront the dark side of human nature...callousness of modern society... capitalism a juggernaut fuelled by its victims...shoulder to shoulder at the barricades...driven into exile... beloved adopted homeland'. Etc.

Hayhoe shuddered.

You want an obit? How about this: D'Arcy Potterton was a writer who got a giant crush on his sister. They went to France and played hide the salami for twenty years. Then a Frog hillbilly mistook him for something four-legged and furry and blew him away.

Did she really need this shit?

FIFTEEN

Tito Ihaka's slide show took place in a conference room at Auckland Central early on Saturday afternoon.

His audience consisted of Detective Inspector Finbar McGrail, Detective Constable Johan Van Roon, and the SIS man, Wayne Cramp. The gathering was a prelude to a full-scale briefing for the 26-strong Aotearoa People's Army taskforce formed following the murder of Chas Gundry MP by live burial in a purpose-built underground oven, a method of assassination largely neglected since the invention of the bow and arrow.

The first slide came up.

'Sergeant Kerry Keene,' said Ihaka. 'He'd been on Gundry-watch for all of twelve hours. The APA would've picked them up when they left the meeting in Mt Roskill just after nine-thirty. They had a feed in a restaurant in Dominion Road; about eleven, Gundry pitched up at a part-time hooker's apartment in Parnell, big-noting that he was so important, he had a personal bodyguard parked outside. They made it easy for the APA: they could take Keene while Gundry was having his knob polished, then just wait for Gundry. Another very slick piece of work – no-one around there saw or heard a thing.'

Cramp asked, 'What about the hooker – could she've been in on it?'

'Wayne, she's a fucking air hostess.'

Slide two: Keene (close-up, deceased).

Ihaka, dispassionately: 'Gundry left her just after midnight. They went over to Greenhithe in his Commodore and another vehicle and parked in the lock-up garage. They put a hood on Keene, taped his hands behind his back, and fed him to Gundry's pit bull. It started on his legs, tipped him over, then went for the kill.' Ihaka tapped the screen with a pointer. 'It got into the jugular, also bit through his Adam's apple and tore up the larynx. Cause of death: air in the jugular.'

McGrail: 'Sergeant, any leads on the other vehicle?'

'No sightings. We're checking all stolen vehicles that come in. We did a sweep of the main car parks for dumped vehicles first thing this morning. They're being checked now. There were no unidentified prints in the Commodore, by the way.'

Slide three: Son of Sam (close up, deceased).

'What was left of the mongrel after they shot it at point-blank range with Keene's gun.'

McGrail: 'Who looked after it when Gundry was in Wellington?'

'A pet-babysitting place in Albany. Gundry would tell them when he was heading back and they'd drop the mutt off so it was there to greet him when he got home.'

'They had a key?'

'Yep.'

'They checked out?'

'Been in business for thirteen years.'

Slide four: Keene's pistol.

'The weapon in question: Smith & Wesson ten-millimetre semi-auto. One shot fired, which decorated Gundry's hall with doggy brains. The only prints are Keene's.'

Slide five: the *hangi*.

'Gundry was big on *hangis*. He had all the gear: stones, sacks, chicken wire and whatnot.'

Cramp: 'The APA obviously knew that, and about the dog.'

'Wouldn't take much,' said Ihaka. 'Pit bulls and *hangis* get a mention in bloody near every story ever written about Gundry.'

Van Roon: '*Hangis* take a fair while, don't they, Sarge?'

'Seven or eight hours' preparation, twelve minimum for cooking. Say they got going around one or two in the morning, they would've popped Gundry in about eight. As you'll see, he wasn't quite done when we dug him out.'

Slide six: Gundry (full-length shot, deceased).

Cramp swore under his breath when Gundry's corpse came up on the screen. It was slightly charred and grotesquely bloated by massive blisters on the stomach, chest, and inside the arms and legs.

McGrail, grimmer than usual: 'Was he alive when they put him in?'

'Yeah, but probably not conscious – he got a whack on the back of the head.'

Slide seven: the APA communiqué.

'And now, a word from our sponsors.'

COMMUNIQUÉ NUMBER THREE

Despite the examples made of Freckleton and Pike and our unequivocal warnings, the politician Gundry launched a blatantly demagogic attack on the Maori people and those who lead its struggle for liberation and sovereignty.

With this action against a member of the ruling clique, the Aotearoa People's Army has demonstrated its ability to strike at the very core of the pakeha power structure. We had no direct interest in Gundry's bodyguard. However, since the state security apparatus is merely the armed palace guard of a reactionary regime, its members are legitimate targets.

The Aotearoa People's Army calls on the state and its security apparatus to abandon its oppressive treatment of those engaged in the fight for justice. There should no longer be any need to spell out the consequences if this call is ignored.

'It was on Gundry's back fence.'

Cramp: 'They must've made your surveillance on the TV girl.'

Ihaka half-smiled at Cramp's US cop-speak. 'Maybe. Maybe they just gave us credit for doing the basics.'

'Do we know why they used her in the first place?'

'I suppose they wanted the media to have the communiqués in case we sat on them. As far as we can tell, they picked her at random and she served her purpose. It's a roundabout way of doing it, but nothing these guys do is simple; it's all tricky and elaborate, like they're playing a game.' He looked at McGrail. 'That's it from me.'

Ihaka sat down; McGrail told Cramp he had the floor.

Cramp moved to the front of the room. 'I don't want to say I told you so but you'll remember I predicted this.' He eyeballed Ihaka. 'Everyone's got an opinion but some have more basis than others, eh Sergeant?'

Ihaka yawned.

Cramp pontificated. 'I flew to Wellington this morning for a special meeting of the advisory committee of all the security departments. There was unanimous agreement on two points: one, that the country is facing a deadly serious threat to its internal security; two, given that, in addition to the factors I've already raised, Gundry's speech was the trigger for his assassination, given the method of it, and the language in the communiqués, it would be a dereliction of duty on our part not to thoroughly test the proposition that the APA is linked to – if not actually a front for – extreme elements in the Maori nationalist movement. A few moments ago, I heard from Wellington that a cabinet subcommittee chaired by the PM has endorsed that approach.' Cramp smiled thinly. 'Our political masters want action, gentlemen. Right now, there's a bunch of MPs changing their underpants every hour on the hour.'

He picked up a marker pen and wrote on the whiteboard, speaking over his shoulder. 'I don't have any slides but there are a few names I'd like to put in front of you. We believe these people are the absolute hard core of Maori radicalism. They're all on record as advocating violence to achieve their ends and, from what our sources tell us, their public comments are tame compared to what they say in private. Our monitoring also indicates a pattern of intensified activity which includes going to great lengths to avoid surveillance.'

Cramp finished writing and stepped away from the whiteboard.

There was a knock on the door. A uniformed constable poked his head in. 'Excuse me, sir,' he said to McGrail, 'the Commissioner's on the phone for you.'

Ihaka scarcely noticed McGrail leave: he was too busy studying Cramp's list. His niece was on it.

No-one spoke or moved. Cramp watched Ihaka, who stared at the whiteboard; Van Roon looked from one to the other, feeling something in the air.

Finally Cramp said, 'What's up, Sergeant – I didn't spell one of these wackos' names wrong, did I? Or are you all choked up because your niece made the A team?' He grinned, pleased with his sarcasm. 'It wasn't very bright keeping that to yourself, then dumping on me every time I argued the case against them. You've left yourself wide open, my friend.'

Ihaka did a slow double-take. 'Your friend? You sure know how to hurt a man, Wayne.'

Cramp kept his grin going. 'Mind you, what else would you expect from Jimmy Ihaka's granddaughter?' He took a sheet of paper from a plastic folder. 'Your old man was hard-core too, wasn't he? Dedicated communist at the age of eighteen; active in the 1951 waterfront strike; broke with Moscow over the invasion of Hungary; expelled from the Socialist Unity Party but remained a convinced Marxist – quote: "Communism hasn't failed, the Soviet Union has." Nineteen sixty-nine, kicked off the Kapuni gas pipeline for general troublemaking; 1970, arrested for assaulting a police officer during anti-Vietnam protests against Vice-President Agnew. And so it goes.'

'Don't tell me you missed the Cuban connection?'

'What Cuban connection?'

'He used to smoke a Cuban cigar every Labour Day – one of those real big mothers, like Fidel Castro.'

Cramp's grin was triumphant. 'I'm glad to see you've still got a sense of humour – you'll need it. Your name came up at that meeting this morning – as a matter of interest, when did you get offside with the Minister of Police? He's not your biggest fan by the sound of it. Anyway, the heavy hitters aren't impressed by your family tree or your conduct. They think you've got a conflict of interest to go with your attitude problem. You're off the team, Ihaka; I'd say McGrail's getting the message as we speak.'

Ihaka got up and headed for the door. 'Suits me. I could do with a weekend off.'

Cramp fell in behind him. 'I know blood's thicker than water but try to remember you're a policeman. Don't contact your niece.'

Ihaka stopped dead and turned in a tight circle. They were face-to-face. 'It's not that you should worry about,' he said mildly.

'What then?'

'This.'

Ihaka shot out his left hand and grabbed Cramp's testicles. Cramp mooed. He started to double up but his face ran into Ihaka's head.

McGrail walked in.

Cramp brayed, 'That fucking maniac just headbutted me.'

McGrail asked, 'Did you, Sergeant?' as if he found the notion a trifle far-fetched.

Ihaka shook his head, more in sorrow than in anger. 'He came up behind me, giving me a gobful. I stopped and he just walked into me.'

Cramp cupped his genitals and snarled, 'What about my balls?'

McGrail swivelled expressionless brown eyes to Van Roon. 'What happened, Constable?'

With his blond, almost white hair, fair skin, and deep-blue eyes, Van Roon looked every bit as wholesome as the Milky Bar Kid, as Ihaka had dubbed him when he'd arrived at Auckland Central. After six years of appearing in the witness box, he was also adept at information management.

'I didn't really see it, sir – I was taking down the names on the whiteboard. But I've seen the sergeant headbutt a few blokes – in the line of duty, of course – and they came off looking a lot worse than Mr Cramp.'

McGrail stroked his narrow nose. 'Well anyway, you're out of each other's hair as of right now. Sergeant...'

'I got the message,' interrupted Ihaka, 'by dildogram. I'm off the case, right?'

McGrail nodded. Ihaka turned to go.

'Hold your horses, Sergeant – that doesn't mean you're on holiday. We've got a knifing murder in Kingsland: you're on it.'

'Can I take Van Roon?'

'Under the circumstances, that's probably sensible.'

Ihaka winked at Van Roon. 'Okay, Snow, let's go beat a confession out of someone. What's the story?'

'The deceased is a white male, thirties, named Brandon Mules…'

'The footy player?'

'Do you know him?'

Ihaka shook his head. 'I saw him play a few times: he was a bit of a gutless wonder – looked like Tarzan, played like Jane.'

Ihaka stood in the toilet doorway contemplating the dead Brandon Mules and wondering if five murders in less than a fortnight was some sort of record. He glanced over his shoulder at the pathologist. 'What do you reckon, Doc? Was he dropping a biggie when he copped it?'

'I haven't had a close look yet; that pleasure is still to come…'

Ihaka ho-hoed and sang, 'Some guys have all the luck.'

'But I haven't seen anything to suggest he was killed elsewhere and moved here, if that's what you mean.'

'What's the ET?'

The pathologist shrugged. 'Twelve hours ago or there-abouts.'

Ihaka bent forward to take a closer look at the wooden handle protruding from Mules' chest. 'What sort of knife do you reckon that is?'

The fingerprinter, hovering in the corridor, said, 'I'd say it's a sharp-pointed stainless-steel cook's knife. Probably his own – there's one missing from the block on the kitchen bench.'

Ihaka twisted around. 'And who the fuck might you be? The galloping gourmet?'

The fingerprinter smiled wanly. 'No; I take cooking classes though.'

Ihaka closed the toilet door and joined them in the corridor. 'All right, Antoine, how long's the blade on that thing?'

'Twenty centimetres or so.'

'Jesus. Takes a bit of grunt to smack that in up to the hilt, eh Doc?'

The pathologist nodded.

Ihaka and Van Roon went out to the front room. 'Okay,' said Ihaka, 'the killer lifts out a pane and opens the door from the inside. He hears the sound effects of a dump in progress. He gets a knife from the kitchen, kicks open the shithouse door, and nails Mules with one almighty thrust before he can get his arse off the seat. I think it's safe to assume we're not dealing with your average burglar here. Then he tears the place apart. Why'd he do that? He could've taken his time – it wasn't as if he was going to be interrupted. You say there's no-one home upstairs?'

Van Roon shook his head. 'They're overseas.'

Ihaka mused, 'This is fucking weird: standard pro B & E access, but what sort of burglar pins a gorilla like Mules to the wall then goes through the kitchen drawers and the linen cupboard? Conan the Interior Decorator? What's missing?'

'The VCR by the look of it but we don't know what was here. Maybe the word was out he had a stash of something.'

'Yeah, could be. Take a couple of boys and do the street. Whoever it was had walked the course, so ask about strange faces, strange cars, anyone poking around recently.'

Van Roon set off then turned back. 'Sarge, can I ask you a question?'

'Shoot.'

'How come you're not pissed off about getting the shove from the APA team?'

Ihaka draped an arm over Van Roon's shoulders and walked him to the door. 'Let me ask you something: what do you think of Cramp?'

Van Roon frowned, surprised Ihaka should have to ask. 'Well, he's a fuckwit.'

'Apart from that,' said Ihaka patiently. 'Is he any good?'

'Well, he seems to know a lot of stuff, but it's like he got it all out of a book.'

Ihaka clapped him on the back. 'Good boy. He's got his anti-terrorist handbook, which would've been written by a twat like him, and he's following it to the letter. If the politicians and the bureaucrats try to run the show from Wellington through Cramp, it'll be the biggest fuck-up of all time.'

'Is that why you got me out?'

'That and the fact you'd always be watching your back: he'd be out to get you.'

Van Roon shrugged. 'He did get off lightly. What about your niece?'

'Jesus, don't worry about her – she'll be as happy as a pig in shit if they pull her in. Those guys want to be

taken seriously, they want to be treated like they're a
threat to the system: that's the whole point.'

When Van Roon left to work the street, Ihaka called
over one of the constables who'd found the body.

'We got a tip-off, right? Man or woman?'

'A man, Sergeant.'

'What'd he say?'

'Just gave the address and said we should get over
here.'

'Sift through this crap,' Ihaka waved at the mess on
the floor. 'Pull out letters, bills, names – anything that
tells us a bit about Mules or connects him to someone. If
you find an address book, you've hit the jackpot.'

Ihaka took the bedroom: zilch. He went to see how
the constable was getting on: double zilch.

Ihaka brainstormed. 'You come across his phone
books?'

'Over there, Sarge, under those tug mags.'

'Go through them page by page: look for names he's
marked or underlined.'

Twenty minutes later, the constable delivered a tentative report: 'I found a few, Sarge, but whether they're
any use...there are a couple of pizza delivery places, a
dial-a-whore, a hardware shop, and a guy, Trousdale, in
Mission Bay.'

SIXTEEN

Leo Strange spent most of Sunday wondering how much strife his sister would be in if Mrs Trousdale didn't get her diary back.

He worked on the basis of 'if' not 'when' because it wasn't beyond the bounds of possibility that the diary would be returned: perhaps Brandon Mules' murder had nothing to do with the diary; even if they were connected, perhaps the killer hadn't found it. In that event, the police would find it, return it, and everyone except Mules would live happily ever after.

It wasn't likely but it was conceivable. Then again, so was peace on earth, a chicken in every pot, and O. J. Simpson becoming president.

A more likely scenario was that the killer had the diary and intended to use it the same way as Mules, in which case there was only one sensible course of action. The reason it took Strange so long to think it through was that, like most devious people, he instinctively distrusted obvious conclusions.

He rang his sister at 7.45 on Monday morning, catching her before she left for a day's temping at an advertising agency in Birkenhead where her duties were answering the phone, making photocopies, sending faxes, and boiling cups of water for the managing director who didn't drink tea or coffee because they gave him erotic dreams about his ex-wife.

Strange got straight to the point: 'Just deny everything.'

'What do you mean?'

'Ring Early and tell him he's got the wrong end of the stick. Say you didn't tell anyone about his affair and had nothing to do with the blackmail.'

'Leo, has it slipped your mind that he's threatening to go the police? It's all very well for you, skulking down there in the Marlborough Sounds, but I'm the one in the hot seat.'

'He's bluffing,' declared Strange. 'If he went to the police, they'd laugh at him – don't forget, he's not the one being blackmailed. The police won't take it seriously unless the woman lays a formal complaint and I bet that's the last thing she wants to do.'

'You didn't see Early, Leo. He didn't look to me like he's bluffing.'

'Of course he is. Apart from anything else, he hasn't got a shred of proof. Okay, he managed to work out that you listened in on his phone call but he can't actually prove it, and he certainly can't prove that you told the blackmailer. He's bluffing all right; and if he isn't, all the more reason to deny it. Trust me; I've given this a lot of thought.'

Adlington doubted she'd ever completely trust her brother again but refrained from saying so. Instead, and not entirely sarcastically, she asked, 'I suppose telling the truth would be out of the question?'

Strange detested that sort of talk. He believed that telling the truth was downright unprofessional: there was no percentage in it, no angle, no room for manoeuvre. If you told the truth and it didn't work, what was your fallback? If you lied, on the other hand, you had options: next time round you could embellish the original lie, tell a new one, or mix it up, one part truth to several parts untruth, so the other side had to decide which was which. Pros only told the truth as a last resort and there were a few stops to go before they reached that dismal destination.

'Renee,' he said, giving it the quiet emphasis of the last word on the matter, 'if you had any idea what the truth was, you wouldn't even think about it.'

Adlington rang Clyde Early and followed her instructions.

'You're lying,' responded Early with daunting certainty. 'You're making a bad call, lady,' he continued over her spluttered protest. 'I offered you a way out but you didn't take it. You won't get another chance.'

Early hung up and swung to and fro in his swivel chair. A quick, clean resolution would've been nice but was never very likely. Adlington and whoever was the brains behind it weren't going to incriminate themselves by handing over the diary, so the real objective had been to scare them off. Time would tell if he'd succeeded.

He thought about bringing Rusty up to date but decided to leave it for the time being: it wouldn't achieve much beyond raising her hopes and his heart rate.

Amanda Hayhoe wasn't in the best of moods that morning. She'd been sweetness and light for most of the weekend, doing penance for biting her flatmate's head off on Friday night. Now the well was running dry.

Maybe I'm not cut out for TV. The stars don't waste their charm on people; they save it for the camera.

She knew from the cuttings file that D'Arcy Potterton's local publisher was Fraser Merritt at Sceptre Press. She rang him to get Potterton's phone number in France.

'You'll need more than that to get hold of D'Arcy.' Merritt's jocularity came as a surprise after the leaden solemnity of his tribute to the late writer.

'Yes, I realise he's no longer taking calls; it's actually his sister I'm after.'

'Belinda's back.'

'Back where?'

'Back here – in Auckland.'

'Really? How can I contact her?'

'Try Fiona Vanarkel's art gallery; she's looking after it while Fiona's in India finding her inner self – yet again. The bloody thing's as elusive as the Loch Ness monster.'

'What's the gallery called?'

'The Gallery.'

Whatever it did for the soul, looking at poor people and water buffalo obviously didn't do a whole lot for the imagination.

Hayhoe rang The Gallery and asked the woman with the plummy voice who answered if she could speak to Belinda Potterton.

'You are.'

'My name's Amanda Hayhoe. I work for Television New Zealand…'

Potterton cut in sharply: 'Are you a journalist?'

'Yes, I'm working on a story –'

'I'm surprised it took you so long – don't they teach you at journalism school that you can't defame the dead?'

Hayhoe was taken aback: mockery was the last thing she'd expected. 'I can assure you I'm not gunning for your brother.'

'What then?'

'I'm doing a story about Jackson Pike, the magazine editor who was murdered last week. I was interested in what happened when he met your brother.'

'As a matter of fact, they got on famously once D'Arcy had recovered from the shock. The man just popped up out of the blue – we hadn't seen hair nor hide of a New Zealand journalist for years. I don't suppose you'd happen to know who put him on to us? I assumed it was Fraser Merritt, D'Arcy's publisher, but he swears it wasn't him.'

Hayhoe smiled to herself. 'I think it might've been Garth Grimes.'

'Who's he?'

'A retired journalist who's either a living legend or a fossil, depending on your point of view. He also dropped in on your brother – in 1979, I think it was.'

'Seventy-nine? That's a lifetime ago.'

'Yes, and he would've been pretty ancient then.'

There was a long pause before Potterton, almost whispering, said, 'God, now I remember him – he stole a photograph of us from a restaurant in the village.'

Whoops.

'Is he really still alive?'

'Very much so.'

'You sound as if you know him?'

'We've met.'

Another protracted silence. 'Come to the gallery at five o'clock tonight. I might have a question or two of my own.'

Hayhoe put the phone down and said, 'Oh, shit,' to her reflection in the kitchen window.

Brandon Mules' next-door neighbour had often seen him in the mud-brown military-style uniform worn by employees of Maximum Security, a security firm with a mixed reputation which operated from a former used-car yard in Great North Road. Early on Monday afternoon, Detective Sergeant Tito Ihaka went there to see Mules' boss, a citizen by the name of Bill Tench.

The first thing Ihaka learned from Tench, who was squat and swarthy and looked like the end product of a cross-breeding program involving several species, none of them *homo sapiens*, was that Mules hadn't been well liked by his workmates.

'Why not?'

'You ever meet him?'

'Once – he was dead at the time.'

'You probably saw him at his best,' said Tench with a lack of sentimentality which Ihaka found refreshing. 'The guy was an arsehole.'

'Everyone around here's an arsehole, including you. What was so different about Mules?'

Tench put on a wounded tone: 'Hey, come on, Sergeant – that's not nice.'

Ihaka studied Tench as carefully as a plastic surgeon who'd just heard the magic words 'money is no object' and shook his head in silent wonder. 'Tench, stop pissing around and tell me something useful.'

Tench might have been concentrating but it was impossible to read anything from his jumble of ill-matched features. 'He thought the sun shone out his arse, buggered if I know why, plus he never had a good word to say about anyone. Shit, he was just a nasty piece of work, that's all there is to it.'

The second thing Ihaka learned was that Mules had been up to something.

'My oath, he was.' Tench wiggled his head like a wind-up toy. 'He was bolshie at the best of times, but fuck me, you should have seen the carry-on last week. He kept saying it was just a matter of time till he told me to stick the job up my jacksie.'

Ihaka felt it was time for some bluff common sense. 'Why didn't you sack the cunt?'

'Beggars can't be choosers, Sergeant. See, Mules might've been a pain in the bum but he was a rare bird in this game: a real big hua who wasn't thick as pigshit. You wouldn't believe some of these drongos. You know they say if you take too many steroids, your tackle shrinks till you end up with a counter-sunk cock? I reckon they have the same effect on the brain.'

This little homily drew another bemused look from Ihaka. 'Interesting theory, Tench; maybe you should pass it on to the medical association. What about dope? You reckon Mules could've been into it?'

'Sure, why not? He was a lazy bastard; he'd do any-thing for an easy buck.'

The third thing Ihaka learned was that Mules' pay was automatically deposited in an account at the National Bank in Karangahape Road.

He spoke to the branch manager who told him that the account balance was $2361.28. The manager provided a banker's perspective on Mules' demise, saying it was ironic that just when he'd finally got out of overdraft, he'd gone and got himself killed. Mules' long-awaited shift into the black had taken place a week earlier when he'd deposited $4500. In cash.

The Gallery was in a mall in the Remuera shopping centre, at the top of Victoria Avenue.

At a couple of minutes after five o'clock, Amanda Hayhoe stood in the foyer awaiting developments. She was joined by a young man in black who looked her up and down and said, 'Yes?', generating as much sibilance as three elocutionists ordering sushi.

Hayhoe told him what she'd come for. He led her through the gallery to an alcove containing two rattan chairs, a low cane and glass table, and Belinda Potterton.

She was about fifty, a faded beauty whose fine bones were diminished by her empty grey eyes and the sardonic set of her wide, thin-lipped mouth. She wore a loose, stylish shadow-check trouser suit with the double-breasted jacket buttoned over a cream silk shirt.

The assistant disappeared. Potterton invited Hayhoe to sit; she lit a cigarette, and blew a stream of smoke at the ceiling.

No beating around the bush. 'So tell me, Amanda, when did you last see Grimes?'

'Just last week as a matter of fact.'

'And how is he?'

'Well, he's as old as Rip Van Winkle but he's still got his marbles.'

'Did he tell you about his visit?'

Unblinking, lifeless eyes watched her; Hayhoe had to make an effort not to squirm.

'He mentioned it.'

'What did he say?'

Hayhoe had known what was coming but it had taken a much more direct route than she'd expected and arrived well ahead of schedule. She opened and closed her mouth, not knowing where to start or how much to say.

Potterton breathed smoke through a cold grin, this time not bothering to avoid Hayhoe's airspace. 'I think you'd better tell me everything, don't you?' she said, as if she'd read Hayhoe's mind. 'And don't worry about offending me – I'm every bit as tough as I look.'

Hayhoe told her Grimes' story.

Potterton listened in silence although her eyes came to life as the narrative unfolded. When it was finished, she burst into laughter which rang slightly brittle. 'That really takes the cake. God, when I think of the lengths we went to…and that old snoop sniffed it out in half a day.' She leaned back in the chair. 'You might as well know that I couldn't give a damn; never did, in fact. It was D'Arcy who lived in dread of being found out. My attitude was that we were two people who loved each other; we were old enough to know what we were doing, and it was no skin off anyone else's nose. I'm having a drink; do you want one?'

Hayhoe said yes. Potterton went into an office opposite the alcove. She returned with a tray containing a bottle of Stolichnaya, a large bottle of tonic, an ice bucket, a lime on a saucer, and a knife.

'Vodka and tonic okay?' Before Hayhoe could answer, she said, 'There's some white wine if you want it – people here don't seem to drink anything else. The proles eat chips with everything; the bourgeoisie drink white wine with everything. You go to someone's place and it's white wine before, during, and sometimes, God help us, even after dinner. Now I just take my own booze; I feel like a bag lady and the hosts get sniffy but it's worth it.'

Hayhoe said vodka and tonic would be wonderful.

As she made the drinks, Potterton asked, 'Did Pike know?'

'I think so; he and Grimes were very close.'

She nodded. 'He did throw me some odd looks; at the time, I thought he was just another anti-smoking Nazi. So what do you want to know?'

'One of Pike's writers told me that he came back from holiday with a bee in his bonnet, but he was so secretive, he wouldn't let on what it was. He did say to Grimes that going to see your brother was well worth it, so I wondered if there was any connection between the two.'

'You mean, did D'Arcy put the bee in his bonnet?'

Hayhoe nodded.

Potterton hummed thoughtfully. 'He was hardly in the door before D'Arce started pumping him about what was going on here. One of the differences between us was that I got over being homesick about fifteen years ago so I pretty much left them to it. I remember them discussing the expat syndrome, which I think was how they got on to the Le Droffs. Does that name mean anything?'

Hayhoe shook her head.

'The Le Droff family owns a lot of land around where we lived; they like to act the landed gentry but I gather they've gone from back street to chateau in a few generations. One of the sons lives here – in Auckland; done very well for himself, apparently. Don't ask me why but Pike was terribly interested in this fellow, so much so that D'Arcy volunteered to find out a bit about him. Whether he ever got round to it is another matter, of course; I suspect he felt obliged to make the offer after having grilled the poor sod for most of the afternoon.'

SEVENTEEN

The next morning, Amanda Hayhoe got Serge Le Droff's file out of the clippings library. There were only a few pasted-up newspaper stories in the manila pouch, which usually meant that the subject's fifteen minutes of fame had led to cell-block C or a hole in the ground.

The first and, as it turned out, most substantial item was from April 1987, when he'd started his Eurotours package holiday venture. Speaking at the launch, Le Droff revealed that he'd been living in New Zealand on and off for several years.

'I came here in 1984 purely out of curiosity,' the quote ran, 'to assess the opportunities created by the opening up of the economy. I found what I consider to be one of the most interesting and rewarding investment environments in the world. As you can see, I believe in putting my money where my mouth is.'

Le Droff was described as 'an Anglo-French entrepreneur with business interests in Europe and the Middle East'. There was a grainy photo of him flourishing the first Eurotours brochure as if it was Jesus Christ's birth certificate. He was mid-thirtyish, with a lean face, dark eyes, curly black hair, and an enviable set of teeth. At first, Hayhoe thought there was something vaguely familiar about him but she decided it was just the Latin look: he had the sort of face which has launched a thousand instant-coffee commercials.

In early 1989, he scored a mention in an investment magazine's story headed 'Riches To Rags: The Big Losers Of The Stockmarket Crash':

It is, of course, much more difficult to get an accurate picture of how the substantial private investors fared but talk around the market suggests that Kiwi-based Frenchman Serge Le Droff took a big hit. The low-profile Le Droff had a reputation as a bold investor partial to entrepreneurial stocks, and market sources believe he was long in some of the crash's major casualties. The encouraging performance of his Eurotours travel business will have provided some consolation.

He also made a few innocuous appearances in *New Nation*'s gossip column, 'Aucklander's Diary', where he went from being 'saturnine' to 'enigmatic' to 'debonair'. It wasn't clear whether the transition was prompted by biorhythms, hormone treatment, or the diarist's thesaurus.

The most recent item was two years old, a snippet in a home-and-garden magazine about his in-progress conversion of the top floor of a downtown high-rise into a 'Manhattan-style' penthouse apartment.

Hayhoe's phone was ringing when she got back to her desk. It was Belinda Potterton doing a passable impersonation of Louis Armstrong.

'You don't sound too good.'

'I feel a damn sight worse and it's your fault.'

'What did I do?'

'You got me stirred up. I went home and opened my last can of foie gras and a bottle of pink champagne; then I had some Armagnac. When I was nicely sozzled and maudlin, I rang a friend in Levignac. God knows how long I was on the phone – long enough to more or less sober up, otherwise I probably wouldn't remember this. I don't know what to make of it – if it wasn't for our conversation last night, I wouldn't give it a second thought. You know D'Arcy was killed in a hunting accident?'

'Yes.'

'Well, the chap who shot him is a farmworker; I'll give you one guess who owns the farm he works on.'

Hayhoe had to think about it, but not for very long: 'The Le Droffs?'

'*Mais oui.*'

'You're kidding.'

'Some things even I wouldn't kid about.'

Detective Sergeant Tito Ihaka stopped in front of the wrought-iron gates of Greywater, the Trousdale residence on the cliff above Mission Bay, and got out of his car. It was 11.51 a.m. on Tuesday, 5 September and, as usual, it was raining. He pressed the intercom button and was squawked at by a foreign-sounding female: 'Yes, who is that?'

He told her and had to prove it by holding up his ID for the closed-circuit TV camera. A few seconds later, the gates began to swing open. He drove in.

Greywater was a three-storey, red-brick Georgian mansion with an imposing portico entrance. In the middle of the circular drive was an ornamental pond with a statue of a young woman wearing an off-the-shoulder number and a remarkably serene expression for someone with one brat clamped to her exposed breast and another climbing her right leg.

A grey Bentley was parked out front; a Mercedes convertible and a four-wheel drive sat in the garage, which still had room for a combine harvester. On the other side of the house, a lush, moss-green lawn, immaculate as newly laid carpet, rolled to the cliff edge.

Ihaka parked behind the Bentley. He walked up the steps to the front door, which was answered by a pretty young Asian in a black maid's uniform. She led him through to a sitting room, saying Mr Trousdale wouldn't be long.

Off the sitting room was a dining room with a massive polished mahogany table laid with silver candlesticks and cutlery and crystal glassware. Ihaka was counting the place settings – there were thirty – when a man came up behind him and said, 'I trust this won't take long; I've an appointment in town at twelve-thirty.'

The speaker was in early middle age, short and rotund with a fat, wobbly face the colour of grilled salmon. He had very fine, bone-white hair, poached-egg eyes, and a tiny, cartoon-character nose. He wore gold-rimmed spectacles, grey trousers held up with braces, a white shirt with French cuffs and pearl cufflinks, a polka-dot bow tie, and a navy-blue blazer.

Shit the bed – first Tench, now this one. It's the Invasion of the Pod People.

Ihaka said, 'Nice place you've got.' He hooked a thumb towards the dining room. 'Having a few mates around for a barbie, eh?'

'I'm afraid we don't do guided tours,' said Trousdale tartly. As is often the case with unsightly individuals whose formative years were spent at boarding schools, his sense of humour hadn't survived the ordeal. 'As I say, I'm rather pressed for time so I'd appreciate brevity.'

'Time is money, right?' said Ihaka knowingly, one tycoon to another. 'The name Brandon Mules mean anything to you?'

Trousdale shook his head decisively. 'Never heard of him.'

A real head-turner in a figure-hugging hound's-tooth check Chanel suit came in from the entrance hall. She gave Ihaka a nice smile. 'I didn't realise we had company.'

Trousdale half-turned to her. 'Darling, this gentleman's from the police – I'm sorry, I didn't catch your name.'

Ihaka sensed rather than saw the woman react. 'Ihaka, Detective Sergeant, Auckland Central. Do you know a guy called Brandon Mules?'

She relaxed. 'Not me. Do you, Maurice?'

'No, I don't. Who is he anyway?'

'Mules is a dead man. We found him in his flat in Kingsland on Sunday morning with a length of cold steel through the left tit. Your name was underlined in his phone book.'

The Trousdales were clearly appalled, either by Mules' fate or his presumption. Her jaw dropped; he exclaimed, 'Good God!' getting his hand up just in time to prevent

his spectacles sliding off his button nose. 'Who on earth
was he? I mean to say, what do you know about the man?'

'Mules? Common or garden low-rent white trash. He
wasn't a crim – at least, not that we know of. His claim
to fame was that he played rugby for Auckland a few
times, back in the early eighties.'

This time Ihaka knew he hadn't imagined the jolt of
comprehension in the woman's eyes. *This is her show,
not the blob's.*

Trousdale said, 'You access phone records, don't you?
You could tell if he'd actually rung here.'

'Done it. All that proves is he didn't call here on his
phone. He could've used a public phone – or someone
else's.'

'Well, I certainly haven't spoken to him. Rusty, have
you had any strange calls?'

'Not to speak of – I mean, there's always the odd
wrong number...' Rock-steady.

*So what? The lies I bet she's told him, she should be
good at it.*

'I don't think our friend's here to investigate wrong
numbers.' Trousdale puffed up as if he'd said something
stupendously witty. 'Look, I really should get going. As
you can see, Mr Ihaka, it's a mystery to us why this
character marked our name, so I don't think we can be
of much assistance.'

Ihaka agreed. 'Doesn't look like it.'

They followed him to the door, co-ordinating their
programs: she was lunching with Jane in Parnell, then
coming back to oversee preparations for his birthday
dinner party; he had lunch at the club, followed by a
session with the accountants.

Ihaka turned into the first sidestreet. After the Bentley and the Mercedes had swished past, he drove back up the street and parked outside Greywater. He opened his newspaper, turned on the car radio, and settled down to wait.

Hayhoe was nibbling a filled roll when she got the idea. She was surprised and not altogether pleased to find that she still remembered her ex-lover's direct line. It hadn't changed and neither, it seemed, had he.

'Gary, it's Amanda. Have you got a moment?'

'Amanda?' Surprise gave way to wariness. 'Where are you calling from?'

'Relax – I'm in Auckland.'

'Oh, right. So how's it going? I've seen you on the box a few times.'

She could picture the scene: Gary and Mrs Gary and the kids settling down in front of TV to watch little old her.

'It's going okay but I need a favour.'

'I've got to tell you, Amanda, this isn't a good time – it's balls to the wall here. I've got a diary like Bill Clinton's…'

'Spare me the corporate-slave routine – I've heard it before. You owe me one, Gary. When the shit hit the fan, I left town and I went quietly. You never heard a peep out of me and you know damn well I could've kicked up a major fuss if I'd wanted to.'

'Maybe,' he said flatly. 'That was then; you don't have a lot of leverage now.'

'Jesus, Gary, don't go all sentimental on me.'

'Eh?'

'I was being sarcastic.'

She waited him out.

'So what's the favour?'

'You told me once that the bank uses some sort of high-powered corporate information service.'

'Did I say that?'

'I remember it distinctly. You said you were clients of this company which specialises in short-notice warts-and-all bios. I think your exact words were, "They can tell us the last time the guy jerked off." '

'We're in the information game,' he said blandly. 'We tap into a range of sources.'

'Come on, Gary: can you have someone checked out for me or not?'

'Would it need off-shore input?'

'Yep.'

'This is a very big ask, Amanda. It means bringing in London or New York and those guys charge like wounded bulls.'

'It should leave us about all square then.'

'Who?'

'Serge Le Droff.'

'The mysterious Monsieur Le Droff?' Gary showed some interest. 'What's got you so interested in him?'

'His name cropped up in a story I'm working on – to tell the truth, it's a long shot.'

'Amanda, if I do this for you, we're square. You'd be wasting your time with another appeal to my conscience.'

'Fair enough.'

'What I'm saying is, you only get one wish, so are you absolutely sure this is how you want to use it?'

She said sweetly, 'I can't think of anything else you could do for me.'

The news broke on the one o'clock bulletin. Ihaka was expecting it; he'd had a sneak preview first thing that morning in the form of a frantic call from his sister.

'New Zealand may be on the brink of a race relations crisis,' recited the newsreader in the tragic tones normally reserved for wars, mass murders, and beached whales. 'That was the widespread reaction to the bombshell announcement that police investigating the Aotearoa People's Army are questioning a number of prominent Maori radicals.

'Following overnight raids on houses in Auckland, South Auckland and Rotorua, seventeen members of Maoridom's radical fringe are being held at Auckland Central police station. Searches of the properties are continuing. The seventeen are being questioned by detectives from the APA task force set up following the murder of MP Chas Gundry and his police bodyguard, and the earlier slayings of radio talkback host Fred Freckleton and magazine editor Jackson Pike.

'Initial responses to the raids from opposition parties, leaders in the Maori community, and church and civil liberties groups range from disquiet to outright condemnation. However, the Minister of Police strongly defended the police actions.'

They had the minister on tape: 'This is a straight-forward police operation with no political implications,' he shrilled. 'The police are simply following up all lines of enquiry, as they are duty-bound to do. I would remind critics that the APA has claimed responsiblity for four cold-blooded murders and made intolerable threats against anyone in public life who opposes their aims. I'm confident that ordinary New Zealanders – as opposed to professional agitators and those with a political axe to grind – understand the gravity of the situation and will fully support the police in their efforts to bring the terrorists to justice.'

Ihaka said, 'Sounds like fun,' and flicked off the radio.

Shortly after two o'clock, Mrs Trousdale's Mercedes came up the street. He got out of his car and waved at her as she swung into the driveway.

She halted and lowered the car window. 'Hello again; did you forget something?'

He leaned against the car, looking down at her. 'We need to have a chat.'

'What for? I told you I don't know that man...'

Ihaka nodded. 'Yeah, but that wasn't the cross-your-heart-and-hope-to-die version, was it?' Her face tensed up. 'Look, I guess you think had a good reason for not coming clean but this is a murder investigation – you're legally obliged to spit out whatever you know. So why don't we go in, get Suzy Wong to make us a cup of tea, and talk it over?' He paused. 'And what the sugar daddy doesn't know, can't hurt him, right?'

She iced him. 'That was fucking rude and completely uncalled for.'

He nodded, deadpan. 'The job makes you cynical – it gets to the stage you can't recognise true love when it's right under your nose.'

Reluctant amusement rippled across her face. 'How terribly sad for you.' She mashed the accelerator and the Mercedes bounded forward. Ihaka muttered, 'Thanks for the lift, you tart,' and walked up the drive as the rain came down again.

He was in an armchair in the sitting room; she strode in, followed by the maid carrying a tray.

He asked, 'I don't suppose you could stretch to a sandwich? While you were having lunch with Jane, I was out there listening to my stomach juices foam.'

'I can see you've practically wasted away since this morning,' she said unsympathetically. 'Cecilia, would you mind rustling up a snack for our guest? Something light – a suckling pig, perhaps.'

Cecilia tittered and departed. Mrs Trousdale crossed her legs with a rustle of black silk and gave Ihaka another amused and slightly patronising look. 'Well, Sergeant, you wanted to talk: so talk.'

Ihaka switched on menace: 'You say you don't know Mules and think that's the end of it. Take it from me, sister, it ain't, not by a long stretch. Right now, that line under your name in Mules' phone book is the only lead we've got, so if I have to I'll tear your world apart to find the connection. I've got a feeling old Horace or Maurice or whatever the hell he's called doesn't know what's going on and you want to keep it that way. Well, that's your problem – I don't give a shit.'

Her green eyes flashed. 'Are you threatening me?'

Cecilia came back with a plate of dainty, cocktail-sized sandwiches. He shovelled a handful into his mouth.

The maid left. Ihaka eased off. 'I'm not threatening you, Mrs Trousdale; I'm trying to explain that I'll find out, one way or the other. If you help me, then maybe it won't need to go beyond this room. But if I have to do it the hard way...' he shrugged indifferently 'So be it. If it comes to that, just bear in mind that when we start beating the bushes, all sorts of strange things can crawl out.'

Ihaka sat perfectly still. He had nothing more to say and nothing showed on his wide brown face. Rusty Trousdale realised that she'd come up against a force which, for all her experience of men, she had no idea how to deal with.

To break eye contact, she reached for a sandwich she didn't want. 'All right, there is something going on. But I've got no reason to think it's got anything to do with Mules.'

'Yes you do – deep down.'

She sighed heavily. 'Believe it or not, it's all because Mules was a rugby player.'

EIGHTEEN

Once Rusty Trousdale's resistance crumbled, she didn't hold back. It was the story of her life.

Assuming Brandon Mules was the blackmailer, then Lusty Rusty's bits on the side also had a motive. Tito Ihaka decided to start with Amanda Hayhoe, because that promised to be the most fun. She wasn't at TVNZ so he drove over to Clyde Early's hardware emporium in Birkenhead. Another wasted trip: Early was in Canberra, attending a coaching seminar at the Australian Institute of Sport. That left the Frog.

The Eurotours receptionist, a beefy woman with a mouth like a half-healed wound, ran a reptilian eye over his scuffed sneakers, faded jeans, and black leather jacket. Despite her natural assets, she was out of her league trading dirty looks with Ihaka. He pulled a scowl which would've killed a cockroach at ten paces and told her who he was and what he wanted.

The combination brought her to heel. She simpered, 'Can you tell me why you wish to see Mr Le Droff?'

He squinted at the wall for a few seconds, pretending to think about it. 'No.'

She snatched the phone to relay the message, then invited him to take a seat.

A minute later, a robust, silver-haired man in a double-breasted suit burst through the door behind the reception desk. He marched up to Ihaka and barked, 'Wyatt Bloodsaw at your service; I'm the security bod.'

Ihaka scarcely registered that Bloodsaw appeared to be a werewolf – every second person he met these days was some sort of freak. They exchanged a crunching handshake; Ihaka made a mental note to introduce Bloodsaw to Wayne Cramp.

'This way, old chap.' Bloodsaw spun on his heel. 'By the right.'

He stomped over to the door, which he opened with a plastic card. They went up a flight of stairs to another security door. Bloodsaw jabbed in a code and it clicked open. At the end of a dimly lit corridor, double doors opened into a crescent-shaped room. A curved ceiling-to-floor window extended the length of it, providing a panorama of the harbour from the mangroves of Te Atatu around to the silver thread of traffic winding along Tamaki Drive through the eastern bays.

The room, by contrast, was subdued: dark tones, sparse furnishings. There was a bookshelf along the wall, and in the foreground a matching pair of black leather chesterfields faced each other across a low table. Beyond the chesterfields was a U-shaped work station, set up as two desks with duplicate functions: each had a computer, a stack of trays, and a phone.

A man in navy-blue chinos and a pale-yellow sweater sat at the work station. He stared out the window, hands clasped behind his head.

'Detective Sergeant Ihaka, sir,' said Bloodsaw. 'One of Auckland's finest.'

Le Droff gave no indication that he'd heard, even though the announcement had been made at parade-ground volume. He held the pose like an artist's model for half a minute then slowly swivelled in the chair. He stood up, studying Ihaka impassively. He was wiry, about 180 centimetres, with curly dark hair, olive skin, and a blue-black shadow bordering a long-nosed, hatchet face. Ihaka put him in his early forties.

'Good afternoon, Sergeant.' The accent was neutral, transatlantic. 'Let's sit down.'

Ihaka and Bloodsaw sat on one side of the low table, Le Droff on the other. He re-clasped his hands behind his head and put his feet up on the table, crossing his ankles.

Ihaka said, 'I've been talking to Mrs Trousdale: she sent someone to see you last week.'

'He spoke to the Colonel.' Le Droff tilted his head at Bloodsaw.

'About how she was being blackmailed?'

Le Droff gave a tiny nod. He seemed completely relaxed but his unblinking, light-brown eyes never left Ihaka's face.

'A guy called Brandon Mules was murdered last weekend – you know him?'

Le Droff answered with the barest shake of his head. 'I saw something about it in the paper.'

'It looks like he was the blackmailer.'

'Just desserts, some would say.'

'The law doesn't see it that way.'

'How do you see it, Sergeant?'

'I'm on duty; I agree with the law.'

Le Droff smiled a brief, private smile.

'If Mules was blackmailing Mrs Trousdale, that obviously makes her the prime suspect.'

Le Droff raised his eyebrows sceptically. 'I seem to remember he was stabbed?'

'With a long-bladed knife; the killer used every inch of it.'

'Not a modus operandi one would readily associate with Rusty.'

'Oh yeah? So how would she do it?'

Le Droff grinned, showing perfect white teeth. 'She'd kill with kindness.'

It was Ihaka's turn to raise his eyebrows. 'Well, Mules sure as shit didn't go out with a smile on his face. You had an affair with her –'

'I wouldn't call it an affair.'

'What would you call it?'

'I call a spade a spade; what we had was a fuck.'

Bloodsaw made a noise like a feral pig having the orgasm of a lifetime. The tight, cold smile was back on Le Droff's face.

'A fuck?' said Ihaka. 'That's it?'

Le Droff looked at the ceiling. 'We met at a party last summer. I suggested she drop in next time she was in town and I'd take her to lunch. A few days later, she did. We came back here after lunch and had sex on a desk in one of the offices downstairs.'

'Why?'

Le Droff frowned. 'Why what?'

'Why on a desk? Haven't you got a bed?'

'Oh, I see. Well, I was already late for a meeting. It was fast and furious and none the worse for that.'

Ihaka's eyes narrowed enviously. 'Then what?'

'Then nothing – that's all there was to it. Hence my view that it didn't amount to an affair.'

'You weren't tempted to go round again – maybe on a photocopier?'

'Oh yes,' said Le Droff almost dreamily. 'Most definitely.'

'Why didn't you?'

Le Droff sighed and rubbed his eyes. 'I got the feeling that Rusty was torn: part of her wanted fun and adventure, part of her wanted to leave all that behind and settle down to be a good little wife. Do you smoke, Sergeant?'

'No.'

Le Droff took a Marlboro from the packet on the table and lit it with a slim gold lighter.

'I have this problem with cigarettes: I like smoking but I hate being a smoker. I've tried to give up plenty of times and I know how hard it is if you're surrounded by people who smoke. You see what I'm driving at? Besides, I'm not much good at adultery – I can't be bothered with all the intrigue – so I decided the best thing all round was to let it go.'

'And she returned the favour by writing it up in her diary? That must've slutted you?'

Le Droff was all worldly nonchalance. 'Womanising has its risks; always has and, I dare say, always will. I could do without it but frankly, Sergeant, it's no big deal. I'm not married; I don't have a steady girlfriend; I don't have shareholders to keep happy; I'm not trying to get elected; and my family's 20 000 kilometres away. I'm in the fortunate position of not having to give a damn what people think of me so, personally, I really couldn't care if Rusty's diary's serialised in the newspaper.'

'Not everyone can afford to take that attitude.'

'Obviously not.'

'Mrs Trousdale, for instance?'

'Definitely not.'

'She's the sort of woman some men would go out on a limb for.'

Le Droff looked down, smiling and shaking his head as if he found the notion absurd. 'Not this man. Rusty's a big girl; she also happens to be the author of her own misfortune, if you'll pardon the expression.'

Ihaka gave no sign that he'd got Le Droff's little joke. 'Where were you in the early hours of Sunday morning?'

Le Droff held his gaze. 'Tucked up in beddy-byes – where else?'

'By yourself?'

'Yes, by myself. Abstinence obviously isn't as safe as it's cracked up to be: if I'd known I was going to be a suspect, I'd have organised a bedmate. Or two.'

'I didn't say you were a suspect.'

'I'm relieved to hear it.'

'I didn't say you weren't, either.'

Le Droff smiled. 'On the subject of the diary, I assume you've recovered it?'

'No, we haven't.'

Le Droff thought about it. 'Then how can you be sure Mules was the blackmailer?'

'We can't. I never said we were.'

'Well, okay, but you seem to be working on that assumption. If it turns out it wasn't him, then neither Rusty nor I have a motive.'

Ihaka leaned forward, putting his elbows on his knees. 'We know Mrs Trousdale was being blackmailed; we know Mules was capable of it; we know he was acting like he'd won Lotto; and there's evidence to indicate he contacted her. I'd say that means one of two things: either Mules was the blackmailer or we've got a mother-fucker of a coincidence on our hands.'

'Coincidences do occur from time to time.'

'Only when it suits us.' There was nothing in Ihaka's expression to suggest he was joking.

Ihaka got home just before eleven. He got a couple of beers out of the fridge and went through to the lounge where he flicked on the TV with the sound down low and flopped into an armchair.

He'd been at his sister's place. His niece was there, fresh from her brush with the law. She seemed to have enjoyed the experience and was looking forward to doing it again. He had a feeling she wanted to be a political prisoner when she grew up.

The raids had been a fiasco. The house searches turned up a rusty .303, a slug gun, a couple of knives, a Dutch bestiality video, and small quantities of the usual drugs, but not one tiny, tenuous link to the APA. No charges were laid. The seventeen activists bopped out of Auckland Central into a media love-in, spitting defiance in pre-packaged sound-bites. The government was shitting itself.

Boo hoo.

Fuck it anyway. He had his own problem – who spiked Mules?

The Trousdales or Amanda Hayhoe? What a line-up –
three natural-born killers if he'd ever clapped eyes on
them. Le Droff? Why would he care? Clyde Early? That
felt a bit more like it, especially if he and Mules had bad
blood going back. Then there was the mystery man
Mules had been seen with in The Globe.

The other scenario was thieves falling out: Mules
might've had a partner who got greedy, which would
explain why they hadn't found the diary. One problem:
Mules was a loner; everyone said so. Why would he
suddenly get a partner if he thought he was going to
score big-time? At least there was a tap on the Trousdales' phone now, if someone else had a go...

Ihaka felt himself drifting into sleep.

*Haul arse, fat boy, before you flake in the chair. You
don't want to wake up at four in the morning stiff and
cold and feeling like shit.*

In fact, it was 3.35 a.m. when Ihaka woke up in the
armchair. He was cold and needed to piss and the TV
was throwing out a static buzz. Before he could attend to
any of those things, there was the small matter of the
gun-wielding figure in the dark boilersuit and ski mask
looming over him.

Ihaka got halfway out of the chair before the pistol
barrel came down across his temple. He grabbed a
handful of boilersuit and fell back, pulling his assailant
down with him. He glimpsed a second dark figure, then
took another metallic crunch on the side of his face. He
saw starbursts. He pawed weakly at the guy on top of
him, who knocked his arms aside and chopped him
again with the pistol, driving his head back into the
chair. Fingers dug into his left arm and the sleeve was

196

yanked above his elbow. He felt a needle sting in the crook of his arm.

He was in quicksand. He craned his neck to suck in air and clawed at solid ground, trying to hold on. The force dragging him down was relentless and his arms burned unbearably with the strain.

He lost his grip and sank like a stone, all the way to the centre of the earth.

NINETEEN

I t was lunchtime. Amanda Hayhoe was contemplating a quick trip to the cafeteria to top up her cholesterol when she got a call saying there was a package for her in reception. She went down to collect what turned out to be an unmarked, unaddressed white A4 envelope.

'How do you know it's for me?' she asked the receptionist.

'Because the guy said so.'

'Did you get his name?'

'Listen, he just shoved it at me, said it was for you, and shot through.'

'What did he look like?'

The receptionist rolled her eyes. 'Get real: we get a zillion people coming in here dropping things off. He was a suit, that's all I can tell you.'

Hayhoe went back to her desk. The envelope contained five typed, numbered sheets. There was no letterhead, no covering note, no signature – nothing whatsoever to indicate the source.

She started reading:

Serge Alain Le Droff was born in Hôtel Dieu Hospital in Toulouse, south-west France, on

11 October, 1949, the second child of Jean-Jacques and Penelope Le Droff. His father was a small businessman who owned several cafés and bistros catering mainly to blue-collar workers. His mother, whose maiden name was Brackett, was English. His parents had met in 1946 when she accompanied her father, a London wine and spirits merchant, on a buying trip to Gers, the Armagnac-producing region west of Toulouse.

Jean-Jacques Le Droff had been a member of the underground Resistance movement during the German occupation. Fiercely patriotic and conservative, he was persuaded to stand for the mayoralty of Toulouse in 1952 but lost heavily to the socialist candidate. Disillusioned, Le Droff moved his family (a daughter, Josette, had been born in 1948; a second son, Dominique, was born in 1954) to the then French colony of Algeria. He settled in Algiers and went into business importing produce from the Gers and Haute-Garonne regions.

In Algiers, Le Droff senior's interest in politics was rekindled. His forceful personality and status as a hero of the Resistance made him a prominent figure among the Algerian French, the Pieds Noirs – 'Black Feet' – as they were known in France. Not surprisingly, he was vehemently opposed to the Algerian independence movement, the Front de Libération Nationale (FLN), which was locked in an increasingly bitter guerilla war with the French security forces.

When Le Droff's political hero, General Charles De Gaulle, returned to power in 1958 vowing that

Algeria would remain French, the Pieds Noirs and the army were euphoric. However, when De Gaulle began negotiations with the FLN, the euphoria was replaced by a profound sense of betrayal.

Le Droff senior publicly supported the 1960 settlers' revolt and the equally abortive 1961 putsch by units of the French army serving in Algeria. While it seems unlikely that he was a member of the Organisation Armée Secrète (OAS), the terrorist group formed following the failed putsch and which made several unsuccessful attempts on De Gaulle's life, it is perhaps significant that the Le Droffs moved to New Caledonia in 1962. Jean-Jacques may have been forced to spend a 'cooling off' period there before being allowed to return to metropolitan France. Deals of this kind were struck with particularly intransigent Pieds Noirs; in return, the authorities dropped investigations into their links with the OAS. The fact that the Le Droffs moved back to Toulouse in 1966 lends some credibility to this theory.

In 1962, at his mother's insistence, Serge was sent to board at Downside in Somerset, England. Even allowing for his bilingual upbringing, he made the transition with remarkable ease. He did well scholastically and excelled in a number of sports, notably cross-country running and fencing.

In 1967, Le Droff enrolled as an Economics student at the Sorbonne in Paris. He later claimed not to have taken part in the so-called 'Days of Rage', the student riots which convulsed France in May 1968, almost bringing down De Gaulle.

While he would have been one of the few students at the Sorbonne not to have participated, that would be consistent with his apparent indifference to politics. In his subsequent career, he has appeared an apolitical pragmatist solely concerned with commercial considerations.

Le Droff left university at the end of 1968 without completing a degree and dropped out of sight for three years. He has occasionally referred to his experiences crewing on charter yachts in the French West Indies, which would account for this gap.

In October 1972, he turned up in the Gulf state of Dubai, part of the United Arab Emirates (UAE), re-establishing contact with junior members of the Dubai royal family whom he'd met at the Sorbonne. He would spend most of the next decade in and around the Gulf, engaged in various trading ventures and middleman activities.

The 1973 Yom Kippur war and subsequent oil-price shock transformed commercial activity in the Middle East. As vastly increased oil revenues flowed into the region, opportunities opened up for skilful middlemen with connections on both the supply and demand side of transactions. With the Arab states investing heavily in military hardware, Le Droff was once again able to tap personal contacts: in this case, officials in the highly integrated French defence establishment – the military itself and the government-owned armaments manufacturers – who had served with his father in the Resistance.

The commissions Le Droff earned from his role in a number of arms deals provided the launch pad for his swift expansion. By the late '70s, he had companies in Dubai, Abu Dhabi, and Bahrain engaged in the importation of luxury goods. In addition, he continued to earn commissions from acting as a middleman or 'spotter' for French companies doing business in the Middle East.

His travels throughout the region included a number of trips to Lebanon, which was embroiled in multilateral civil conflict, and Iraq, during its protracted war with Iran. The reasons for these trips are not known.

In October 1980, the classified appendix to a staff study on terrorist activity prepared for the US House of Representatives Committee of the Judiciary was leaked to the publisher of a military-intelligence newsletter. Le Droff's name appeared on a list of known or suspected procurers of sophisticated weaponry for the various groups operating under the umbrella of the Palestine Liberation Organisation (PLO). However, he was not mentioned in the appendix to a full report on the subject which was prepared for the committee several months later and also leaked. A footnote attributed discrepancies to the fact that the earlier study had contained information from a since-discredited source.

The nature of Le Droff's business activities precludes confident estimates of his wealth but there can be little doubt that by 1980 he was a millionaire, probably several times over. He installed his family in a twenty-room chateau near the village of Levignac, outside Toulouse, and bought several farms in the area. When not on the move around the Middle East, Le Droff himself generally stayed at his home in Cap Ferrat on the Côte d'Azur.

However, the early eighties were not kind to Le Droff. He was involved in several civil aircraft sales campaigns in Africa and the Middle East, acting on behalf of the European manufacturing consortium, Airbus Industrie. Virtually all these deals went sour when the airline industry slumped in 1982, a slump which coincided with a sharp fall in the price of oil. Most of the customers were the state-owned airlines of nations with oil-based economies and they reacted to these twin blows by reducing, indefinitely postponing, or cancelling their orders.

Le Droff is believed to have invested heavily in these deals in the form of bribes paid to airline executives, government officials, and members of the ruling group or family, in the expectation of earning substantial commissions when the sales were finalised. Even those sales which did eventuate were effectively oil-for-aircraft barter transactions, meaning Le Droff was forced to take his commissions in kind, i.e. oil, which he then had to sell at a loss on the spot market. He was also rumoured to have invested in Middle Eastern arms dealer Adnan Kashoggi's catastrophic Sudan venture.

With the Middle East no longer such a profitable environment, Le Droff looked for fresh fields. Having scaled down his holdings in the Gulf, he visited Latin America in 1983 and Australia and New Zealand in 1984. Impressed by what he saw as the potential for growth in the New Zealand financial sector as a result of the deregulatory policies embraced by the Labour Government, Le Droff moved to Auckland in mid-1984. He rented a house in Kohimarama and acquired a shelf company, Craxus Holdings Ltd, which he renamed Brackett Investments Ltd. He took office space in Air New Zealand House in Queen Elizabeth II Square and began trading shares.

When the market boomed in 1985–86, Le Droff's focus shifted from blue chips to high-yield entrepreneurial stocks, a switch which left him heavily exposed when the market crashed in October 1987. Although no hard information is available, market watchers believe the losses wiped out a good percentage of his gains of the previous three years. He is believed to have resumed share-trading within the last two years, although on a smaller scale.

In April 1987, Le Droff launched Eurotours, a wholesale travel company specialising in middle- and up-market package holidays to lesser-known regions of France and Italy. The Eurotours product was seen as offering quality and value-for-money and was well received. As a result, the company was able to weather the post-1987 recession and capitalise on the surge in offshore travel when the economy eventually picked up and the New Zealand dollar strengthened.

Once again, however, events conspired against him. Eurotours was caught in the consumer backlash against all things French triggered by the resumption of nuclear testing at Mururoa Atoll and is understood to be trading on sharply reduced volumes.

Le Droff is seeking to diversify. He has approached the New Zealand aviation authorities with a proposal for a charter airline operation linking New Zealand (and possibly Australia) and Europe. He is believed to have agreed terms with Airbus Industrie's used-aircraft division for the lease of up to three A310 wide-body jets and secured in-principle approval from the French authorities, as well as stopover/pick-up rights in Singapore. The New Zealand authorities are favourably disposed towards the proposal but the minister has put further consideration on hold until the furore over French nuclear testing has abated.

In 1986, Le Droff obtained the right to continuous residence in New Zealand. In 1993, he bought the top floor of the First Pacific Bank building in Quay Street and converted it into a penthouse apartment. The property is mortgaged to the Banque Nationale de Paris for $NZ2.5 million. He also leases the ground and nineteenth floors for Eurotours' sales and corporate offices respectively. His various other commercial operations are also located on the nineteenth floor.

For a wealthy man, Le Droff has very little in the way of an entourage. His personal staff consists of a cook–valet, a Corsican named Pascal, and Colonel Wyatt Bloodsaw, who could best be described as his right-hand man. Le Droff met Bloodsaw, formerly of the British Army's 13th Parachute Regiment, in Sharjah in 1982. Bloodsaw was an old Middle East hand, having served in Oman and Qatar while on attachment to the SAS. He left the army in 1979 to take up a position as a military advisor and trainer in UAE. In 1982, Bloodsaw joined Le Droff's organisation as an executive assistant with responsiblity for security. He appears to be Le Droff's closest associate.

Little is known about Le Droff's personal life. He is private to the point of reclusive but is said to be relaxed and adept when he does socialise. Those who have had business dealings with him describe him as an accomplished performer in meetings and negotiations. His social contact is largely confined to a small group of acquaintances in the financial community who date from his early share-trading days.

He has never married but the inevitable rumours of homosexuality appear to be baseless. Indeed, he earned a reputation as something of a ladies' man among the expatriate community in UAE and is known to have had a number of short-lived relationships with Auckland women.

He owns a house on the eastern side of Waiheke Island in the Hauraki Gulf, where he spends most weekends, and a 12-metre yacht, *Lady Penelope*, which is moored at Westhaven marina. He has always been fitness-conscious and reportedly remains in good physical condition. He visits his parents at least once a year and also makes regular trips to Tahiti and New Caledonia, where his family retains ties.

Hayhoe finished the report and announced, 'The plot thickens,' in a dramatic voice.

She saw the producer coming her way, looking even more harassed than usual. When he reached her desk, he put his hands on his hips and said ominously, 'If I was in your shoes, I'd unthicken it. Double quick.'

'Why, what's up?'

'I've just heard that news is preparing a one-hour special on the APA to go to air next Monday – fronted by Ainsley Tarr.'

'Eeek.'

'Exactly. If our story isn't a quantum leap forward from whatever they come up with, two careers will crash and burn. My kids are relying on you, Amanda.'

Massive bladder pressure finally woke Tito Ihaka. The dense, throbbing pain in his head reminded him that he was in the shit.

He was fully clothed, lying on a thin rubber mat with a blanket over him. When he rolled onto his back, he felt a tug on his left wrist and left ankle. He threw off the blanket: his wrist and ankle were handcuffed to what proved to be a leg-press weight training machine. He tried to shift it but only succeeded in confirming the obvious – it was too heavy – and making his head pound like a fishing-trip hangover.

He sat up and looked around. He was in a windowless room, a basement maybe, about six metres square with white-washed plaster walls and old carpet. The leg press and another weight machine, a bench press, were against the wall facing the door. On his right was a wine rack which must have held a hundred bottles; on his left, an old chest of drawers, a few cartons, and a stack of magazines. The room was chilly and dimly lit by a single-bulb light.

He looked at his watch: 2.43 on the sixth. He'd only missed two meals.

Well, maybe not. On the floor beside him were two plastic buckets, a bottle of mineral water, a roll of toilet paper, a packet of aspirins, and some sandwiches in Gladwrap.

Well, fuck me, I've been kidnapped by the Salvation Army.

He got a bucket, manoeuvered himself into a semi-kneeling position, and had the longest day-time piss of the twentieth century. It was the biggest thrill he'd had for a while.

He checked the damage: the left side of his face was swollen and he had three lumpy welts between hairline and cheekbone. The skin was broken and there was dried blood on his fingers when he took his hand away. He popped a couple of aspirins, washing them down with water.

He hollered a few times but nobody came and it just made the thumping in his head worse. He decided to have lunch. There was a choice of cheese or ham; he went for ham.

The first swallow came back up a lot faster than it had gone down. It triggered a power-spew, accompanied by epileptic shudders and sound effects which would've made a torturer gag.

Ihaka lay propped up on his elbows, waiting for the nausea to recede and surveying the mess. He knew he'd had a lot to eat at his sister's place the night before but he was surprised and mildly embarrassed to see just how much.

A little later, he sat up and reached for the rest of the sandwich with a trembling hand.

TWENTY

Detective Constable Johan Van Roon thought nothing of it when Tito Ihaka didn't turn up at work on Wednesday morning.

There were any number of possible explanations. Ihaka was unconventional: he didn't always go to bed at night and get up in the morning and brush his teeth after meals like most people.

But when Ihaka failed to show for the two o'clock Mules investigation briefing, a faint alarm bell rang. You could accuse him of a lot of things – and he'd give you one of his 'up your's' grins and admit to most of them – but at the end of the day he was a pro: he fronted up. Ihaka didn't miss murder briefings come hell, high water, or the sort of hangover which drove lesser men to their first AA meeting.

There was no answer at Ihaka's house and his mobile was switched off. Van Roon checked with the switchboard. He hadn't reported in, but as the operator pointed out, so what's new? He had a look on Ihaka's desk, which was as neat as could be because Van Roon himself had spent an hour the previous day creating order out of chaos, as he did every few weeks. The fact that it was still in that state meant Ihaka hadn't been near it since. Van Roon didn't go through the drawers: he was concerned but not that concerned.

Van Roon went back to his desk and tried to do some work. *What am I worrying about? Any minute now, he'll barge in and abuse me for not reminding him about the meeting.*

Ihaka would've been out in the badlands, sidling up to back doors for whispered conversations or putting the squeeze on some loser in the back bar of a dead-beat pub. He'd look round with that sour expression, as if he'd just walked into someone's fart fog, and say something charming like, 'Hi there, homos. Am I too late for the circle jerk?'

But no matter how hard Van Roon tried to put it to rest, it just kept nagging away at him. Finally, for his own peace of mind, he decided to take a quick run out to Ihaka's place.

Ihaka's car was in the drive but the curtains were drawn. That was odd: if he was home, he would've opened the curtains; if he wasn't, why was his car there? The front door was unlocked: he never bothered to lock it when he was there but usually remembered to when he went out.

The house was clean and tidy. A few months earlier, Ihaka had got sick of living in his own private black hole of Calcutta; he'd decided to get a cleaning lady in once a week. A couple took one look at the place and declined the gig; the third one agreed to take it on at time-and-a-half and on condition that he started showing a little house pride.

Van Roon called out but didn't even get an echo. He checked the house room by room and looked in the car and around the backyard: Ihaka definitely wasn't in residence. He went back inside to use the phone and saw the envelope slipped under the receiver. It was unsealed; he flipped it open with a ballpoint and slid out the note.

The news could have been worse but only just:

COMMUNIQUÉ NUMBER FOUR

The police harassment of seventeen Maori patriots was an outrageous provocation and clear proof that the state is now on a war footing vis-à-vis radical elements. The Aotearoa People's Army herewith vows to stand shoulder-to-shoulder with those threatened by the police state's onslaught and to resist it with all the means at our disposal.

The police state should understand that retaliation for any future actions of this kind will be swift and decisive. To demonstrate this, the APA has seized the policeman, Ihaka. He is a traitor to his people and will be treated accordingly, should there be any repeat of the indiscriminate, rascist and fascist police action against those in the vanguard of Maoridom's struggle for liberation and sovereignty.

It is not too late for the state to abandon its totalitarian course. If the authorities are prepared to apologise for their action and give an undertaking that it will not be repeated, Ihaka will be released unharmed. If, however, they are intent on violent confrontation, he will merely be the first of many casualties.

212

Van Roon, who'd had a religious upbringing and didn't take the name of the Lord or any of his immediate family in vain, said, 'Holy Mother of God.'

At 5.39 that evening, the SIS man Wayne Cramp paused outside Detective Inspector Finbar McGrail's office. He loosened his fat Windsor knot and breathed hard through his nose, then knocked and entered.

McGrail was ready to call it a day: he had his jacket on and, as he did every evening before leaving the office, he'd cleared his desk, except for a copy of the APA's fourth communiqué.

As Cramp lowered himself into a chair, McGrail tapped the communiqué with his index finger. 'Well, Mr Cramp, it seems our little exercise on Monday night achieved something after all. I think you'd concede it's not quite the outcome you predicted.'

Cramp loosened his tie some more and cleared his throat. 'If you remember, Inspector, I did predict they'd strike at police officers. I think it shows we're on the right track.'

McGrail studied Cramp as if he had a mildly interesting deformity. 'Oh really? And how did you arrive at that sanguine conclusion?'

Cramp, with a hint of bluster: 'Well, why else would they've grabbed Ihaka? Okay, we mightn't have hit the target on Monday night but this tells us we got too close for comfort. It's obvious from the communiqué what they're up to – they're trying to make us back off.'

'I see.' McGrail nodded slowly. 'Can I take it then, that your department's advice to the minister will be "carry on regardless"?'

Cramp thrust his chin out. 'Absolutely. In fact, we'll advocate turning up the heat.'

'Well, if nothing else, that should eliminate the slightest chance Sergeant Ihaka has of remaining in one piece.'

'Look, Inspector, I'm gutted about Ihaka but you know as well as I do he's a goner. We can't cave in to these bastards: there's no way in the wide world the government can let a gang of criminal subversives dictate terms to them. The APA know that too; that stuff about letting him go is just posturing.'

McGrail nodded dolefully.

Sensing he was winning the argument, Cramp pushed on. 'With all due respect, we'd be kidding ourselves to think otherwise. They wouldn't dare turn him loose now. The guy's an experienced officer – he'd know far too much about them. I'm sorry to say this, I really am, but my guess is he's already dead.'

McGrail sighed. 'Thank you, Mr Cramp. I think I'll go home now.'

The conversation had confirmed what McGrail already suspected: the government had written Ihaka off. Only his friends could help him now. The question was, would they?

McGrail didn't go home. He drove out to Sandringham, to Ihaka's place, where he wandered around trying to keep out of the way of the lab boys who were going through it with a fine-tooth comb. When he'd found what he was looking for, he drove back towards the city, crossing Newton Gully and Great North Road, and went into Grey Lynn the back way, up the hill.

He parked outside a restored villa in a short street off Richmond Road, went up the steps to the veranda and knocked on the door: no-one home. He got back in his car and called his wife to say he'd be late. Then he sat and waited, still and contemplative as a mystic.

It was almost eight before his patience was rewarded. A Peugeot 305 zipped past, its showroom sheen reflecting the streetlights. It halted in front of the garage; the man McGrail was waiting for got out, opened the garage door, and drove in.

McGrail stayed put. The man locked the garage. Without looking left or right, he walked towards the steps up to his front door. Instead of going up the steps, he circled around the rear of McGrail's car on cat's feet and wrenched open the driver's door.

McGrail looked up at him, a glimmer of amusement in his bleak brown eyes. 'I'm pleased to see you're still on the ball.'

Duane Ricketts smiled quizzically. 'Detective Inspector McGrail, as I live and breathe. What are you doing lurking outside my humble abode?'

'It's a long story. If you could spare me half an hour…'

'Why not? I can go to the opera any old night.'

They went inside. Ricketts offered McGrail a drink; he said a cup of tea would be nice. Ricketts put the kettle on and got himself a beer. He sat down opposite McGrail and made a perfunctory 'cheers' gesture with the bottle.

. 'It must be a year,' said McGrail. 'You look healthier.'

The last time they'd met, Ricketts wasn't long out of a Bangkok jail. He'd been on the scrawny side and sunken, wary eyes and hollow cheeks had accentuated his sharp, slightly foxy features. Now he'd bulked up to lean and had an expensive haircut to go with the smart suit and the boldly-patterned silk tie. Add the new house and the new car and Duane Ricketts seemed to be doing quite nicely, thank you.

The packaging was different, flasher, but McGrail was sure the product hadn't changed: the mind behind the knowing grey eyes would be just as quick and calculating. Not for the first time, he reflected that Ricketts would have made a very good policeman if he hadn't been expelled from the force all those years ago. It was before McGrail's time and he'd never really got to the bottom of it: a newspaper was slipped a police photograph from an unsavoury sex case and somebody – presumably not the horse – kicked up a fuss...

'Yeah, well, staying out of jail helps.'

'Work's going well by the look of things?'

Ricketts nodded. 'I'm getting heaps of work from Trubshaw Trimble and a couple of other law firms. Your recommendation certainly didn't hurt.'

'It might've got you in the door, that's all.'

Ricketts went to make the tea. McGrail called through to the kitchen: 'Have you been following the exploits of our home-grown terrorists?'

'Pretty hard not to.' He came out with a tray. 'They don't muck around, do they? You on to them yet?'

'We're still chasing shadows, I'm afraid.' McGrail sipped his tea. 'They struck again last night.'

Ricketts decided he was about to find out why McGrail had come a-calling. He put down his beer and paid attention.

'They've got Sergeant Ihaka.'

Ricketts stiffened. He opened and closed his mouth, as if McGrail wasn't a suitable audience for the comment he had in mind. 'You mean they're holding him prisoner?'

'Yes.'

'What are his chances?'

'Poor to non-existent.' McGrail could've been predicting the weather. 'He may be dead already. His release is conditional on government compliance with demands which can't and won't be complied with. Unless they're completely crackers or completely naive – and I don't believe they're either – they know that perfectly well, so the offer isn't worth the paper it's written on.'

Ricketts shook his head. 'So what are you doing, ripping the town apart?'

'We're doing the usual things with an unusual degree of urgency. There's a complication. The APA says it's retaliation for the other night's blitz on Maori activists and he's for the chop if it happens again.'

'Why would you do it again? It was a big fat zero, wasn't it?'

'That hasn't deterred our anti-terrorism experts...'

'Who're they?'

'Some gentlemen from the SIS. They're convinced that the APA are Maori extremists and that view seems to hold sway in Wellington. They see what's happened to Ihaka as a vindication – it shows we're getting warm.'

'What do you think, Inspector?'

'Initially, I was inclined to go along with it, if only for a lack of alternatives: who else out there displays the obsessive rage which drives people to political violence? I know from my Belfast days that, over time, terrorist organisations attract romantics and psychopaths and bandits, but they're founded on single-minded fanaticism which derives from a burning anger over some real or perceived historic injustice. Who else in the community does that apply to? Sergeant Ihaka was sceptical from the outset, but, as you know, he tends to operate on gut instinct, which the bureaucratic mindset doesn't value. As you probably also know, he believes a fool should be allowed to suffer the consequences of his foolishness, so he didn't pursue the argument with any great degree of persuasiveness. In fact, it reached the point that his attitude got him dropped from the investigation. Now, the APA wouldn't have known that, but if they are some sort of Maori extremist faction, you'd think they'd know about his niece.'

'What about her?'

'She was one of the strident seventeen hauled in for questioning. Don't you think that abducting her uncle is an odd form of retaliation? The niece certainly does: I spoke to her mother late this afternoon – the girl's beside herself.'

'Maybe the APA didn't know…'

'Maybe – she does have a different surname. I'd be surprised though – when all's said and done, they're a pretty select group and I would've thought word would get around.'

Ricketts poured McGrail another cup of tea and got himself a second beer and a packet of potato chips.

McGrail apologised for keeping him from his dinner; Ricketts told him not to worry about it, he wasn't looking forward to it that much anyway.

'Something else bothers me about the Maori radicals theory,' said the policeman. 'The APA has carried out four operations without leaving a trace. No-one's seen anything, no-one's heard anything – we haven't got a single, solitary lead, not even a sketchy vehicle description. That's the hallmark of experienced professionals, not a bunch of beginners.'

'So why the hell grab Ihaka?'

'That's the sixty-four-thousand-dollar question, Mr Ricketts, and I don't have the answer. Perhaps the sergeant stumbled across something on one of his solo forays.'

Ricketts stared thoughtfully at McGrail. 'Okay, Inspector, what's on your mind?'

McGrail stared back. 'When I was churning over this earlier, it occured to me that you're probably the best people-finder in the business. If anyone can find him, you can.'

Ricketts started feeding chips into his mouth, nodding as he crunched through them. 'Sure, I'll have a go. I owe the fat bastard: if it wasn't for him, I wouldn't be in this place...'

McGrail coughed. 'Yes, I'm not sure I really want to hear about that.'

Ricketts grinned. 'What have you got?'

McGrail flipped open his briefcase and brought out a plastic folder. 'That's everything worthwhile on the APA, which doesn't amount to much. I even included Ihaka's case notes...'

'Jesus, since when did he make notes?'

'In the loosest sense of the word – they're more a collection of rather disturbing doodles. There's also some background on the case he was transferred to...'

'You're sticking your neck out, aren't you?'

McGrail frowned. 'I suppose so. Not as much as you are though. You do realise that, whoever these people are, they're completely ruthless?'

'It's a fine fucking time to bring that up, now that you've talked me into it.'

'The art of salesmanship, Mr Ricketts.' If he hadn't known better, Ricketts would've said McGrail's expression verged on affectionate. 'Don't draw their attention to the fine print until they've signed on the dotted line.'

TWENTY-ONE

I t was well past Finbar McGrail's bed-time.

McGrail liked to be at his desk by 7.45 a.m. having jogged, made his toilet with an attention to detail which suggested a degree of vanity, had a tasteless but reliably laxative breakfast, and chaired a family discussion on the day ahead. This routine meant getting up at 5.30. Seeing he wasn't one for burning the candle at both ends, his head normally hit the pillow at half past ten.

That Wednesday night was an exception. If his arithmetic was correct, there was a seventeen-hour time difference between New Zealand and the state of Georgia, on America's east coast, so midnight in Auckland was seven o'clock in the morning there. Seven in the a.m. was as early as most people cared to get phone calls.

McGrail dialled a number from the address book which he'd taken from Tito Ihaka's house earlier that night. After half a dozen rings, a man answered in a down-home drawl: 'I'm listening.'

'Good morning, I'm trying to get hold of C.C. Hellicar.'

'You got the next best thing, bubba. This here's C.C.'s daddy.'

'Mr Hellicar, I'm Detective Inspector Finbar McGrail of the Auckland police – that's Auckland, New Zealand. I'm sorry to be ringing so early…'

'Hell, that's okay, the whisky ain't biting too hard this morning. And call me Willard. What time you got where you're at?'

'It's shortly after midnight.'

'Midnight, huh? Would that be midnight last night or midnight tonight?'

'Tonight – we're seventeen hours ahead of you.'

'Is that right? Well, if you're seventeen hours ahead, you must be a long ways away; and if you're a long ways away, you'll want to be getting down to the nitty-gritty: C.C. ain't here. Matter of fact, this ain't been home to C.C. for nigh on ten years.'

'I wonder, could you tell me where I can get hold of her? As you know, she came down here last year –'

'Hold your fire, Finbar – did I get that right?'

'Yes.'

'That a New Zealand name?'

'No, Irish. I'm from Northern Ireland originally.'

'I could tell you had an accent of course, but hell, anyone from outside of Walton County sounds a little strange to me. What I was fixing to say, Finbar, was it's news to me my little gal's been down in your part of the world. See, the thing is, C.C. wasn't inclined to tell me a damn thing about her job. I remember one time not long after she'd gone to work for that outfit in Arizona, she came visiting and happened to leave her passport lying around. When I picked it up, it just kind of fell open, you know the way they do, and I couldn't help but notice she had a stamp for Mozambique. I said, "C.C., what in the hell you been doing in Mozambique?" Well, sir, she just looked at me with those pretty blue eyes and said, "Daddy, I can't tell you on account of it's a matter of national security." So ever since then, we've had ourselves an arrangement: I don't ask and she don't give me the high hat.' His voice dropped: 'Not that I didn't have a good goddamn idea what she was doing: I mean, the government didn't send her to Fort Bragg to learn touch typing, right?'

While C.C. Hellicar was undeniably attractive, McGrail felt that only a fond father would refer to her pretty blue eyes, since they were the coldest, palest shade of blue imaginable, like frozen meths. But that wasn't the comment which really made McGrail prick up his ears: 'Willard, you said "what she *was* doing"…'

'Check.' His voice got flat. 'C.C. quit – she don't do that stuff no more. It's a sad story: about midway through last year she started stepping out with a fellow in Phoenix, professor at the college there. I'll tell you, Finbar, you wouldn't have looked at C.C. and this boy and said straight off they were made for each other. I'd always figured that any man she got serious about would have to be like her and then some, you know what I mean? This Oliver, he was a gentle guy, real earnest – shit, he was a professor, what can I say? But he sure was sweet on her and I guess that counts for a lot. Anyway, to get right along, something bad happened when they were on vacation in England last fall – the professor bought the farm. C.C. don't talk about it; all she said was her past caught up with her. She quit and went off to Hawaii; she's working in a fitness club there run by an old friend of hers. The point is, Finbar – and I apologise for taking the long way round – if you had in mind for C.C. to do a job for you, the plain fact is, she's retired.'

'I see.' McGrail didn't try to hide his disappointment.

'Why don't you give that company she worked for a call? They must have other folks who do whatever the hell it was exactly C.C. did.'

'The problem with that, Willard, is this isn't an official call. It's a personal matter: someone C.C. got to know when she was here is in a terrible bind.'

'Well shit, why didn't you say so? The way she is these days, there's no telling which way she'll jump, but C.C.'s always been one to side with her friends. You hang there two shakes and I'll find her number for you.'

C.C. – for Candice Clara – Hellicar dozed in the single bed in her pokey mid-town Honolulu apartment. The apartment bore a passing resemblance to a cell in one of the looser nunneries. Like a lot of things, it had seemed like a good idea at the time.

As she often did in the dreamy haze of her slow awakenings, Hellicar was retracing the sequence of events which had brought her to Hawaii. She'd decided some time ago that the connecting thread, if there was one, was sex.

It began in late fall 1993. She was working for a security company based in Scottsdale, Arizona, which provided advice, training and protection to a range of international clients. The company was a CIA front – 'a proprietary' in agency terminology – and Hellicar was a CIA agent. A very special type of agent: she belonged to a unit so shadowy that its very existence was a matter of conjecture within the US security and intelligence apparatus. The unit's members were known as 'the cleaners'; they were the US Government's instruments of last resort for ridding itself of rogue agents who, in intelligence jargon, had 'gone bamboo' – become the menace they had been charged to combat.

Drew Hobbs was one such rogue. He was tall and blond with an appealing 'aw shucks' country boy manner and good enough at the game to have gone a long way. Instead, he'd gone seriously off the rails, teaming up with Cuban intelligence to run dope into Florida. The Cubans had been doing it ever since the revolution. It was just about the perfect anti-Yanqui operation: they piped poison in and sucked greenbacks out. Hobbs didn't see himself as a criminal, let alone a traitor. The way he looked at it, any fool could see that Cuba posed as much of a threat to the US as the Canary Islands. He was just meeting a demand and getting rich in the process and wasn't that the American way?

When Hobbs' superiors at CIA headquarters in Langley, Virginia finally caught on, they took a diametrically opposed view. They assigned Hellicar the task of conveying their extreme disapproval in any way she saw fit providing it a) caused Hobbs' death; b) couldn't be traced back to the agency; and c) didn't exceed budgetary guidelines.

The set-up was a variation on the honey-trap. Hobbs was in Miami, staying at the Bellevue Hotel on South Beach. He was a compulsive skirt-chaser so around ten o'clock he'd hit the Bellevue's cocktail bar, one of the hot spots along the beach, where a 21-year-old Cuban-American calling herself Carmelita would be sitting alone at the bar.

It was a sure thing that Hobbs would zero in on Carmelita, whom Hellicar had recruited from one of the ferociously anti-Castro Cuban exile groups in Miami, because she made every other babe in the bar look like Courtney Love on a bad smack day. She had a mane of glossy-black hair, a heart-shaped face, hot eyes, and a soft-lipped, crimson pout. She wore spray-on black leather pants and a skimpy white singlet which barely restrained bulging, centrefold breasts and exposed a swathe of flat, satiny midriff. When Hobbs got a load of Carmelita, he'd be putty.

She'd let him come on to her. When he suggested adjourning to his room for some meaningful interaction, she'd reply that they knew her in the bar and she didn't want a reputation as an easy lay. Why didn't he go on up to the room and set out a few lines of coke? She'd go powder her nose and be up in a few minutes.

Hobbs would drift off; Carmelita would give Hellicar the nod on her way to the ladies' room. When she knocked, Hobbs would open the door with a flourish to find a silenced Heckler & Koch VP 70 9-mm semi-automatic pointed at the small gap between his front teeth.

Except it wasn't Hobbs who opened the door of Room 1053. It was a brunette wearing a see-through black peignoir and an expression of glazed expectancy. Hellicar knew her from a photo in Hobbs' file: she was his wife, Diann. What wasn't in the file was the information that Diann didn't mind her husband playing around as long as she could join in. She'd flown into Miami late that afternoon for some three-way action.

Diann screamed a warning and tried to slam the door but Hellicar punched the pistol butt into the side of her jaw and squeezed into the room. Naked except for his stainless steel Rolex Oyster Sea-Dweller, Hobbs was squirming across the king-sized bed trying to get to the gun in the bedside table drawer. Maybe his erection got snagged in the bedclothes because he'd only just got the drawer open when Hellicar's first round hit him below the left armpit.

Hellicar tore up a sheet to tie and gag the new widow. She hung a 'Do not disturb' sign on the doorknob, took a cab to the airport, and caught the midnight flight to New Orleans.

Diann Hobbs might have been a tad kinky but she wasn't stupid; in fact, the joint venture with the Cubans had been her idea. So when the Miami police department started dragging its feet, despite having a fairly accurate description of the shooter, she assumed they'd filed Drew's killing under Spook Shit. The question was: whose spooks?

The Cubans got word to her that it wasn't them. Three weeks after Drew's termination, an elegant middle-aged woman followed Diann into the restroom at a Georgetown café and told her it had been a CIA hit. Their sources inside the anti-Fidel movement said the hitwoman had a southern accent and used the name Clara Monroe.

Diann thought it over. 'If I find out who she is, will you waste the bitch?'

The middle-aged woman looked offended. 'You mean me personally?'

Diann rolled her eyes. 'Your people. Cuba.'

'I doubt it,' said the woman, 'but you can always ask.'

Diann Hobbs knew that several of Drew's colleagues had a permanent hard-on for her. She casually asked the best-looking of them to see what he could find out about a statuesque operative with eerily pale blue eyes and a southern accent who used the field name Clara Monroe. He was happy to oblige.

He reported back a couple of weeks later that the description appeared to fit a Candice Clara 'C.C.' Hellicar, current status and whereabouts unknown. Trawling through the computer, he'd come across a biog listing which described her as an electronics specialist and mentioned the fact that she'd attended high school in Monroe, Georgia.

That was good enough for Diann. She flew down to Mexico City and went to the Cuban embassy where she asked to see an intelligence officer. They said, 'Come back tomorrow.' The next day she asked the fat man in the safari suit who'd flown in from Havana if his government would avenge Drew's murder. The fat man smiled politely and craned his neck to get a better look at her bare, brown thighs.

When the fat man realised that she was serious, he said his government was very sorry about the death of her husband, who was an enlightened man and a valued ally, but was unable help her. She asked why not. He explained that Cuba was seeking to improve its relations with the United States so inserting an assassination squad, even in such a worthy cause, would be viewed as counter-productive. He stood up, took a lingering, regretful look at her legs, and said that if she could alert them in advance, with detailed information, when Hellicar ventured beyond US borders, then...he shrugged expressively...perhaps the matter could be re-assessed.

Diann re-enlisted her late husband's colleague, urging him to find out everything he could about Hellicar. That amounted to next to nothing. Hellicar obviously worked in a highly sensitive area, probably covert operations, because accessing her full file needed a whole lot more security clearance than he had. Diann threw him a motivational fuck and asked him to try again. He didn't get any further and warned her that if he kept trying, someone would notice him poking his nose where he wasn't authorised to poke it.

She took him to bed again and went through the manual. Afterwards, she gave him a tear-jerking and largely fictitious account of her husband's death. It went in one ear and out the other: he didn't give a foaming fuck who'd aced Drew or why. The important thing was that Diann was alive and kicking – and scratching and biting for that matter. He was prepared to play along with whatever dumb-ass scheme she had going if it meant some more of that wild sack-time. He had a buddy in the office of personnel in the Support Directorate; maybe he could find out something.

By early summer, Diann was running out of patience with her lover's inability to deliver the goods in either sense when his buddy came through with Hellicar's itinerary for the overseas holiday she had planned for the fall. It was routine procedure for agency staff going on vacation to submit an itinerary and contact details to the office of personnel so they could be reached in an emergency. Covert ops were an exception, as they were to most things, but the Plans (Clandestine Services) Directorate had sent Hellicar's program through anyway. There was no particular reason for it: it was just another of the countless bureaucratic screw-ups which occur in Washington DC – and every other government town – on a daily basis.

Diann returned to Mexico City for another audience with the fat man in the safari suit. He studied Hellicar's itinerary and remarked that Britain was hardly the ideal country in which to mount such an operation but he'd see what could be done. In the meantime, perhaps she might like to give some thought to what she could do in return for Cuba's assistance. Diann shrugged and said she picked up lots of stuff from her CIA friends and their wives which she was happy to pass on; apart from that, she'd consider any reasonable proposition.

The fat man smiled until his face creased like a baby's. He pushed his chair back so he could see her legs under the table. She'd worn an even shorter dress this time.

Hellicar and her beau, Oliver Kirsopp, flew to London in the first week of October. For Kirsopp, a professor of English literature at Arizona State University, the trip was both a romantic interlude and a pilgrimage. His Mecca was the Welsh seaside town of Laugharne where his hero, the poet Dylan Thomas, had lived and, having cemented his reputation by drinking himself to death at the tender age of thirty-nine, been buried.

They spent a few days sightseeing in London, then drove down the M4 and across the Severn bridge into Wales. They rented a cottage near Worm's Head on the Gower peninsula and after the visit to Dylan's grave and the boathouse where he'd worked, they explored the soft, green countryside. They drove down impossibly narrow lanes, tramped across fields, picnicked on the banks of the Towy, wandered in dark woods, and climbed Sir John's Hill in the mild twilight. Kirsopp knew much of Thomas's work off by heart. In each location, he'd recite an appropriate poem, imitating the dead poet's celebrated bardic chant. His light Louisiana tenor was a far cry from Thomas's rich baritone but Hellicar didn't care: she could've listened to him all day long.

On their way home, they'd stop for a drink in rural pubs where they were mostly welcomed as guests, occasionally shunned as tourists and Yanks to boot. Back at the cottage on the cliff, they'd have dinner, drink wine, make love, and fall into deep, country sleep.

Kirsopp had no idea what Hellicar really did. She'd told him that she designed and supervised the installation of state-of-the-art electronic security systems. So when a noise woke them at 3.13 one morning, he insisted that she stay put while he went to investigate. Against her better judgement but feeling that it was a little late to admit to knowing more ways of killing a man with her bare hands than Ezra Pound had mental breakdowns, she acquiesced. He got up, pulled on his black kimono with the dragon rampant on the back, and stepped out into the corridor.

About half a minute later, there was a noise like a suppressed sneeze followed immediately by a baffled grunt, another suppressed sneeze, and a series of thuds. The average person might have assumed that Oliver was having a sneezing fit, had tripped in the dark and fallen over; Hellicar knew the sound of a lover being shot dead with a silenced pistol when she heard it. She sprang out of bed, hoisted the window, and dived through it. She did a forward roll as she hit the ground, bounced to her feet, and sprinted into the night. Behind her, doors slammed, footsteps pounded, and voices were raised in a gabbled exchange.

It wasn't freezing but it was too cold to be playing hide and seek in nothing but a pair of Calvin Klein underpants. She was wearing underpants because she had herpes and because Oliver slept naked and was inclined to get amorous in his sleep. With exquisite timing, the herpes had made one of its infrequent appearances the previous day, ringing the usual bells: the joke – 'What's the difference between love and herpes? Herpes is forever'; the scumsucking ex-boyfriend; and the vow to track the scumsucker down and tattoo the joke on his dick with a jackhammer. Not that there was room.

The rented cottage was a good killing ground: the nearest house was a kilometre away and the cliff twenty metres from the back door cut off escape. It was dark though – low cloud blocked out the night sky – and there was cover from the overgrown garden dotted with clumps of trees and a low stone boundary wall.

Pin-drop quiet. *Don't run; hide, wait. Let them come. You'll hear them; they'll have to see you.*

Hellicar crouched in a stand of trees by the wall, about forty metres from the house. Someone was coming. She dropped onto her stomach and inched backwards into the knee-high undergrowth which grew along the wall. Thorns raked her bare back.

A squat figure shuffled up to the trees, right arm extended, swinging to and fro like a windscreen wiper. He edged through the trees and bellied up to the wall. She could smell the cigarette smoke on his clothes.

He was almost on top of her when she erupted from the undergrowth, like a missile from an underground silo. She caught his right wrist, wrenching it down, and pulped his nose with the heel of her other hand. His head whiplashed. She slipped a leg behind his and flipped him. His skull pinged off the wall as he went over. She ripped the pistol from him, jammed the silencer into his ear, and pulled the trigger.

The gun was a Colt Woodsman .22. Hellicar tossed the silencer: they were into stealth, she was more concerned with accuracy. She tore at the buttons of the dead man's jacket until a gravelly crunch told her the other gunman had crossed the drive. She forgot the jacket. Exposure was the least of her worries.

The dead man lay half in, half out of the undergrowth. As she lifted his feet into the long grass, his trouser leg rode up his calf. He had an ankle holster with a Harrington & Richardson Young America .22 revolver: seven more rounds. She stuck it in the waistband of her underpants, at the small of her back.

Hellicar crawled on her belly through the under-growth to the line of trees and shrubs along the cliff edge. The Atlantic Ocean boiled over rocks fifty metres below. She knelt behind a tree, in the firing position, straining her ears and eyes for a rustle or flicker of movement.

Then the tree trunk exploded, blasting wood fragments into her face. She lurched backwards, losing her footing and the Colt. The ground dropped away and she slid on her stomach. She wrapped her right arm around the base of a sturdy bush growing out from the lip of the cliff. Her feet swung into space and she pawed frantically for a toehold on the cliff face.

She had both arms around the base of the bush hauling herself up when the second gunman appeared above her. He wore a dark tracksuit with a woollen cap pulled down to his eyebrows and dangled a pistol in his right hand. He lowered himself onto his haunches, elbows on thighs, wrist uncocked, the fat tube of the silencer pointed downwards.

He said, 'Well now, darling,' in a broad Irish accent, 'and how long would you be thinking you can hang on there?'

'Not for long.'

'You look a bit cold.' A low chuckle. 'Your nips are standing to attention like grenadier guards.'

'Who are you?'

'Ah, now that would be telling.'

'Why did you do this?'

He showed off a toothy grin. 'Let's just say we're doing some friends a favour...' He broke off, noticing the Colt: 'That's Davy's – I don't much like the look of that. What have you done with him?'

'He's over there.'

The Irishman looked over his shoulder. 'Where now?'

Hellicar dropped her left arm and plucked the revolver from the waistband of her underpants. When he looked back at her, she shot him twice through the left eye. The Harrington & Richardson must have pulled right because she'd aimed at the bridge of his nose.

The dead gunmen turned out to be members of a deactivated Provisional IRA hit squad. The Provos had taken on the job at the request of the Libyans who, after all, hadn't asked for much in return for the moral and material support they'd provided over the years. The Libyans, for their part, were doing a favour for the Cubans. Hands across the water.

Hellicar's rehashes always led to the conclusion that Oliver was dead because of her. Sometimes, she wondered whether she'd feel any worse if she'd been in love with Oliver, as opposed to very, very fond of him. Occasionally, she'd reflect that if it hadn't been for the herpes attack, she'd probably be dead too.

She never dwelt on that notion for long: the ironies were too bitter.

Hellicar looked at the bedside clock. Five after eight: she'd be late for work – again.

In Auckland, about 8000 kilometres to the south-west and across the international date line, it was 6.05 the following morning. Finbar McGrail had treated himself to a half-hour sleep-in after his late night.

The phone rang. Hellicar's past was reaching out for her again.

TWENTY-TWO

As a rule, Rusty Trousdale didn't bother keeping up with the dreary parade of trivia, humbug, acts of God, and man's inhumanity to man which we call 'the news'.

Massacres in the Kwa-Zulu, tidal waves in the Bay of Bengal, bone-pits in the Balkans, baby-faced crack whores on the South Side, family fatals on the motor-way – shit happens, as they say; always has done, always will. Rusty wished it was otherwise but as the old prune who'd taught her French at boarding school used to say: 'You can wish till you're blue in the face, *ma petite*; that won't make it so.'

This morning was different. Today's top billing victim-wise was someone she knew: Detective Sergeant Ihaka. A couple of days earlier, he'd sat in the next room wolfing sandwiches and bullying her ragged; now there he was on the front page. The photo, a blow-up from a news shot taken at a crime scene, captured Ihaka in all his sensitive New Age glory. It cried out for a cartoon balloon: something like, 'Get the fuck out of my face.'

The accompanying story reported that Ihaka had been abducted by these terrorists whom Maurice and every-one else she came across insisted were wild-eyed Maoris.

While Rusty didn't actually know any Maoris personally and didn't pretend to understand what made them tick, she found it hard to fathom why a bunch of angry, disaffected Maoris would take it out on one of their own. Surely there were plenty of pakeha policemen to choose from?

She was reading the Police Minister's statement and thinking that the stuff about not making deals with terrorists didn't sound too promising for Ihaka when her mobile phone rang. It was Clyde Early, in a better mood than last time they'd spoken.

'I got your message. Sorry I didn't get back to you sooner – I've been in Australia.'

'That's okay. The reason I called, there's been a development.'

'I've got some news too.' He sounded positively cheerful.

'Good news?'

'I'd say so.'

'Well?' she coaxed. 'Don't keep me in suspense.'

'Have you heard from the blackmailer this week?'

She hesitated. 'No, why?'

'I reckon I've scared him off.' He told her how Renee Adlington, the temporary secretary, had found out about their affair by listening in on the phone call, how he'd figured it out and put the wind up her.

'So she's in it with the creep who rang me?'

'Yeah, obviously. I don't know who he is but...'

'Did she confess all?'

'Course not; she lied through her teeth, just as you'd expect her to. You should have seen her though – she was packing shit.'

Rusty went, 'Hmmm.'

'What's the matter? You don't sound all that pleased.'

'Well, it's just that...you know that ex-rugby player who was murdered?'

'Mules? I'll say. I sacked him once, in Italy. I could've told you he'd come to a sticky end. What about him?'

'Remember I said it sounded like the blackmailer knew you?'

'Yeah.'

'The police think Mules was the blackmailer.' She told him about Ihaka's visit and the underlining in Mules' phone book.

There was a long silence as Early digested this information. He asked slowly: 'Does that mean the cops know about us?'

'Afraid so.'

'But they didn't find the diary at Mules' place?'

'Afraid not.'

'This cop...'

'Detective Sergeant Ihaka.'

'Right – he thinks whoever murdered Mules has got the diary?'

'I suppose that's a reasonable assumption.'

'Shit.' Early was struck by another unpleasant thought. 'Jesus, what about Maurice? Does he know?'

'No. Ihaka's more subtle than one would think.'

'Well, thank Christ for that.'

'Getting back to your temp for a moment: Ihaka made Mules out to be a nasty piece of work, which is certainly how the blackmailer came across. It's not that I don't think you've been very clever, because I do, but is that how you see Renee Whatsername?'

'Probably not but then I didn't see her as the sort who'd listen in on phone calls. You know, we should tell Ihaka about her: she might know something about the murder.'

'As a matter of interest, Clyde, have you read today's paper?'

'Just the sports section, why?'

'Have a look at the front page. You'll see that Ihaka's got rather a lot on his plate just now.'

In fact, Tito Ihaka hadn't had as much as a crumb on his plate for eighteen hours.

Gnawing hunger was just the start of it: he still had a booming headache, still felt the queasy after-effects of whatever they'd injected him with. He was also cold and his body ached from enforced discomfort.

Then there was the smell. During the night, room service had emptied the buckets and left him a sponge and an old towel to mop up what had missed and what had splattered but he couldn't clean up what he couldn't reach. He'd woken up that morning with an urge to surge and ended up sludging on an industrial scale. Now that was mingling with the residual puke and really starting to hum.

Then there was the boredom. He was running out of things to think about, ways to pass the time.

Analysing his plight hadn't taken long. The APA had got him. They'd known where to find him because he was in the phone book, bravado he now regretted. Why him? He'd been named in a couple of early APA newspaper stories and they weren't to know he'd been arseholed from the task force. The fact that he was still alive might mean they planned to use him as some kind of bargaining chip. Then again, it might mean they were dreaming up a really warped way of sticking it to him.

Stewing on it wasn't going to help so he'd turned to other subjects. He'd chosen the best and worst All Black teams of the past twenty-five years. He'd picked his top ten films, top ten albums, top ten Bruce Springsteen songs, ten biggest fuckheads on TV, ten sleaziest people in town, ten sportsmen who could be closet homos, and the ten people he'd most like to beat to within an inch of their lives – give or take an inch. Interestingly, that list had almost as many cops as criminals. He'd gone for Steve McQueen in *Bullitt* as his favourite movie cop, ahead of Gene Hackman in *The French Connection*. Ellen Barkin in *Sea of Love* bolted home in the cop's squeeze category.

From there it was a natural progression to the ten women of his acquaintance he'd most like to fuck. Over half of them – including Rusty Trousdale, who made a strong late run, coming in at six with a bullet – were married or de factos. Not a very healthy state of affairs but that was the way the cookie crumbled. He tried the ten women he'd most like to fuck again but that proved overly ambitious; even five was tough going. His ten most fuckable movie actresses reflected the enduring influence of his uncle's *Playboy* magazines, with which he'd whiled away many a happy hour in his youth. Claudia Cardinale just pipped Brigitte Bardot for top spot.

Now what? Ten policewomen you'd like to fuck? Settle down. Try 'wouldn't knock back on a wet Sunday afternoon' and you could probably scrape up a few. How about ten known or suspected dykes you'd like to...No, I don't think so. Okay: ten women you know or have reason to suspect don't wear undies? Well, for a start there's...

A key rattled in the lock. The man who stood in the doorway was in his mid-fifties, tall and wiry, with receding grey-black hair, olive skin, and deep-set, unblinking black eyes in a thin, lined face.

Psycho.

Ihaka said, 'What's for lunch?'

The man ignored him. He sniffed, wrinkling his nose in disgust, and produced a wide-bladed commando knife from behind his back. After he'd given Ihaka a good look at the knife, he put it away and removed the crap-bucket. He came back with a bucket of water, sluiced away what was left of the vomit, and threw the empty bucket at Ihaka.

'Who are you?'

The tall man's forehead furrowed as if he'd been asked the square root of 187 trillion. Then he casually kicked Ihaka in the stomach and walked out. He returned a few minutes later with a bottle of water and some food: a few slices of salami, a lump of cheddar cheese, buttered bread, and an apple.

Ihaka said, 'Pig's bum.'

The tall man grinned unpleasantly, revealing uneven yellow teeth. He kicked Ihaka again – in the ribs this time and quite a lot harder – and exited, locking the door.

Ihaka looked at the food: all of a sudden, he wasn't that hungry. The fact that the mute with the cut-throat eyes had showed his face meant that they were going to kill him. It was just a matter of time.

The words every journalist dreads hearing are: 'There's someone out here who wants to talk to you.'

Members of the public who hawk their wares around newsrooms generally fall into one of two categories: those who've been gang-banged by little green men from the planet Zorb and those who think their petty obsessions – a wrangle with the gas company over the sum of $28.76, for instance – are of cosmic significance.

For female journalists, particularly those who appear on TV or have picture by-lines, there's a third category: the admirer.

The admirer is almost never a well-adjusted hunk with a fascinating past and more frequent flyer points than the Duchess of York. He's more likely to live with his mother and wear woolly orange socks with leather sandals; or to belong to a cult which worships the midget from 'Fantasy Island'; or to smell like a badger and break out in medieval skin disorders at full moon; or to have the world's largest private collection of ladies' bicycle seats.

Most of them will get a hearing though, on the same basis that people buy lottery tickets: sooner or later someone will walk in off the street with an earth-shattering story. Maybe this is the one; maybe this guy isn't a loony; maybe he really did see Lord Lucan roller-skating along King Edward Parade.

Thus Amanda Hayhoe was wary when she got the call to say there was a man in reception wanting to see her. His name meant nothing so she asked the receptionist to find out what it was about. Answer: Detective Sergeant Ihaka.

'What about him?'

Another hiatus. The receptionist came back on the line: 'He said, "What sort of question is that? I thought she was a journalist." '

Hayhoe said, 'I'll come down.'

At first sight, Duane Ricketts seemed normal. They sat on a settee in the reception area.

'Okay,' she said briskly, 'what about Ihaka?'

'I'm trying to find him; I was hoping you could help me.'

'Don't you think you should leave that to the police?'

'There's nothing I'd like more.'

'So what's stopping you?'

Ricketts didn't answer straightaway. 'Ihaka's a mate of mine. More to the point, a senior cop came round to my place last night to ask me to have a crack at finding him. That's what I do for a living, by the way – I find people. He thinks the task force is barking up the wrong tree. He gave me some background on the APA, which is how I got on to you.'

Hayhoe couldn't believe her ears. 'Are you telling me that a senior police officer thinks the task force doesn't know what it's doing?'

'Put it this way: they're working on the assumption that the APA are a bunch of radical Maoris; he doesn't share that view.'

'Jesus, this is all pretty...irregular, isn't it?'

'You can say that again: his arse is hanging out, big-time. Keep that in mind.'

'What's that supposed to mean?'

'It means that if word gets out, he'll be in deep shit.'

'Well, excuse me,' snapped Hayhoe. 'I don't remember asking you to come in here and tell me about it. And in case you've forgotten, I do happen to be a journalist.'

'I haven't forgotten,' said Ricketts mildly. 'I haven't forgotten Ihaka either.'

They locked eyes for a few seconds.

Ricketts said, 'I told you about it because I'm asking you for help and I figured you were entitled to know the background. But if I'd thought it was going to cost the guy his job, I wouldn't have told you, would I?'

Hayhoe was sure she'd find a flaw in his logic when she got round to putting her mind to it. 'Well, I'm not making any promises. Anyway, what makes you think I can help?'

'I had to start somewhere. And I was intrigued that you bobbed up in both Ihaka's recent cases.'

'What do you mean, both? What's the other one?'

'A guy called Mules was murdered last weekend. Ihaka reckoned he was blackmailing a Mrs Trousdale over her sex life – which apparently you featured in.'

The ghost of a smile which flitted across Ricketts' face only added to Hayhoe's fury. 'Where the fucking hell did you get that from?'

'I told you, the cop filled me in on what Ihaka was working on. Relax – I can keep a secret. I'm sure you can too.'

Hayhoe's eyes flashed dangerously. 'You're pushing your luck, buster.'

Ricketts smiled.

It was a nice enough smile, as smiles went, but Hayhoe was in no mood to be charmed. 'Look, I'm flat out right now, doing a story on the APA as it happens, so could you get on with it? Whatever it is.'

The smile vanished. 'Why do you think the APA left those communiqués on your car?'

She shrugged impatiently. 'Ihaka asked me that. I didn't have a clue then; still don't.'

'How long have you been chasing the APA story?'

She frowned. 'Since Freckleton. Why?'

'What've you come up with?'

'How do you mean?'

'Ihaka seemed to think you were pretty smart. I just thought that if you've been on it since the start, you might have some bright ideas.'

That didn't sound like Ihaka. 'When did he say that?'

'In his notes. He did add "for a TV reporter" but hey, a compliment's a compliment – especially from him.'

Hayhoe started to say something, then stopped. 'The cop who came to see you – he doesn't think they'll find Ihaka?'

Ricketts shook his head slowly. 'The way he sees it, I've got forty-eight to seventy-two hours. After that, he's history.'

Hayhoe didn't want to seem callous but she had her own problems: she was under big pressure to come up with something new, break a major story, scoop all comers. She had her hunch but standing it up wasn't going to be easy...

Brainwave: *Why not do a deal with Ricketts? Use him – wind him up and let him go, see what happens.*

You've got nothing to lose. Ihaka's got even less.

She said, 'This has got to be a two-way street: I get something in return.'

'What?'

'Everything you pick up, you pass on to me, right? And I mean everything, whether it's from following my lead or not.'

'So you can put it on TV?'

'If it's any good, you bet. It won't go to air until the weekend after this, at the earliest. If your cop friend's right, by then it won't matter either way.'

Ricketts nodded. 'True.'

'So: do we have a deal?'

'We do.' He put out his right hand. Hayhoe thought a handshake was overdoing things but she went along with it.

'Okay,' she said. 'Can you find out if the cops found any floppy disks at Jackson Pike's place and, if so, what was on them?'

'Yep.'

'What about what was on his home computer's hard disk?'

'Yep.' After a pause: 'Did you say something about a two-way street?'

Hayhoe finally smiled. 'Have you heard of a guy called Serge Le Droff?'

TWENTY-THREE

Duane Ricketts: closing in on forty, unattached, looking like staying that way.

It wasn't that he was under-powered in the sex-drive department or quirky – at least, not by late-twentieth-century sexual etiquette. But he was choosy. Contrary to the usual trend and, perhaps, common sense, the older he got, the choosier he became. These days, he just never seemed to meet suitable women.

Instead he met: wives who gave him the eye while hubby wrote the cheque; solo mothers floundering in cask wine and self-pity, looking for a saviour or someone to take down with them; lady lawyers whose wish lists didn't stretch to a man with a past but without a degree, a man who only knew three types of pasta and fell asleep during *The Piano*; law-firm secretarial chicks.

Holy shit.

Last summer, he'd gone to the mat with a 22-year-old secretary at Trubshaw Trimble. She made his mouth water, she wore a fake diamond in her belly button, she thought he was cool. So far, so good. And she kept it real basic. So what do you want to do, Nicole? Nicole shrugged. 'Grab some Thai, check out the Empire, then

go back to your place and pump it, baby – what else?'
Well, if you insist. Ricketts gave it his best shot; then he
gave it what he had left. Then he rolled over and went to
sleep, thank you and goodnight. Nicole smoked a joint,
sank a can of Beam 'n' Coke, then shook him awake:
'Hey man, don't flake on me, I'm just getting warmed
up.' *Honey, have you got a licence for that thing?*

So Ricketts was sleeping solo when the bedside phone
went ape at 6.57 on Friday morning. He groaned, raised
his head to look at the alarm clock which was set to go
off at 7.30, groaned again, and flopped his face on the
pillow, mumbling filth. A few rings later, he lunged for
the receiver.

'I don't remember asking for a wake-up call.'

'Have I read you wrong, Mr Ricketts?' enquired
Detective Inspector Finbar McGrail. 'I picked you as an
early riser.'

'I thought I was.'

'I wanted to be sure of getting hold of you,' said
McGrail, as if that settled the matter. 'Any progress?'

'Maybe.' Ricketts sat up and shook himself awake. 'I
need a favour – could you run a check on one Serge Le
Droff, a Frog businessman resident in our fair city?' He
spelt out the name and gave McGrail a taste of him.

'You think he's got something to do with it?'
McGrail's politeness couldn't muffle his scepticism.

'It's clutching at straws time, right? Think of Le Droff
as a straw.'

'Point taken. Now then, have you got much on this
morning?'

'This and that,' said Ricketts unhelpfully.

'Could you pick someone up from the airport?'

'Hang on, Inspector: I signed on to find Ihaka, not run a fucking limo service...'

McGrail cut him off but without heat: 'Don't be daft, man – it's someone to watch your back.'

'Oh.' Ricketts knew he should have known better. 'Who?'

'C.C. Hellicar.'

'Jesus.'

'She's on the Air New Zealand flight from Honolulu, arriving at ten past ten.'

'So for once in his life, Ihaka wasn't bullshitting.'

'Come again?'

'He always said they started a fire.'

McGrail's description was typically terse: late twenties, pale-blue eyes, short dark-blond hair, serious accent.

Hellicar would meet her pick-up at the Air New Zealand ticket desk. Ricketts worked on half an hour to disembark, retrieve luggage, and queue for immigration but didn't allow for a closed lane on the motorway and a two-kilometre crawl. It was after eleven when he got there. A woman with a straight back and a gymnast's bum had her elbows on the counter, reading a paperback. The hair was shoulder-length though, and more blond than dark.

The guy manning the ticket desk was standard-issue airline camp: blow-dried hair, signet ring, manicure, fluttering hands. Ricketts asked him if he'd sighted a

Ms Hellicar, just in from Honolulu. The blonde looked up. 'I'm C.C. Hellicar.' Butter-wouldn't-melt drawl.

Check those eyes. Hellicar was tall, maybe 170 centimetres, long-legged, square-shouldered. She had great cheekbones and wore black jeans, a denim shirt over a white t-shirt, and canvas sneakers.

'McGrail said you had short hair.'

'It grew.' Not rude, just jet-lagged into indifference.

He offered his right hand. 'Duane Ricketts.'

She goggled. 'The dope fiend?'

Now that's rude.

Ricketts froze for a couple of seconds, then let his hand drop. 'Nice to meet you too.' He picked up her large metal suitcase, felt his testicles retract, and looked around for a trolley.

'Leave it,' she said, 'I can carry it.'

He put it down. 'That makes one of us.'

They exited the terminal. He asked, 'What was that in aid of?'

'Dope fiend? That's a direct quote from Tito,' she replied coolly. 'You ought to know I seriously disapprove of that shit.'

Ricketts stopped dead and gave her what was intended as a cold stare. The one she sent back was the real McCoy. He did an eyes-front and kept walking. When they reached his car, he flipped open the boot and stood aside as she heaved the suitcase in.

He eyed her across the roof as he unlocked the car. 'Seeing we're going to be working together, can I make a suggestion? If you find yourself disapproving of me, try minding your own business. It works for most people.'

250

She drilled him with another ice-coated laser beam.
'Well, excuse me all to hell. You want to screw around
with hard drugs, don't expect folks to pat you on the
back.'

They got into the car.

He said, 'Once upon a time' – laying it on – 'I smoked
half a heroin cigarette. It ended up costing me fifteen
grand and three weeks in a Bangkok piss-tank. Isn't that
enough for you?'

'I don't enter into it. The point is, it obviously wasn't
enough to put you off.'

'What are you talking about?'

She sniffed contemptuously. 'You know goddamn
well – that big mess of coke you and the rest of that trash
were panting after.'

Ricketts frowned. 'Didn't Ihaka tell you what
happened?'

'I haven't been in contact with Tito since the day I flew
out of here.'

'Not even a postcard?'

'You do the job, you move on.' She looked straight
ahead. 'Besides, he didn't strike me as one of nature's
pen pals.'

'Now you're back – so what's changed?'

'A shitload.' Read: mind your own business. 'Did my
ears deceive me back there or did you make mention of
us working together?' The honeyed accent somehow
added sting to the implication that the prospect made her
skin crawl.

McGrail had obviously told her the bare minimum,
which didn't include a character reference.

'Guess whose back you get to watch?'

She raised her eyebrows. 'You're the one's going to find him?'

'I'm going to try.'

Neither spoke till they hit Mangere Bridge. 'I've got to tell you' – shaking her head – 'this is a real kicker.'

Ricketts said nothing, kept his eyes on the road.

'I have this very clear recollection: we're driving back from Tito's beachhouse and he's cussing you out... goddamn, I ain't heard nothing like it, ever. Where it all led to was, once you were behind bars, he was going to induce the biggest, ugliest, meanest dudes in the joint to...well, I guess you can figure it out.'

Playing dumb: 'No, what?'

'You know...'

He shook his head.

Hellicar gave him a look, not sure if he was for real. 'Hose you,' she said eventually. 'Often.'

'Oh, I get it: the old prison diet – pork every day and twice on Sundays. And you approved of that?'

'It seemed reasonable at the time.' She giggled like a schoolgirl. 'But seeing as how you and McGrail are holding hands these days, I've got to assume you walked? Picked your moment and cut a deal, huh?'

'Something like that.'

'That figures. I have to admit, in between the many less flattering comments, Tito did concede you were smart.'

Ricketts remembered the lie he'd told Amanda Hayhoe. 'Let's hope he's right.'

Coming down Manukau Road, he asked her where she was staying. McGrail had booked her into the Centra.

'Who's picking up the tab, if it's not a rude question?'

'Me so far,' she said, 'but the Inspector said he'd fix it.'

252

'Is that right?' By reputation, McGrail was as tight as a bull's arse in fly season.

'Why, would that be a problem for him?'

'He's got a young family; I doubt he's rolling in dough.'

She shrugged. 'It's no big thing.'

'Why waste money – yours or his – on a hotel? I've got a spare room; I've got a spare bathroom, come to that.'

She thought about it. 'Makes sense, I guess, seeing as the reason I'm here is to wet-nurse you. And if it turns out you ain't a gentleman – well, I can't get too shook up over a guy who couldn't hardly budge my suitcase.'

By the time they got to Ricketts' place, Hellicar was fading fast. First though, she wanted to hear what they were up against. He told her about the Aotearoa People's Army and McGrail's doubts about the investigation.

She said, 'Let's say he's right and this all ain't about the natives getting restless: what percentage of the population does that eliminate?'

'Talking about the real hot-heads? Depends on who you believe.'

'Just roughly.'

'Less than one per cent.'

Hellicar went, 'Uh huh. Well, it's a start.'

'This guy interests me.' He showed her the material on Serge Le Droff, the spoils of his horse-trading with Amanda Hayhoe.

She skim-read it. 'Well, there's no denying he's interesting – unusual even – but it sure doesn't read like the profile of a left-wing terrorist.'

'There's more.' He covered the Mules case and the Jackson Pike–D'Arcy Potterton connection.

Hellicar rubbed red-rimmed eyes. 'So not long after they got together, the writer gets whacked in a hunting accident – by someone who just happens to work on this boy's farm – and the editor has his neck broke by the APA. That the way it was?'

'Yep.'

'Shit, I can't make head nor tail of that.'

'Let's call it a coincidence. Here's another: on Tuesday afternoon, Ihaka goes to see Le Droff about Mules and the blackmail; that night, the APA grabs him.'

Hellicar nodded thoughtfully. 'That's a little better.'

She went to get a sweatshirt. 'You wouldn't have a gun by any chance?' she called out, 'because I don't.'

'No. What did you do last time?'

'Last time, I was on assignment – from DC with love; my piece came in in the diplomatic bag.'

'I'll mention it to Uncle Finbar.'

She came back into the living room yawning like a big dog.

Ricketts stood up. 'Why don't you get some sleep?'

'I could use some – we flew out of Honolulu at one o'clock in the morning and I don't sleep on planes the way I used to. What about you?'

'I've got some things to do but I should be safe enough in the Lands and Titles Office.'

As he was showing her around, he asked how she'd managed to make it at such short notice.

'There was nothing much to stop me.'

'How come?'

She got sombre. 'I was in your shoes, I wouldn't want to know.'

It was shaping up as one of Amanda Hayhoe's better days.

In the morning, she persuaded Belinda Potterton to talk on camera about her brother and Jackson Pike. Then she took a camera crew over to Takapuna to film Garth Grimes' eulogy to the late editor. She also extracted an adulterated version of why he'd put Pike on to D'Arcy Potterton in the first place. As she'd expected, the old perv proved to be great talent.

In the afternoon, she and the crew went to the *New Nation* office for some footage and a few 'the Jackson Pike I remember' sound bites. Afterwards, she had a coffee with Justin Hinshelwood, the staff writer.

Hinshelwood bolted his and ordered another. He was acting like a man with something he wanted to get off his chest. When he'd made a start on the second cup, he got to it: 'You know something? I feel like shit every time I hear his name.'

'Pike's?'

He nodded. 'I didn't tell you this but Pike and I had a huge falling-out. In fact, we weren't on speaking terms when he was murdered.'

'What happened?'

Hinshelwood squinted anxiously. 'This is between you and me, right? I mean, you're not going to use it?'

Hayhoe sighed and gave him a smile which was both reassuring and gently reproachful. She said nothing.

'A few months ago, he got me to do a story on the tenth anniversary of the *Rainbow Warrior*. I threw a tantrumette – I mean, when it reaches the stage of *Rainbow Warrior, The Musical*, it's a pretty good sign there's not much flesh left on the carcass, wouldn't you agree? It didn't get me anywhere. So I rocked up to the *Sunday Star* – we've got access to their clippings library – pulled out the files, and did what I thought was a reasonably comprehensive overview: a cut-and-paste job, in other words. Well, Pike spiked it – with extreme prejudice.' Hinshelwood put on a grating voice; she assumed he was mimicking the dead editor: "No self-respecting cadet reporter on a suburban free-sheet would submit this sort of crap; I should've known that if I want something done properly, I have to do it myself." Et cetera, ad nauseam. Not long after that, he swanned off to Europe for a couple of months. While he was away, I did this piece on Ron Rangi –'

'Who?'

'An All Black in the sixties – a rough-round-the-edges Maori boy. He blotted his copybook: it was real so-what stuff, you know, routine rugby boofhead carry-on, but they sent him to Coventry on a slow train. He hit the bottle, hit the skids, died a semi-derelict at the ripe old age of forty-five. It was a bloody good read, if I say so myself – pissed all over the usual sports profile herogram. When Pike got back, he pulled it on the grounds of who gives a fuck? It was obviously meant to teach me a lesson: this is what happens when you take short-cuts on my story ideas. I thought it was vindictive, not to mention unprofessional. It was our last conversation, if you could call it that. The very last thing I ever said to him was, "You wouldn't know a decent story if it shat on your lap."'

Back at TVNZ, Hayhoe got a call from Ricketts. He was keeping his end of the bargain, letting her know that the cops hadn't found any floppy disks at Pike's place. He'd seen a police summary of what was on the home computer's hard disk: it was innocuous stuff, mostly admin – budgets, staff files, planning for upcoming issues. Nothing to die for.

She tried the *Sunday Star* clippings library but they'd knocked off for the day.

Ricketts got home just after six. Hellicar, in bicycle pants and a *Pulp Fiction* t-shirt, was exercising on the living-room floor. The t-shirt featured Samuel L. Jackson doing his bad motherfucker thing, about to blast someone into baby food. The caption said: 'And you will know my name is the Lord when I lay my vengeance upon you.'

He asked how she was feeling: a little fuzzy. She followed him into the kitchen, wanting to hear his news.

Ricketts leaned against the bench and popped a beer. 'You know that stuff on Le Droff mentioned he had a yacht moored at Westhaven marina? I got his mooring from the boating register and went and had a look at it. I got chatting to this old guy mucking around on the boat on the next mooring; turned out he's retired and goes down there most afternoons. I asked him how much use *Lady Penelope* got. He said about every second weekend but funny you should ask: just this week, he'd gone down first thing one morning and it wasn't there. When he went back after lunch, it was.'

He paused to sip his beer.

She said, 'You're going to tell me that when you jogged that old boy's memory, it transpired that it was Wednesday morning? Am I right?'

Ricketts grinned. 'I didn't have to jog his memory. He plays in a golf four at Devonport every Wednesday morning and sometimes drops in at the marina on his way over. It's the only time he's ever there in the morning.'

'You're thinking maybe they put Tito on the yacht and took him over to that island?'

He got a map of the Hauraki Gulf from his workroom and spread it out on the bench. 'I did a search at the Lands and Titles Office.' He put his finger on a small bay on the eastern side of Waiheke. 'Le Droff's place is here, Sutcliffe's Bay – he owns the whole bay. This is the unfashionable end of the island: it's pretty rugged, access by water or four-wheel drive; this time of year, there'd be hardly anyone around anyway. It's a big, old house, built in 1905, so there'd be a few nooks and crannies to stash someone away – even a lard like Ihaka.'

'You've been a busy boy.'

'One other thing…'

'You do keep saying that.'

'A friend of mine lives over there. This afternoon, he took his Pajero down that end of the island and got up on top of a hill with a pair of binoculars. He didn't see anyone but there was smoke coming from the chimney.'

'You talked to McGrail about this guy?'

Ricketts nodded. 'As far as the cops are concerned, he's a model citizen.'

'What does he think?'

'Same as you: Le Droff's interesting but there's nothing to justify kicking down his door. He's also rich, which tends to make cops tread extra carefully.'

'He's getting more interesting all the time. It might be worth a call to the States.'

Ricketts pointed to the phone. 'Help yourself.'

He had a shower and was watching the news when she came through from the kitchen.

'That was my old boss in Phoenix. He's going to ring round a few of his buddies inside the company, see if any of them have heard of Le Droff.'

'The company?'

'The C...I...A.'

'Oh, that company.'

'No harm in trying. This boy's been around – hustling God knows what in the Middle East, getting himself named in that report. He'll get back to me in the morning. So what now?'

'Well, I thought we could go out, have dinner somewhere...'

Hellicar planted her hands on her hips. 'I meant, what now in the race against time to save our friend Tito's ass?'

'I don't know about you but I plan to have a nice dinner and get a good night's sleep, because tomorrow we go exploring.'

'I don't want to harp on it but as of right now, we ain't equipped for a showdown.'

'We will be by lunchtime tomorrow – Uncle Finbar's on the case.'

TWENTY-FOUR

Saturday came in on a warm wind, like a change of seasons.

Duane Ricketts and C.C. Hellicar were having breakfast on the rear deck when the phone rang. Ricketts answered and got a sagebrush twang: 'How's it hanging, amigo? You got a house-guest by the name of C.C. Hellicar?'

'Hang on, I'll get her.'

'Tell her Bobby G. in Phoenix has got some news for her.'

Ricketts put her on, then strolled down the path to inspect his vegetable garden: it was out of control, a mission for Agent Orange.

Hellicar joined him. She zoomed in on the horticultural freak show through her Ray-Bans: 'Jesus, Duane, Johnny Greenfingers you ain't.'

Ricketts grunted. 'What'd Bobby G. have to say?'

'Just that Le Droff used to be a spook.'

'A what?'

'A French intelligence agent. That middle-man stuff – pushing hardware to the rag-heads – was a cover: he was really working for the DGSE. It explains why his name disappeared from that Congressional report: Langley would've slipped word to the committee that old Serge was fighting the good fight for Christianity and cheap oil.'

'What did he actually do?'

She shrugged. 'The usual. The French are forever playing spook games in the sub-Sahara, places like Chad and Guinea. I never met anyone could explain exactly what the point of it all was, aside from the fact it pissed Gaddafi off, which made it just dandy far as Uncle Sam was concerned.'

'How'd he rate?'

'Not bad,' she nodded. 'Smart, capable, played hard-ball when he had to.'

'Now he's retired – you're two of a kind.'

'Ain't we just?' said Hellicar sardonically. 'A couple of ex-spooks living the good life in well-earned retirement. It kind of makes sense him coming all the way down here, though: you don't put in ten years' fieldwork in camel country without getting on a few hit-lists.'

'Why would a retired French...'

'Intelligence agent be tied up with a way-out terrorist outfit? You got me. It's hard enough to figure a big-shot businessman moonlighting as a left-wing terrorist with-out adding the fact he used to be a spy. The French secret service culture is hard-line right-wing – okay, tell me one that ain't – but boy, they are out there. On top of that, his family background's ultra-conservative.'

'Sounds to me like you think we're sniffing the wrong lamppost?'

'Shit, who knows? I sure hope you got a Plan B though.'

At ten o'clock that morning, Amanda Hayhoe rang the *Sunday Star*'s head librarian to ask if Jackson Pike had used the library in the few months prior to his death.

'Yes, I think he came in not so very long ago, the poor man.' The head librarian sounded middle-aged and gentle.

'Do you remember what he was researching?'

'I wouldn't have the foggiest, dear, but Amy might. She was a friend of his; she always looked after him when he dropped in.'

Amy came on the line, saying she was more a friend of Pike's ex-wife, the first one, that was. Not that she had anything against the guy, but then she'd never been married to him. Hayhoe asked which files he had used.

'All the old *Rainbow Warrior* stuff.'

'Anything in particular?'

'It was to do with the tenth anniversary. I remember him saying he might end up with egg on his face because he'd bawled out one of his writers...'

'Justin Hinshelwood?'

'That's right. Justin had been in a couple of weeks earlier. Spitting tacks he was too – he didn't want a bar of it.'

'So Pike went through the files: then what?'

'Then he went away happy.'

'Why?'

'Oh, he'd found an angle. That was Jackson: if there was something there, he'd find it.'

'Did he say what it was?'

'No offence, but that's a pretty silly question.'

'I work for TV, remember? They're always telling us, don't be afraid to ask dumb questions.'

Amy laughed. 'A few of your colleagues deserve VCs. No, all he said was something like, if you dig deep enough, you'll always find a nugget.'

Hayhoe asked if she could come over and dig through the *Rainbow Warrior* files; Amy couldn't see why not – no-one else was likely to want them.

The man who ignored the doorbell to pound on Ricketts' front door was tall, thin, mid-thirties. He had blond hair, greasy and ponytailed, a wedge of white fluff hanging off his lower lip, and tattooed forearms. He wore ear-studs, wrap-around sunglasses, cowboy boots, black gloves, too-tight jeans, and a white t-shirt which said 'Nuke the Whales'. He had a big gym bag, the sort pro tennis players use, slung over his shoulder.

Ricketts' take: low-life slime.

He said, 'You Ricketts?'

'Yeah.'

'I got something for you.'

'Who are you?'

'Blair.'

'Is that your first name or your second name?'

'What fucking difference does it make?'

Ricketts shrugged. 'I might want to send you a Christmas card.'

He led Blair through to the rear deck where Hellicar sat in the sun, looking good in white shorts, white polo shirt, and Waikiki tan.

Ricketts told her, 'This is Blair. I think he's going to solve our equipment problem.'

Blair panned from Hellicar to Ricketts. 'I have come to the right place? I mean, you two look like tennis-club geeks.'

Hellicar hummed softly. Ricketts said, 'And you look like you fuck dead cats, so what? What've you got?'

Blair showed pointy teeth. He dumped the gym bag on the jarrah table and unzipped it. 'We have: one Remington semi-auto 12-gauge shotgun, two boxes of cartridges, one Browning semi-auto handgun, and two mags – nine-mill, parabellum load.'

Ricketts asked Hellicar, 'You want to have a look?'

She checked and loaded the guns with casual assurance. 'They'll do.'

Blair stared at her; she smiled lazily, unreadable behind dark glasses. He shook his head. 'Weird fucking set-up, man.'

He put the guns and ammunition back in the bag and zipped it up. 'All yours, Ringo. I don't know what you've got in mind and I don't want to know. But should the unfortunate occur and you wind up down at Pig Central having to explain some major fucking carnage, you got this gear from a short, dark, Italian-looking dude you met in a K Road skin joint. Let's call him...Frank. Okay?'

Ricketts wasn't sure if he was serious. 'Frank, eh?'

Blair scanned the back yard. 'You know, mate, you could really do something with this place: start by ripping out the crap you got in those flower-beds, make a nice little rose garden…'

Hellicar drawled, 'There's a real impressive vegetable patch down yonder, behind that tree.'

'I'm a flower man myself: any retard can grow vegies.'

'You want to bet?'

'Well, I'll leave you kids to it,' said Blair affably. 'Remember: eat what you kill and vice versa.'

Ricketts walked him out. Blair stopped in the doorway and turned around. 'I've tagged you now – you're the guy who stitched up Bryce Spurdle.'

Ricketts nodded, thinking, *Undercover cop*.

'That was slick work. I guess you and Emmy Lou know what you're doing after all.'

Hayhoe drove over to Eden Terrace. The *Sunday Star* building was a three-storey box in New North Road, on the city side of the Dominion Road flyover. Amy collected her from reception and took her down to the library, which was tucked away at the back of the building, off the car park – out of sight and out of mind, like an idiot step-child's bedroom.

The files were in ceiling-to-floor walk-in movable cabinets. Amy pulled a stack of thick manila envelopes and told Hayhoe to have fun. She found a desk in the corner and got started.

Tenth of July 1985, Marsden wharf, Auckland harbour: just before midnight, two explosions blow the arse out of Greenpeace vessel *Rainbow Warrior*, about to lead a flotilla to French Polynesia to protest nuclear testing at Mururoa Atoll. Collateral damage: one dead Portuguese photographer.

Boat-owners spending the night on their boats in Hobson Bay to deter thieves see a man pull an inflatable rubber dinghy ashore and run to a Toyota Hiace camper-van in Tamaki Drive. The dinghy gets left behind.

Suspicion falls on the crew of a New Caledonian charter yacht, the ketch *Ouvea*, which left Auckland for Norfolk Island after the bombing. Police fly up there to interview them. The Australian Attorney-General's department gives them twenty-four hours to issue extradition warrants, not enough time to get the results of forensic tests of suspected – later confirmed – traces of explosive in the bilges. The *Ouvea* is allowed to leave Norfolk and promptly disappears, believed scuttled.

Sixteenth of July: police detain Alain and Sophie Turenge when they drop off the Toyota Hiace at Auckland airport. They're Swiss; she's a professor, he's a manager. Well, that's their story.

The passports are false; Sophie turns out to be Captain Dominique Prieur, attached to the French Ministry of Defence; Alain is Major Alain Mafart, an officer at a training centre for DGSE frogmen. DGSE equals Direc-torat Général de la Sécurité Extérieure equals French intelligence.

In Paris, President Mittérand tells his prime minister to conduct a rigorous inquiry, internationally recognised bureaucratese for: whitewash this shit out of my hair.

In Auckland, the evidence points to an elaborate operation by the French intelligence services. The abandoned dinghy was bought in North London by one of the *Ouvea* crew, three of whom turn out to be NCOs from the DGSE underwater combat school on Corsica. By now, they're supposedly lying low in the former French colony of Guinea.

A map found on the *Ouvea* was drawn by Frédérique Bonlieu, a dykey mademoiselle who'd shown up at Greenpeace headquarters in Auckland a few months previously with a letter of introduction from a French antinuclear activist. She turns out to be Christine Cabon, a French army lieutenant attached to the DGSE. She sends Greenpeace a postcard from Israel.

The theory is that Prieur and Mafart collected the limpet mines off a French container ship, *Hélène Delmas*, and passed them to the *Ouvea* crew. The bombers got away clean while the support team sits in Mt Eden prison sweating on a murder/arson/conspiracy rap.

Twenty-second of November: Mafart and Prieur plead guilty to manslaughter and wilful damage, sentenced to ten years' hard time.

Conspiracy theories are a dime-a-dozen:

That the British knew about it, let it happen, then tipped off New Zealand to get even with the Frogs for selling Exocet missiles to Argentina during the Falklands War.

That the CIA and ASIO, Australia's spy outfit, knew in advance but didn't tell because New Zealand was out of the ANZUS information loop over its no-nukes policy.

That the French did it because Greenpeace was infiltrated by the KGB, who had spies and surveillance equipment on the *Warrior*.

That the French did it because they feared the protest flotilla would trigger insurrection in French Polynesia.

That Prieur and Mafart and the *Ouvea* crew were decoys to distract attention from the real strike team.

That the French had sent a hit-team to silence Prieur and Mafart.

That it was all a plot to compromise France's intelligence apparatus, a plot to drive France out of the South Pacific, a plot to stop Gérard Depardieu winning an Oscar.

Hayhoe rolled on.

The French defence minister resigns; the French prime minister resigns; France heavies New Zealand over butter access to Europe; the NZ government says no deal on Mafart and Prieur come hell or high water. The deal goes down – Mafart and Prieur are transferred to a Pacific atoll for three years; the Frogs welch – Mafart and Prieur are sprung from Club Med after less than eighteen months.

Fuck the deal, fuck New Zealand, *vive la France*.

Whatever Pike found, she'd missed it. She started again.

She'd been skimming clippings for five hours and her brain was cutting in and out like a bad satellite feed when she found it. It was buried in the second to last paragraph of a Reuters story out of Paris, dated 8 February, 1986:

'This week's issue of *Paris Match* reported that an unidentified businessman living in New Zealand had collected the mines from the container ship *Hélène Delmas* and passed them to the sabotage team, a role previously thought to have been taken by Prieur and Mafart.'

Now what?

A monster story was lurking out there but could she corner it and get it to air? Did she have enough time? If not, what was the fallback? Pike/APA – the unanswered questions: who broke into the *New Nation* office and went through the computers? What were they looking for? Why didn't the police find floppy disks at Pike's place? Bring in the bee in Pike's bonnet; bring in Potterton and Le Droff – if the lawyers would let her. Would Le Droff do an interview? Unlikely, given his publicity-phobia. So what would she do for pictures? Christ, she didn't even have a proper still of him, just a two-column pic from an eight-year-old newspaper clipping.

The papers ran a lot more business news than TV did: maybe the *Sunday Star* had a pic. She asked Amy, who checked the picture library: negative. Amy said the business section had its own picture library upstairs, mainly mugshots sent in by PRs.

They went up to the newsroom. Deadline fever: frazzled people in fast-forward; sub-editors raging at computer screens; reporters hunkered down behind grey partition screens, beating their keyboards like bongo drums.

The business section was deserted – they had an early deadline. Amy showed her the gunmetal filing cabinet and left her to it.

Hayhoe looked under names beginning with L and drew a blank. She tried D; strike two. The filing system was haphazard, sometimes using the person's name, sometimes their company's. She tried E. Bingo: a paperback-sized black-and-white print of Serge Le Droff, chairman and chief executive of Eurotours Ltd.

The photo was similar vintage to the one in the newspaper clipping but much better quality. Once again, Hayhoe had the nagging feeling that she'd seen the face before. She willed herself to make the connection but it was like Rubik's cube: the fragments of memory wouldn't click into place.

She wrote 'For pic of Serge Le Droff of Eurotours, see Amy in library' on a piece of pad paper and left it in the E folder. She took the photo downstairs and asked Amy to keep it in a safe place until she'd got permission to use it.

Hayhoe drove home. Going down Ponsonby Road, she passed a liquor store advertising a French champagne special: 'Prices slashed on top brands – Veuve, Moët, Bolly'.

The memory flash hit like an electric shock.

A Saturday night in late February; a friend from her investment-banking days called to invite her to a birthday party. She dragged her heels: she didn't know the people. He said they wouldn't mind: Amanda was on TV – that made her somebody. She'd never get a better chance to see how the other half lived – these people were loaded. He talked her into it.

Remuera Road: the rustle of wind in tall trees, the rustle of old money. In through big gates, down a winding drive to seventy squares of red brick and gables.

Round the back, a huge patio with a harbour view and steps down to a pool, a hundred people swilling Bollinger. The host was a stockbroker whose wife and daughter shared a birthday. That explained why the guests came in two packages: young and pretty, middle-aged and well-preserved.

Hayhoe spotted a couple who didn't fit in either – they were worldlier than the young crowd, sexier than the old.

The woman had striking chestnut hair. What was revealed by the plunging neckline of her caramel-coloured Donna Karan dress wasn't ho-hum either. When the woman noticed Hayhoe watching them, she smiled enigmatically and locked eyes until Amanda looked away. When she glanced back half a minute later, they were watching her. The woman still had the enigmatic smile but her green eyes glittered; the man looked amused.

Before the night was out, Hayhoe would discover that the woman's name was Rusty Trousdale and she was every bit as worldly as she looked.

The man, she now realised, was Serge Le Droff.

TWENTY-FIVE

He was so clean-cut and earnest, he had to be a missionary – direct to your doorstep, all the way from Salt Lake City. Renee Adlington wasn't buying but she couldn't help feeling sorry for him: what a way to spend your Saturday afternoons.

The young man with the peaches-and-cream complexion and neat blond hair said, 'Mrs Adlington? I'm Detective Constable Van Roon.'

Adlington hadn't come that close to wetting herself in twenty-five years. Then: an unbearably hot January night in the Bay of Islands; toss the blanket, toss the sheet, strip off the shorty nightie, peel off the knickers – finally cooled down enough to sleep. She'd woken up goosebumped at first light to find a giant weta nesting in her bush.

Van Roon asked if he could come in. Adlington nodded, catching flies.

Inside, a florid heart-throb going to seed had his feet up watching TV. He saw Adlington's spooked expression and said, 'Trouble at mill?' in a Monty Python voice. Van Roon would've bet on him having a repertoire of them.

He was Henry Pye, Renee's admirer from the mature singles night. The clock had ticked down on their month-long moratorium the day before, not a moment too soon for Adlington: Pye had her pawing the carpet by portraying himself as a sex wizard who worked women over in ways Masters and Johnson hadn't documented.

As so often happens, the bigger the build-up, the bigger the let-down.

Henry had come over for an intimate dinner. He'd 'had a few' at the pub with the people from work; after the lion's share of two bottles of Chardonnay and a barrage of Tia Marias, his nose had more of a glow than the candles.

They'd adjourned to the bedroom. He'd promised to blast her into orbit but she never even got off the launching pad. To top it off, he had the hide to suggest that a spot of 'throat' would be just the ticket. She'd feigned ignorance and grimly fumbled between his legs. Getting him to half-mast almost gave her tennis elbow.

But to hear him tell it in the morning, he'd been a pork-pumping ball of fire; he'd left her chewed, screwed, and unglued. She retreated to the kitchen in a daze, trying to decide if he'd had a booze black-out or was simply a shameless bullshit artist.

Van Roon introduced himself. Pye's eyebrows formed question marks. He zeroed in on Renee, mock-teasing: 'What have you been up to, saucepot?'

She blushed beetroot. Van Roon picked up the vibes. 'Would you be Mr Adlington?'

Pye leered: 'No, we're just good friends, as they say.'

'Well, Mrs Adlington and I have a few things to discuss, if you wouldn't mind leaving us to it for an hour or so.'

'I won't get in your way...'

Adlington said, 'Henry, please.' Van Roon unbuttoned his sports jacket and put his hands on his hips.

'All right, I get the message.' Pye snatched his car keys and headed for the door. 'You'll see me when you see me.'

Van Roon asked, 'May I?' before sitting down. He produced a pocket notepad and ballpoint.

'Is this something to do with Clyde Early?' she asked nervously.

'He's been in touch with us.'

She blurted: 'Honestly, that man – he barged in here accusing me of listening in on his phone calls. I sent him away with a flea in his ear.'

'Yes, he said he'd talked to you. Mrs Adlington, do you know a man called Brandon Mules?'

She screwed up her face to show she was doing her best.

'The ex-rugby player who was murdered last weekend,' prompted Van Roon. 'You might've seen something about it?'

'Oh, yes, I thought I'd heard the name – I saw something about it on the news.'

'We think Mules was blackmailing Mr Early's friend.' He paused to see if she'd caught on but nothing moved on her face. 'Obviously, him getting murdered makes it a whole new ball game.'

Bull's-eye: Adlington went toilet-bowl white. She could hear Leo lecturing her in his big-brother-knows-best voice: 'Renee, if you had any idea what the truth was...'

'Let's start from scratch, Mrs Adlington. Did you overhear Mr Early talking to his girlfriend?'

She lowered her eyes. 'I didn't mean to; I wasn't sure if he'd picked up the phone...'

'That's not important. What is important is whether you told anyone about it.'

'I swear I didn't tell a soul.'

Van Roon no longer bore such a resemblance to a mummy's boy hot gospeller from Squaresville, USA. He drummed his ballpoint impatiently on the notepad. 'Mrs Adlington, I wonder if you realise how serious this is. It's gone way beyond your dispute with Mr Early: you're in the middle of a full-scale murder investigation. Now, if you can't convince me you've told the whole story, I'm going to have to ask you to come into Central and go through it by the book.'

'I am telling the whole story,' she pleaded. 'I had nothing to do with any blackmail and I'd never heard of Mules until he was on the news.'

'You'd never met him, never spoken to him?'

She waggled her head. 'On the Bible.'

Van Roon flipped through his notepad. 'What about this bloke? He'd be in his fifties, well dressed – suit, tie, cufflinks – pink complexion, a bit overweight, going bald. He goes round with a brown leather satchel and a white raincoat – oh yeah, and he drinks top-shelf Scotch. Any of that ring a bell?'

Adlington gulped air. Van Roon saw her hands shake. 'No, I don't know anyone like that.'

'He was seen with Mules a week ago yesterday; Mules was murdered that night. Think hard: are you absolutely sure you've got no idea who he might be?'

She clamped her hands between her legs. 'Positive.'

Van Roon stood up and went to the sideboard where a set of framed colour photographs of Renee Adlington's nearest and dearest were displayed. One of them featured an owlish, middle-aged man with round, pink cheeks and thinning hair.

He took the photograph back to where Adlington sat squirming and thrust it under her nose. 'So who's this joker?'

Amanda Hayhoe was hyped.

She buzzed on the story, on the implications of Rusty Trousdale's party huddle with Serge Le Droff, on the ambiguous feelings stirred by memories of the girls' night fizzle. She tore home, found the number, and made the call. Rusty answered.

'It's Amanda Hayhoe here.'

Crackling silence ended by a brittle titter: 'Oh dear, how embarrassing. What can I say, Amanda, except that I'm abjectly sorry? I know I should've made contact myself but to be perfectly honest, I wasn't up to it. Caspar said you took it very well.'

Quedley, shit. She'd almost managed to wipe that epic fiasco from her consciousness. 'Did he now? What else did he say?'

'Only that you were kind enough not to tell the world about me.' She sounded on the level: maybe Quedley had taken pity on her. Maybe he really was a changed man.

'I wanted to ask you something. That guy you were with at the party was Serge Le Droff, right?'

'Well, I wasn't with him as such. I didn't arrive with him and, as you know, I didn't leave with him. But yes, that was Serge. Why?'

'Does he know who I am?'

'I beg your pardon?'

'Yes or no, Rusty.' The words came out clipped. 'Does Le Droff know me?'

Another silence. 'Why do you ask?'

Hayhoe snapped. 'Why can't I get a straight fucking answer? Is that too much to ask?'

Rusty said, 'Don't get mad at me, Amanda.' She made it sound like tears were just another snarl away.

Hayhoe soothed, marvelling, *What a scene-player.*

'This is what happened.' The tremor had gone from Rusty's voice; now you hear it, now you don't. 'That night at the party, I mentioned to Serge – à propos of what I'm not quite sure; general boudoir goss I suppose – that I'm partial to the occasional roll in the hay with someone of the female persuasion. Part of life's rich tapestry and all that. He was fascinated: for some reason, girl-on-girl stuff gets most men fizzing. He wanted to know if there were any women there who got me hot and bothered. That's when I saw you.'

'And?'

'And I said, "Yes, Mandy Pandy over there" – I knew you from TV, remember? I told him who you were.'

'Have you talked about me with him since then?'

'God, I don't know. I couldn't swear not but I can't remember it. At the risk of getting told off again, can I ask what this is in aid of?'

Hayhoe ignored her. 'Did he know you were going to...make a move?'

'Did he ever – he practically suggested it.'

'Then surely he wanted to know what happened?'

'That's a point: he wanted a full account – anti-climaxes all round.'

Hayhoe hardly heard her. She was being jolted by another memory flash. *Rusty dropped me home the next morning.*

'Rusty, this is important: did you tell Le Droff where I live?'

'Gosh, maybe. I mean, I might've. Come to think of it, I probably did. I drove you back to your place in the morning, didn't I, so I expect that's how I finished my report. Don't say he's been hassling you?'

'No, it's not that.'

'Thank God for that. Mind you, it would be a feather in your cap. Normally Serge is the one ducking for cover. I hope I haven't put my foot in it – you haven't fallen for him, have you?'

Hayhoe couldn't help smiling. *Talk about a one-track mind.* 'No, it's not that either.'

'Don't do it, darling. He's charming when he puts his mind to it but he doesn't feel a thing.'

Duane Ricketts and C.C. Hellicar got the three o'clock ferry to Waiheke Island. Ricketts' friend 'Bum' Yandall met them at the Matiatia Bay wharf. Bum had an unusual shape and a salesman's body language.

They climbed into his Pajero. Hellicar said, 'It's probably one of those questions a body shouldn't ask but how'd you get stuck with a name like Bum?'

'I'm not stuck with it.' Yandall admired himself in lurid sports sunglasses in the rear-vision mirror. 'Ricketts is. You can call me Derek like everyone else.'

He drove through Oneroa and Onetangi, which swarmed with weekending yuppies and day-trippers making the most of the balmy weather. They swung inland. Sealed road gave way to gravel; hillside paddocks gave way to jungly native bush.

Ricketts' mobile phone rang.

Amanda Hayhoe said, 'You did give me the number.'

'I'm not complaining.'

'You sound like you're en route to Pluto in a concrete mixer.'

'Not quite: I'm on Waiheke.'

'Waiheke? Are you going to Le Droff's place?'

'Yeah. Thought I'd have a sniff around.'

'This should interest you then. I've just found out that Le Droff knows who I am and where I live; has done for months.'

Ricketts focused, made the jump: 'Which could explain why you got the communiqués.'

'Couldn't it just? Want to hear my latest theory? It's a real…'

They crested a ridge and dropped down into a hollow. Hayhoe went off the air. She came back on, along with a blizzard of static, as they climbed out the other side. Ricketts said he'd call her back later.

He looked over his shoulder at Hellicar. 'Le Droff just firmed in the betting.'

Tito Ihaka's guts churned when he heard the key in the lock. It was too soon for room service: the psycho had just slung him a sandwich and emptied the bucket.

The psycho stood silhouetted in the doorway. He flicked on the light and stepped deferentially aside. Serge Le Droff sauntered in, hands in pockets, a cigarette slanting from the corner of his mouth.

Ihaka gaped; he goggled; he – reflex action – scratched his balls.

Le Droff enjoyed the reaction. 'Cat got your tongue, Sergeant? A simple hello would be nice.'

Ihaka propped himself up on his elbows. 'Where the fuck am I?'

'Let's just say you're my guest.'

'Well, thanks for nothing. The service is ratshit and every time I open my mouth, Herman Munster there puts the boot in.'

Le Droff blew smoke. 'I gather you've made life un-pleasant for him. As for conversation, you're not missing much. Pascal speaks very little English – for that matter, he's not exactly a chatterbox in French.'

'Where'd you find him – the serial killers' hall of fame?'

Le Droff dropped the butt and stood on it. 'You're being disrespectful to a brave man. Pascal served with distinction in the French Foreign Legion for almost three decades. He has a wide range of expertise, including, as you may soon discover, interrogation.'

Ihaka's colon writhed like an eel but he managed to keep his voice steady. 'You mean he's a sadist?'

Pascal's ears were burning. He peered at Le Droff: '*Quoi? Qu'est-ce qu'il a dit, le flic?*'

Le Droff glanced at him. '*Il pense que vous soyez sadiste.*'

Pascal shrugged indifferently. '*Et alors?*'

Le Droff liked it. 'Roughly translated, that means, you'd better believe it.'

Ihaka lay back and stared at the ceiling. 'So what's going on?'

'If I told you that, I'd have to kill you.' Le Droff was a laugh-a-minute.

Ihaka turned his head and beamed poison: 'You're going to kill me anyway, cockbreath.'

Le Droff threw his head back and hooted. 'Well, now that you mention it…'

They were on a hilltop, two hundred metres above the road. Beyond the road, the hill slid steeply down into Sutcliffe's Bay where *Lady Penelope* bobbed at anchor. A barbed-wire fence ran alongside the road and a cast-iron cattle-stop gate barred entrance to a drive which wound down through tall pines to the waterfront house and a few outbuildings.

Ricketts lowered the binoculars. 'So there are at least two of them, assuming whoever lit the fire yesterday's still around.'

'There'd be more than two, wouldn't there?' said Hellicar. 'You couldn't sail that thing solo.'

'Why not? People sail round the world single-handed. The old guy at the marina said *Lady Penelope* was state-of-the-art, auto-everything.'

Yandall piped up: 'I could find out for you.'

Hellicar and Ricketts exchanged raised eyebrows. He said, 'And how do you propose to do that, Bum?'

'I'm a real estate agent, remember? I know people who'd kill for a place like that: an old four- or five-bedroom kauri house in a private bay, off the beaten track. I've got one guy who's ready to kick loose up to two and a half mill for the right place.'

'Get to the point, Bum.'

'The point is, I can go down there, knock on the guy's door, hand over my card, and tell him if he's ever thinking about selling to give me a yell because I've got a serious buyer lined up. Shit, I do it all the time. He might say piss off, in which case we're no worse off; or, when I spill the magic words "two point five million", he might cream his jeans. The second rule of real estate, Duane: everyone's a seller at the right price.'

'What's the first?'

'Position, position, position.'

'I still don't see what...'

'Where's the downside?' Yandall was already into his sales pitch. 'He'll either shut the door in my face or he won't. If he doesn't, I'll ask for a quick look inside so I can give the client a feel for the place. Then I can have a bit of a ferret and see how the land lies.'

'Can you get in that gate?' asked Hellicar.

'It's not padlocked – I checked yesterday.'

Ricketts asked her what she thought.

'What I think is, a little recon wouldn't go amiss. The case against this guy still ain't exactly iron-clad – I wouldn't want to go in blazing and find him serving milk and cookies to the local orphans.'

'The local orphans eat grass and shit standing up.'

'You know what I mean. For all we know, he could have friends over for the weekend or there might be a posse in there. We could ride with Bum – I mean Derek: put the seat down and stretch out. If he parked between those buildings out back, they wouldn't see us coming. The alternative is, we wait till it gets dark and go in blind. Darkness works both ways: it gives us cover but they know the terrain.'

Ricketts was edgy but it made sense.

'Okay, Bum, we'll do it your way. Just remember what this is all about: if you fuck up down there, you could be waving goodbye to a lot more than a commission.'

'Duane, look, just relax, would you? Christ, I've been a real estate agent for almost twenty years – I can talk my way out of anything.'

Ricketts punched numbers on his mobile phone. Hellicar said, 'Who is it this time?'

'Uncle Finbar.'

She nodded. 'Just remember to switch the goddamn thing off when you're done.'

TWENTY-SIX

Serge Le Droff got down to business.

Pascal fetched a director's chair and plonked it down in the middle of the room. Le Droff sat, legs crossed. Pascal leaned against the wall, giving Tito Ihaka the evil eye.

Le Droff said, 'Let's begin with an assessment of the APA investigation.'

'Suck shit.'

'A word of advice: don't play the hero.' Le Droff's tone was almost avuncular. 'If you invite Pascal to do his worst, he'll be happy to oblige. You look tough enough and that go-to-hell manner may be the real thing; on the other hand, the ones who wear their toughness on their sleeves often break like little girls. Why make it hard on yourself?'

'Why don't you make it easy?'

'How?'

'Uncuff me – I've been lying here like this for four days.'

Le Droff shook his head.

'Well, what about taking one of them off? At least let me sit up.'

Le Droff thought about it, shrugged, rat-tat-tatted French at Pascal. He handed over a set of keys, then held his knife under Ihaka's chin while Le Droff unlocked the ankle-cuff.

Ihaka hoisted himself into a sitting position and flexed his legs. 'Shit, that's better. Tell you what, I could go a drink.'

Le Droff rolled his eyes. 'I should've just left it to Pascal. What do you want?'

'You got any bourbon?'

'Don't drink the stuff. There's some good cognac.'

'That'll do.'

Pascal was dispatched.

Ihaka asked, 'Are we in Auckland?'

'You're answering the questions, Sergeant.'

'How the fuck would I know what's happening? I got the shove from the task force a week ago and I've been here, chained up like a rabid dog, since Wednesday.'

'What was the state of play then?'

'It was going nowhere fast – you'd know that better than anyone.'

'Why was that?'

Pascal returned with a tray: Hennessy XO cognac, Pernod, a small ice bucket, a jug of water, and three glasses. He mixed Pernod, ice and water in tall glasses for Le Droff and himself and poured a dollop of cognac into a brandy balloon. Ihaka gulped and felt the spirit roar through his bloodstream.

'We had no leads and no witnesses, plus we were chasing our tail because the anti-terrorism experts in the SIS had sold the government on the APA being a front for Maori extremists.'

'What did the police think of that?'

Ihaka shrugged. 'Some thought it made sense; others didn't like being told how to do their job by armchair experts. That shit comes and goes – you go along with it until it runs out of juice.'

Le Droff sipped. 'Explain.'

'Until whoever's driving it loses interest or gets cold feet.'

'When will that happen?'

'Yesterday. Maybe the day before.'

'Why?'

'Because we would've turned over every Maori tub-thumper in the country and had fuck-all to show for it.'

Le Droff smiled. 'You haven't factored in the latest communiqué.'

'What was that about?'

'You, of course.' His superiority complex was showing.

'I can see you're dying to tell me about it.'

'The communiqué announced that your abduction was retaliation for the harassment of the seventeen Maori patriots and that you'd be released if and when the government apologised and promised not to do it again.' The smile became a grin; Le Droff was having fun. 'I'm afraid we called you a traitor to your people – a little poetic licence.'

Ihaka aped the grin. 'I don't know why you're looking so pleased with yourself, Napoleon: no-one's going to believe that.'

'And why not?'

'One of those seventeen Maori patriots was my niece.'

Le Droff's face rearranged itself. '*Merde*.' After a few seconds he said, 'That might need some finessing. What about the Mules business?'

'What about it?'

'Just curious – I'm a bit player in the drama, after all.'

'I'd say Mules had a partner and they fell out. The partner zapped him and grabbed the diary. He'll wait for the heat to die down, then put the bite on Lady Hotpants again.'

'Any leads?'

'We've got a description of a guy Mules met – and had a row with – on the day of the murder.' Ihaka finished his drink. 'I wouldn't mind a few answers myself.'

Le Droff studied him. 'You want a reason, right?'

Ihaka stared back. 'It'd help.'

Le Droff nodded. 'The condemned man's last wish – to comprehend his fate.' He lit a cigarette. 'First of all, I'm an officer in the Directorat Général de la Sécurité Extérieure, the French intelligence service; secondly, there's no such thing as the Aotearoa People's Army. Once you know that, it all falls into place.'

Le Droff told his story as if they both had all the time in the world. Ihaka didn't complain.

France, May 1968 – revolution in the air. Students riot, workers strike, the government teeters on the brink. Knowing his family background, the DGSE approaches and recruits Le Droff.

Marseille/Corsica/French Guiana, 1969–1972 – training. He learns that the enemies of France are everywhere;

he learns to be a chameleon; he learns to sense weakness, to corrupt, to seduce, to terrorise, to destroy.

He learns that the ends justify the means.

The Middle East, 1972–1983 – agent in the field. His cover: trader/middleman, seeded with DGSE money. He exhibits networking skills and entrepreneurial flair; his superiors encourage his money-making. They let him keep 20 per cent, he skims off another ten; the rest goes into a slush-fund for off-the-books operations – emergencies, last-minute scrambles, the desperate, dirty jobs that no-one wants to sign off on.

The seventies are good years but the eighties start badly – a few business ventures turn to shit.

Lebanon, 1983. A dirty job: spring a hostage before his captors – the Popular Front for the Liberation of Palestine, extremist PLO splinter group – discover he's a French agent and blow France's intelligence network in the region. Le Droff's team snatches a PFLP big-wig and tortures the hostage's whereabouts out of him. The big-wig cracks just in time; he dies a few minutes later.

The ends justify the means.

Do the usual – blame it on Mossad. One slight hitch: the dead Palestinian was a Mossad mole who'd worked his way through the ranks to sit at PFLP head honcho Dr George Habash's right hand – a priceless intelligence asset. The Israelis howl for blood.

Two members of Le Droff's crew, Maronite Christians, are car-bombed into small pink pieces in Beirut. A DGSE agent is garrotted with piano wire in Nicosia. Time to get the fuck out of Dodge.

He tells his bosses he wants to quit, disappear, get rich. They offer a deal: go south but stay inside – there's work to be done down there. The money you make from here on is all yours.

Auckland, 1985. Greenpeace prepares to lead a flotilla to French Polynesia to protest nuclear testing at Mururoa Atoll. Paris is Paranoia City. DGSE head Admiral Pierre Lacoste revives a 1978 plan to ratfuck Greenpeace by sinking its flagship, *Rainbow Warrior*. Defence Minister Charles Hernu says GO.

Inside Service Action, DGSE's dirty tricks brigade, the plan gets a few refinements.

President Mitterrand brought communist filth into his government; President Mitterrand dumped public shit on the DGSE for poor intelligence – on the Falklands War, on the USSR, on the 1984 Libyan invasion of Chad. The refined plan: sink the *Warrior* but blow the operation – humiliate Mitterrand, force him to defend the DGSE against international criticism, maybe even bring down the government.

Three teams are assembled: the patsies, the decoys, the hit team. Target-zone operation co-ordinator: Major Serge Le Droff.

It works. The *Warrior* is sunk, the police home in on the decoy team on board the *Ouvea*, the patsies get caught, the conspiracy is revealed. The louder New Zealand protests, the more intransigent France becomes. Mitterrand throws Hernu and Prime Minister Laurent Fabius to the wolves and is forced to bring right-wingers into the government. Gaullist Jacques Chirac, his archrival, becomes prime minister. Major Le Droff goes back to making money, in between keeping an eye on pro-independence troublemakers in France's South Pacific colonies.

Ihaka said, 'So the two we caught...'

'Prieur and Mafart.'

'Had nothing to do with it?'

'They were the on-shore support for the decoy team. They never knew they were set up to be fall-guys.'

'Weren't you worried they'd finger you?'

'A, they wouldn't talk; B, they didn't know I was involved – that was my precondition. They reported direct to Paris – remember they actually rang a Ministry of Defence number from their hotel?' He shook his head. 'Unbelievable.'

'Did you rat them?'

'I made an anonymous phone call to pass on the number of their campervan but I think half of Auckland beat me to it. Whoever selected that pair of imbeciles did a good job.'

'Did it feel good when they got put away?'

Le Droff shrugged dismissively. 'Intelligence agents, even incompetents like them, understand the principle of expendability.'

Cut to: *New Nation* editor Jackson Pike researching a *Rainbow Warrior* tenth-anniversary story, finds a *Paris Match* reference to a New Zealand-based businessman allegedly involved in the bombing. (The leak came from inside the national gendarmerie's Sixth Section anti-subversion unit, which was monumentally hosed off with the DGSE for turning Paris into the mercenary recruitment capital of the world.)

Pike works a contact in the immigration department, gets details of French-passport-holding businessmen resident in New Zealand in 1985. He concentrates on the Auckland-based ones, eliminates those not in New

Zealand when the bombing took place, those who'd been in New Zealand for more than ten years, those over sixty. That leaves three names. He asks around; bad vibes spread *rapidement* through Auckland's tiny French community.

Le Droff alerts Paris. New president and hard-core big bang man Jacques Chirac is about to press the button at Mururoa – seriously bad timing for a new *Rainbow Warrior* scandal. Any time is a bad time for a DGSE scandal. Monitor and report.

Pike goes to France. The process of elimination has made him hot for Le Droff. He hangs out with D'Arcy Potterton, expat Kiwi writer living near Toulouse, soaks up scuttlebutt on local boy made good, Serge Le Droff. Potterton hears that Serge's borderline-gaga old man, Jean-Jacques, has been known to boast about 'my son the master spy'.

Humungous bingo.

Back in Auckland, Pike requests an interview with Le Droff, gets stonewalled by his security man, Colonel Wyatt Bloodsaw. Pike tells Bloodsaw, 'I'm going to nail your boss.'

Consult Paris. Does this pest know anything about Service Action's domestic political agenda in 1985? Any airing of that could seriously compromise the DGSE.

Le Droff breaks into *New Nation*, searches Pike's office, scrolls through his computer files. No joy.

The family takes out Potterton. Pike still doesn't get the message.

Consult Paris. This is unthinkable; the story must not appear.

Think: two birds with one stone – stop Pike, deflect public/politicians' attention from Mururoa tests. Think:

classic black propaganda – commit atrocities and frame the enemy. Think: the Aotearoa People's Army.

The end justifies the means.

Launch the Freckle from a high place; snap Pike's spine and burn his floppy disks; bake Gundry. Put out communiqués full of Red freedom-fighter mumbo-jumbo. Sit back and enjoy the fun: watch them blame the Maoris, watch Pike get lost in the confusion.

'So pinning it on Maori radicals was the idea all along?'

'I know how the counter-intelligence mind works, Sergeant. When the Cold War ended, your counter-intelligence people would've focused on the Maori nationalist/separatist fringe as potential subversives. I mean, let's face it, how else were they going to justify their existence? The tendency to take the perceived threat's chest-beating at face value is the counter-terrorist's occupational hazard. Eventually, your people would've convinced themselves it was only a matter of time. I simply pandered to that mind-set.'

Ihaka rubbed his face. 'You mean that's all it ever was – a way to stop Pike exposing you in his magazine?'

Le Droff sighed. 'Haven't you understood a word I've said? This has got nothing to do with me, personally; it's about defending the integrity of the most vital elements in France's security and defence structure.'

'You're fucked in the head, pal.'

'How very profound. Contemplate this, Mr Small-Town Policeman: within a decade, a fascist madman will come to power in Russia; Islamic militants will complete their takeover of the Arab world and launch an undeclared war on the west; we shall enter the age of atomic and biological terrorism. America's response will be isolationism: seal the borders and retreat behind the missile shield. Without the world's policeman to maintain a semblance of order, international affairs will become chronically unstable. There will be wars involving nuclear weapons on the Eurasian land-mass, in north Asia, and on the Indian sub-continent, causing unimaginable refugee crises. The world is sliding into chaos – it may even reach this beautiful backwater. Only nations with the will and the means to defend themselves will escape it.'

'So you've read Nostradamus,' said Ihaka with maximum rudeness. 'Big fucking deal.'

Le Droff got up. 'It's all very well for you,' he said, quite unruffled. 'You don't have to worry about the future.'

'You still haven't explained why you picked on me.'

'Ah, well, that's another story – you can thank Rusty Trousdale for that.'

Le Droff had lied about his relationship with Rusty – there was more to it than one desk-top wham bam, although that pretty well set the tone. He would've passed a carnal-knowledge test with flying colours but there were lots of other things he didn't know about her – like the fact that she could read French.

About once a fortnight, usually after lunch, she'd show up at his office/penthouse expecting him to drop everything, including his trousers. One afternoon, before they'd had a chance to lock on, he got called down to the nineteenth floor. She was flicking through the magazines on his desk looking for something to read when she noticed a fax in the top tray. It was in French, from his brother in Levignac, reporting that D'Arcy Potterton was sniffing around asking questions, obviously on behalf of Jackson Pike. Le Droff had scrawled a reply on it and faxed it back: '*On m'a dit que l'écrivain fait souvent le promenade à la Forêt de Bucon – c'est dangereux pendant la saison de chasse, n'est-ce pas?*' I hear the writer often goes for walks in the forest – that's dangerous in hunting season, isn't it?

A week later, Potterton was shot dead while walking in the forest: a hunting accident. When Rusty read about it, she wrote in her diary:

'Freaky or what? At Serge's the other day, I saw a fax saying that D'Arcy Potterton, the writer, is stirring up trouble in France – something to do with Jackson Pike, presumably the same one who runs the mag. Confused? Moi aussi. S wrote on the fax – à propos of beats me – that DAP's hobby of going walkies in the forest is a trifle high-risk during hunting season. Hey presto, Potterton gets potted. A case of many a true word spoken in jest? I don't suppose DAP saw the funny side of it.'

The affair cooled. A month later, Rusty was in her Merc with the radio on. The news was full of Pike's murder. At a slow set of traffic lights, she scribbled a diary entry:

'First Potterton, now Pike – creepy coincidence, non? Alternatively, Serge is up to something sinister. Not sour grapes, but I almost think he's capable of it – that cold, detached side to him. Maybe I'm better off out of it. I'll miss him a tad though – on a different level than the rest. Not to mention très GIB!'

The lights went green; Rusty shoved the diary in her handbag and drove to her next meals-on-wheels drop. She hardly glanced in her rear-vision mirror, didn't notice the blue Laser which had dogged her since she'd left home that morning.

Brandon Mules was intrigued by the diary references to Potterton and Pike. Once he'd read up on their violent deaths in the public-library reading room, he had no doubt that Le Droff was up to something sinister. He saw neon dollar signs ten metres high.

Mules rang Le Droff. 'I've got the slut's diary; there's stuff in it that could cause you a fuckload of grief.'

'What do you want?'

'A million dollars.'

Le Droff asked for proof. They rendezvoused in Twin Oak Drive in Cornwall Park; Mules handed over photocopies. It was a Friday afternoon. Le Droff said he couldn't get the money till after the weekend. Mules said, Monday – same time, same place.

Mules waited till Le Droff had gone before he walked to his car parked up by the tea-rooms. He drove west out of the park, into Royal Oak, through Onehunga and Te Papapa, then left into Great South Road, looping back around Cornwall Park. Bloodsaw and Pascal tailed him in separate cars linked by mobile phones, swapping positions every couple of minutes. Mules led them right to his lair.

They broke in that night. Pascal skewered Mules; they found the diary and trashed the place. No more Mules, no more blackmail.

Then Ihaka turned up. Le Droff was impressed at how quickly he'd got Rusty to own up to the blackmail, and worried that if he kept at her, she'd start squawking Pike/Potterton.

Think: Two birds with one stone. Think: Stop Ihaka, tweak the APA/Maori connection by linking it to the police raids. Think: Fake hostage snatch.

The end justifies the means.

Ihaka asked, 'Why didn't you just whack her and be done with it?'

Le Droff deadpanned: 'Exactly the question I'd expect someone in your position to ask. Whatever Rusty's vague suspicions, I very much doubt that she'd dwell on them long enough to draw any conclusions. And even if she did, I doubt she'd act on them. It may yet come to that but I'd much prefer it didn't. I have a weakness for beautiful women who don't give a damn.'

Ihaka clicked his tongue. 'You know your problem? You're just too soft for your own good.'

Le Droff laughed. 'You're quite right. I'd prefer to spare you too, Sergeant, sentimental fool that I am. Sadly, it's just not within the realms of practicality.'

'Shit, don't worry about me – I can keep a secret.'

Colonel Wyatt Bloodsaw, wearing dark-green corduroy trousers and a cream Pringle golf sweater, walked in.

He said to Ihaka, 'Hullo, old son. How's the noggin?' He noticed the cognac. 'I say, jolly old XO – don't mind if I do.' To Le Droff: 'There's a real-estate johnny at the door; says he's got a punter ready to fork over a king's ransom for a place like this.'

TWENTY-SEVEN

Real-estate salesman's jabber.

'...as I was telling the other gentleman, I know a few people – one bloke in particular – with very deep pockets who're in the market for a property like this. What they're after – well, you know the story: they'd rather have their own little shelly beach down the quiet end than share half a mile of sand with the rest of the island, not to mention the ferry-fodder.'

Rave on: privacy, space, houses like this, kauri timber, they did things properly in those days, cowboy builders, architects with pony-tails...*Christ, didn't the man ever stop to draw breath?*

Bum Yandall was on a roll but Serge Le Droff had stopped listening. He was thinking about the ticklish state of his finances. Eurotours was cash-flow negative; the charter-airline venture was stalled; the mortgage on the penthouse was burning money like an heiress's coke habit...If this clown really could wheel in a serious, top-dollar buyer, it'd take the pressure off.

Le Droff said, 'I'm sorry, I didn't catch your name.'

'Derek Yandall, Island Realty.' He dealt Le Droff a business card.

'Well, Mr Yandall, the short answer is yes, I would entertain a serious offer in that price range.'

Yandall rubbed his hands together. 'That's what we like to hear.'

'When would your client want to inspect?'

'Just on that subject, I was wondering if it'd be convenient for me to have a quick walk-through now? Knowing this client, he'll bombard me with questions, and the more I can tell him, the more fired-up he'll be.'

'Go ahead. Take your time.'

Le Droff had no particular reason to distrust Yandall, but he was suspicious at the best of times and this wasn't one of them. He went out onto the verandah to summon Wyatt Bloodsaw, who was practising chip shots on the lawn. After he'd instructed Bloodsaw to stick close to Yandall, he sent Pascal to scout around out the back; while Pascal was at it, he could check Yandall's car for flyers, 'Open House' signs – anything to show he was who he said he was.

There was a double garage behind the house. Visitors usually parked on the turning area in front of it: not this one. Pascal set off down the shingle drive towards the guesthouse.

The drive ran between the guesthouse and a garden shed before beginning its climb up to the road. Yandall had parked there so the raiding party couldn't be seen from the house. C.C. Hellicar had circled around the shed, skirted the large vegetable garden, and come down the side of garage; now she was in position on the far side of the house, behind a pair of immense oleanders. Duane Ricketts was behind the shed, waiting for Yandall.

The day had dwindled to a crisp, still twilight. Ricketts heard someone coming and gripped the Remington tighter. The car door opened: Bum was back, in one piece. Ricketts hurried around the corner of the shed.

Jesus fuck.

Pascal was in the Pajero, going through the glove box. He saw a flicker of movement out of the corner of his eye and looked up. Ricketts froze; he held the shotgun across his body, radiating uncertainty.

He doesn't know what to do next, thought Pascal. *Get on top of him before he snaps out of it.*

He got out of the Pajero, waving, and walked round it. He didn't hurry, just kept coming.

Ricketts put the shotgun to his shoulder, legs braced. 'Stop there.'

Pascal stopped – the gap was seven metres. Ricketts told him to lie on the ground, face down.

Pascal heaved an exaggerated shrug – no speaka da lingo. He said, '*Comprends pas,*' and took another step. Six metres.

Ricketts waggled the shotgun. 'Fucking...get...down.'

Pascal moved again. Five metres.

His right hand was out of sight, behind his back. A voice in Ricketts' head screamed, If he blinks, shoot him.

Pascal bared his teeth; yellow fire raged behind his deep-set black eyes. *Wild man. SHOOT HIM NOW.*

Steel glinted by Pascal's right thigh. He charged.

Ricketts squeezed and Pascal was airborne. He hung in mid-air for an instant, coming apart like a bug exploding on a windscreen.

Ricketts pumped the shotgun and ran for cover.

Le Droff heard the shotgun blast from his study. He took a Glock 17 semi-automatic pistol from the desk drawer and went into the corridor.

Bloodsaw came out of the dining room dragging a hollering Yandall by the hair. He swung him over to Le Droff and got out of the way: the colonel didn't want exit-wound splatter on his Pringle sweater.

Le Droff jammed the Glock under Yandall's chin. 'How many are there?'

Yandall trembled and stammered; he looked far too frightened to lie. 'One.'

'Who?'

'A mate of the cop's.'

'Is he a cop?'

'No.'

'Do the police know he's here?'

Bad shakes. 'No.'

Le Droff's eyes slid to Bloodsaw. 'Pascal didn't have a gun.'

'Rather unsporting.'

Le Droff stepped back and put the Glock in Yandall's face, holding up his left hand to block head-shot blowback.

Yandall's eyes were screwed shut. He chanted, 'Oh God, please God, please God.'

Le Droff hesitated.

Yandall moaned, 'Please don't kill me...'

Le Droff pistol-whipped him unconscious.

Bloodsaw raised his extraordinary eyebrows. 'I'd call that hedging your bets – has it come to that?'

'Maybe. Someone certainly knows far too much about us.'

'You'd better make tracks. I'll cover you and clean up here.'

Le Droff rummaged in his pockets for Pascal's keys. 'I'll dump Ihaka.'

Drumbeat footsteps on the stairs; the cellar door wrenched open; Le Droff, galvanised, pointing a pistol and throwing Ihaka keys.

'Uncuff yourself, snap the cuff on the other wrist, throw the keys back.'

Ihaka, gagged, made big eyes.

'Do it or you're dead.'

Ihaka did it.

'Move.'

Ihaka stood up. His legs were jelly: he took a couple of steps, lurching like an amputee.

'Up the stairs,' barked Le Droff. 'Move it.'

Ihaka staggered up the stairs. Bloodsaw, cradling a compact black sub-machine gun, called down to him: 'Get those knees moving, old son – chop, chop.'

Ihaka came up through a trapdoor into the hallway. Bloodsaw grabbed him by the shoulder, spun him, and sent him stumbling towards the front door.

Le Droff caught up with him. 'We go down to the beach and get in the dinghy; you row us out to the yacht. Do anything I haven't told you to, I'll kill you on the spot. Go.'

He pushed Ihaka out onto the wide verandah and followed him down the steps to the lawn. They were halfway across the lawn when Ricketts, on his belly in the line of trees which curved from the guesthouse down to the beach, yelled, 'Drop the gun.' He was about twenty metres away, aiming the shotgun.

Fuck me sideways, thought Ihaka, *that's Ricketts*.

Le Droff pressed up close, holding the Glock to Ihaka's temple. 'I don't rate the Sergeant's chances in a fire-fight,' he yelled back. 'If I don't get him, you will.' He hissed at Ihaka, 'Keep moving.'

Ricketts, stymied, lowered the shotgun and watched them go.

The aluminium dinghy was a couple of metres above high-water mark. Le Droff told Ihaka, 'Get it in the water: I get in, you get in, you row.'

Ricketts was watching the beach; he didn't see Bloodsaw in the shadows of the unlit verandah.

Hellicar had slipped in the back door. She moved down the corridor as carefully as a tightrope walker, two-handed grip on the Browning. She stepped around Yandall: he had dents in his face but his jugular pulsed.

Hellicar heard the verandah creak. She eased through the last doorway off the corridor, into a sitting room with a view of the bay through french doors. A big silver-haired man stood on the verandah, his back to the windows. He turned side-on and she saw he had a Heckler & Koch MP5 with a back-up mag Scotch-taped upside down to the magazine: eighty 9-mm rounds, rapid-fire. Heavy duty.

Ihaka got out of the tide into the dinghy; Ricketts got to his feet and stepped out of the trees; Bloodsaw brought up the MP5.

302

Hellicar put four rounds through the window. The impact slammed Bloodsaw through the railing, out onto the lawn. There were three red holes in his cream sweater, a fist-sized crater behind his left ear.

Le Droff was in the bow, watching the shore. Ihaka saw him recoil at the gunshots, saw his face twitch and jump. He glanced over his shoulder; Le Droff chopped his knee with the pistol, told him, 'Row, shithead.'

Ihaka was in the stern: he had to row in reverse, push instead of pull, but it was only forty metres to the yacht. He brought the dinghy up alongside. Le Droff made the transfer in one smooth, gymnastic motion; Ihaka didn't.

Le Droff made Ihaka handcuff himself to the yacht's railing. He looked back: in the gloom, he could make out two figures on the lawn. One was Ricketts.

There, in front of the house: someone down. It had to be Bloodsaw – the other guy must've popped him.

The other guy took off his black baseball cap and shook loose shoulder-length blond hair.

Shit, that's a woman. It couldn't be her, surely to Christ...

Le Droff auto-raised the anchor and started the engine. *Lady Penelope* chugged out of Sutcliffe's Bay.

It was blowing a nor'-wester, about fifteen knots. Once they'd cleared the bay, Le Droff press-buttoned up the mainsail, cut the engine, and pointed *Lady Penelope* north, out into the gulf.

He removed the gag. Ihaka said, 'We going fishing?'

Le Droff sat across the cockpit from him, one hand on the tiller. 'Think of it as a cruise.' He was his old, coolly ironic self again.

'Where to?'

'New Caledonia's nice this time of year.'

'You're dreaming, pal. You won't get as far as Kawau.'

Le Droff started to say something confident, then thought of Yandall. *That dogshit real-estate agent probably lied about the police too.*

They crossed Man O' War Bay. Night fell; so did the temperature. Le Droff went below and came back up wearing a three-quarter length oilskin. He tossed one to Ihaka who pulled it over his shoulders as best he could.

Off Kauri Point, Ihaka sat up straight, cocking his head.

From behind the dark hills away to their left came a faint thump-thump-thump of rotor blades. The sound got steadily louder until blinking lights appeared over the Waiheke skyline. A searchlight blazed; the helicopter went into a left-hand swoop and came pounding over the water, straight at them. Then it was overhead and blinding light strafed the yacht. A loud-hailer boomed: '*Lady Penelope*, this is the police. Turn around and return to Sutcliffe's Bay, otherwise you will be intercepted and boarded. I repeat, this is the police: alter course to return to Sutcliffe's Bay. Signal your compliance immediately.'

Le Droff stood up, waving. The searchlight dimmed and the helicopter backed up. He tacked and the yacht swung through 180 degrees.

Ihaka taunted him: 'You're not giving up that easily, are you? Why don't you swim for it? You could hide out on Ponui and fuck donkeys.'

304

Le Droff shook his head. 'As appealing as that sounds, it's simply not practical – I sail a lot better than I swim.'

He ejected the Glock's magazine and flipped it overboard. He wiped off the gun and tossed it to Ihaka, followed by the keys to the handcuffs. 'I surrender into your custody, Sergeant. For your information, the pistol's never been fired in anger.'

Ihaka uncuffed himself: he was going to live after all. Just when he'd convinced himself that being dead wasn't as bad as it was made out to be.

He pulled on the oilskin, eyeing Le Droff suspiciously: he was a fucking sight too relaxed for a man staring down the barrel of humiliation, disgrace, and twenty-five years' wear and tear on the chocolate speedway.

'You don't seem too worried.'

'Why should I be? My conscience is clear; I've got nothing to answer for.'

Ihaka did a silent-movie double take. 'Well, there are a few what we law enforcement types call technicalities – to wit: five murders and an abduction.'

The superior-being expression was back on Le Droff's face. 'Not my doing.'

'That's not quite what you just told me.'

'You're imagining things, Sergeant. If not, produce my signed confession.'

Ihaka's eyes slitted. 'You're fucked: there's no way you're going to weasel out of this.'

'I can see I'll have to be more careful what I say to you – you're obviously prone to getting the wrong end of the stick.'

'No jury will believe I made it up – all that stuff about the *Rainbow Warrior* and your spy games in the Middle East.'

'The Middle East was long ago and far away. As for the *Rainbow Warrior*, it sounds to me as if my employees told you some tall stories while I was in town working my derrière off. Should I say, my late employees – I don't think Pascal will be telling any more tales either.'

'Oh, I get the idea – blame the dead.'

Le Droff chuckled. 'Succinctly put.'

'Prieur and Mafart all over again, eh? Did the loyal dogsbodies know they were being set up?'

'That scarcely matters now, does it?'

'You had a fall-back rigged up all along, right?'

Le Droff oozed smugness. 'One thing about intelligence work, it teaches you to plan for contingencies.'

Ihaka stood up, stretching and flexing. 'I've got to hand it to you – you're a smooth operator.'

Le Droff's grin gleamed. 'You don't know the half of it.'

The chopper had dropped further back; its dimmed searchlight illuminated the white bubble in the yacht's wake.

Le Droff stared into the night, whistling softly. Ihaka shrugged off his oilskin and swung. Le Droff glanced up, turning his face into the punch. It hit like a wrecking ball: the shock ran up Ihaka's arm to jangle nerves deep in the socket. Le Droff slumped, his head flopping. Ihaka hauled him upright and shook him to and fro, as if they were wrestling. The searchlight was cranked up to high-beam again; when it flooded over them, Ihaka sucked air and rolled overboard with Le Droff hugged to his chest.

The sea was breathtakingly cold but that was okay: he was built for it.

He was going to be down there a while but that was okay too: he'd been diving for crays and shellfish without a tank since he was a kid. What's more, he'd never smoked, not even a puff on one of his old man's Cuban cigars.

Ihaka had a very efficient set of lungs.

EPILOGUE

On Sunday morning, Detective Constable Johan Van Roon flew to Nelson. A local cop picked him up from the airport and drove him out to Honeymoon Bay to see Leo Strange.

Strange had his story worked out: his sister, Renee, had told him about the Clyde Early/Mrs Trousdale affair. He was in the information business: knowledge was power and power was money. Put together adultery, the Trousdale fortune, and Early's high profile, and it spelt opportunity. He'd hired Brandon Mules to get proof. When he realised that Mules had his own, shady agenda, he'd baled out. Next thing he knew, Mules was dead.

As far as Strange was concerned, it was just a speculative venture which hadn't paid off. You win some; you lose some.

Van Roon asked, 'How much did you pay Mules?'

'Five thousand.'

The policeman whistled. 'Where did the money come from?'

'Out of my own pocket or, to be precise, out of a safety deposit box at an offshore bank – my special projects fund.' Strange smiled ingratiatingly. 'I assume you have a reciprocal arrangement with inland revenue – they tell you nothing and vice versa?'

Van Roon ignored the feeler. 'Mr Strange, can you explain to me exactly how you expected to make a profit on that five grand without breaking the law?'

Strange got pinker. 'I don't pretend to be a saint, Detective Constable, but I can assure you I'm not a criminal. The scenario I had in mind was this: I believe the Trousdale marriage was ill-advised and I don't expect it to last. Given what's at stake, I'd expect the break-up and settlement to be contentious, to put it mildly. Had things gone to plan, I would've been in a position to provide Mr Trousdale with information which might've given him some, shall we say, leverage in the negotiations.'

Van Roon saw no reason to go on being polite to Strange. 'Some people would call you a parasite.'

Strange could handle that. 'I've been called worse.'

With both the blackmailer and the blackmailer's killers dead, there was no interest in prolonging the investigation by pursuing Strange on comparatively minor and probably unprovable charges.

Case closed.

On Monday morning, the police team searching Serge Le Droff's Waiheke Island home found an envelope taped to the back of a drawer in the bedroom used by Pascal. It contained Pascal's account, typed in slang-ridden, ungrammatical Corsican French, of how he and Wyatt Bloodsaw had planned and carried out four murders and an abduction in the guise of the Aotearoa People's Army.

According to the document, Pascal belonged to a French neo-fascist secret society, Les Fils de Charlemagne. The Sons of Charlemagne's sacred mission was to 'cleanse' France of foreigners, whom Pascal lumped together under the roughly translated heading 'sand niggers'. They were also big on the need to preserve France's empire, as they characterised its motley handful of overseas territories. The Sons were convinced that New Zealand was hell-bent on driving France out of the South Pacific; the long-running anti-nuclear testing campaign was just part of that master plan.

The APA was intended as a pay-back and a warning that two could play the destabilisation game. The Sons of Charlemagne's leadership in France had devised the strategy; the tactics and implementation had been left to Pascal. He'd enlisted his fellow employee, Bloodsaw, as advisor, back-up and wordsmith.

It transpired that after each APA operation, $US10 000 had been deposited by electronic transfer in Bloodsaw's account at the National Westminster Bank in The Haymarket, London. The money trail was traced back to the Union Bank of Switzerland in Zurich and thence to a nominee company in Vanuatu. The nominee company's directors, two partners in a local law firm, declined to reveal whose nominees they were.

That afternoon, Tito Ihaka and Duane Ricketts recorded exclusive interviews with Amanda Hayhoe. Ihaka and C.C. Hellicar then headed north, to his family's beach

310

house at Tauranga Bay, on the south head of Whangaroa
Harbour.

They had supper on the deck. Afterwards, Hellicar put
on a Lloyd Cole tape and shimmied over to Ihaka. She
draped her arms around his neck and got in close.

'Okay, big boy, where were we before we were so
rudely interrupted?'

Ihaka got instant, jumbo tumescence.

She looked up at him, wide-eyed: 'Goddamn, you
really are pleased to see me.'

After being heavily promoted all week, Amanda
Hayhoe's story went to air on Sunday night. It created a
predictable sensation.

The next day, the French Embassy in Wellington
issued a press release:

The Government of France wishes to make the following
points in response to last night's 'Sixty Minutes' program
concerning the so-called Aotearoa People's Army:

1. Serge Le Droff resigned from the Directorat Général de la
   Sécurité Extérieure (DGSE) in 1983.

2. In December 1984, M. Le Droff was asked to co-operate
   with an internal investigation into possible misuse of DGSE
   funds entrusted to agents stationed abroad during the
   1970s. He refused. The investigation subsequently
   uncovered evidence which suggested that M. Le Droff had
   diverted DGSE funds into his private business ventures. In
   May 1985, M. Le Droff was advised of the investigation's
   provisional conclusions and invited to respond. He declined

to do so. There has been no contact between M. Le Droff
and any agency of the French Government since that time.

3. The dispute between France and New Zealand arising
from the sinking of the Greenpeace vessel *Rainbow
Warrior* was resolved by arbitration in 1986. Under the
terms of the settlement, France paid New Zealand
substantial compensation. It is the French Government's
view that dubious attempts to revisit that regrettable
incident do not serve any useful purpose nor are they
conducive to friendly and productive relations between
the two countries.

4. The French Minister of the Interior has asked the New
Zealand Minister of Police to pass on any information
obtained by the New Zealand authorities relating to an
organisation called Les Fils De Charlemagne. While this
organisation is not known to France's law enforcement
agencies, the French Government undertakes to fully
investigate any firm evidence linking Les Fils de
Charlemagne to the Aotearoa People's Army.

5. The French Embassy has asked the relevant New Zealand
authorities for a full account of the circumstances
surrounding the recent deaths of French citizens Serge
Le Droff and Pascal Borgo.

Naturally, the Government of France deplores the criminal
acts committed in the name of the Aotearoa People's Army
and extends its sympathy to the victims' families.

Late on the morning of the first Monday in December,
Caspar Quedley was sitting at the dining-room table in
his Cambridge cottage working on a business plan for

the public-relations consultancy he aimed to set up in the new year.

Quedley had regained weight and cut back his facial hair to a neatly trimmed moustache and Van Dyke beard. He felt that the moustache/beard set, together with his roughed-up good looks and longish, grey-flecked hair, gave him the air of a well-bred if somewhat jaded pervert in an arty continental film. It was an image to which he'd long aspired.

There was a knock at the door. His visitor was a plump, owlish, middle-aged man wearing a navy-blue linen suit and a white Panama hat. He removed the hat and said, 'Good morning, Mr Quedley.'

Quedley said hello.

The visitor put out his right hand. 'This is a real pleasure. If I may say so, sir, you're a legend in our profession. My name's Leo Strange.'

They shook hands. Quedley said, 'I thought you'd retired.'

Strange seemed to find that amusing. 'You never really retire from this game, do you? Take yourself – I hear on the grapevine that you're poised for a comeback.'

'Word gets around.'

'Indeed it does. Can I have a moment of your time to talk business?'

Quedley said sure. They went in and sat facing each other across the dining-room table.

Strange said, 'I also heard that Maurice Trousdale's wife enlisted your help during her little blackmail imbroglio.'

'I stood in for her at a couple of meetings – it didn't amount to much.'

Strange cleared his throat. 'I have to admit to being partly responsible.' He told how he'd set Mules on to her.

'Why?'

'My interest was in Clyde Early, not her. One of my clients wanted dirt on him.'

Quedley frowned slightly and leaned back in his chair. 'Why are you telling me this?'

'Because it relates to the proposition I'd like to put to you.'

'I'm all ears.'

'A year or so ago, I was reading about yet another British politician coming to grief in a sex scandal. It struck me that I knew some pretty fruity stuff about a number of our leading executives. It further struck me that, from time to time, there are situations in the normal course of commercial activity – hostile takeovers, say, or boardroom power struggles – in which that sort of information, judiciously used, could influence, if not determine, the outcome. I discussed it with a long-standing client of mine who gets involved in a fair amount of corporate argy-bargy – between you and me, it was Benny Strick...'

'The boy wonder?'

Strange nodded. 'He's hardly a boy any more but the tag seems to've stuck. Anyway, Strick was interested. As is his wont, he requested a free sample: he set me the challenge of derailing Early's coaching career.'

'Why the hell would he want to do that?'

'Various reasons. Apparently, when he really was a boy, Early spurned his request for an autograph. Young Mr Strick is not the forgiving kind.'

'I take it you're joking?'

'Well, that was a minor factor. Strick's a fanatical rugby fan with a deep – one might say mysterious – emotional attachment to his home town of Wellington. More to the point, perhaps, he also has a considerable financial stake in our capital city. I'm not a rugby man myself so excuse me if this is a bit hazy, but Strick was – still is, I presume – convinced that Wellington would benefit significantly if a Wellingtonian became the All Black coach. He assured me there's ample precedent for it: the centre which supplies the coach tends to get more players in the All Blacks and is the venue for more big matches; the big matches bring in spectators from out of town who spend lots of money; promising players from around the country gravitate to the centre thinking they'll have a better chance of making the big-time; that boosts the local team, whose success in turn has various commercial spin-offs. I'm sure you get the idea. Strick's premise is that it would do wonders for Wellington rugby and give the place a shot in the arm morale- and business-wise. He's got a candidate lined up – bear in mind, he's looking a couple of years down the track. He's also identified and assessed potential rivals and considers Early the biggest threat.'

Quedley shook his head. 'Now I've heard everything.'

'Unfortunately, using Mules was an error of judge-ment on my part and the trial run was a flop. I'm con-vinced, though, that the principle is sound.'

'So what's the proposition?'

'A joint-venture niche-market corporate information service: you and I, Mr Quedley, joining forces to supply red-hot, absolutely reliable scuttlebutt to big corporate players engaged in no-holds-barred fights. Twice the contacts, twice the dirt. What do you think?'

'Well, it's certainly an intriguing concept.'

'I thought you'd like it – and the beauty of it is, if we keep our arrangement secret, we could supply both sides. I can see it being a most rewarding little sideline for us.' He slid a card across the table. 'Think about it and give me a call. While you're at it, why not bend your mind to the question of how we might capitalise on Mrs Trousdale's penchant for adultery? I haven't given up hope of recouping that investment.'

'I'll give it some thought.'

Quedley saw Strange out.

He went through to the kitchen, where Rusty Trousdale was standing over the stove stirring a cast-iron casserole. She wore cut-off jeans, battered sneakers, one of Quedley's old shirts, and a new apron.

They clinched like honeymooners.

Quedley bent over the pot. 'That smells fantastic. What is it?'

'Risotto alla sbirraglia – chicken risotto to you.'

He pulled her to him again. 'Still no second thoughts?'

Rusty glowed. 'Does it look like it?'

He sat down at the kitchen table. 'Did you catch much of that?'

'Enough. Does he look as sleazy as he sounds?'

'Not really. That's probably how he gets away with it.'

'What are you going to do?'

'Well, first of all I'll ring Early and warn him he's going to have a fight on his hands.'

'Then?'

'Then I'll ring Benny Strick to let him know Leo's been telling tales out of school.'

Rusty knew her man. 'And then?'

Quedley got a dreamy look in his eyes. 'Then we'll weigh up their offers.'